JOURNEY OF JOSEPHUS

ETHIOPIAN CHRONICLES II

G. J. PHOENIX

ALSO BY G. J. PHOENIX

Ethiopian Chronicles

Seat of God

Journey of Josephus: Ethiopian Chronicles II
Copyright © 2011 G. J. Phoenix
Published by Avalerion Books, Inc.

Cover design by Dracontias

ISBN e-book: 978-0-9834119-6-3
ISBN paperback: 978-0-9834119-5-6

Library of Congress Control Number: 2014951610

Cover Photo: Wellcome Library, London - Ascent of the lower ranges of Mount Sinai. Coloured lithograph by Louis Haghe after David Roberts, 1849.

Avelerion Books Inc.
Miami, Florida
avalerionbooks.com

For the many souls who dance to the beat of their own drum and follow the path not taken ... you're the ones who change the world.

JOURNEY OF JOSEPHUS
Ethiopian Chronicles II

G. J. Phoenix

PROLOGUE

Yonah watched as Josephus, his beloved *Mamush*, skirted the shadows trying to avoid his grandfather's notice. The child knew how to set his sights on a goal and achieve it. Yonah hid his smile behind his hand, determined to send the boy back to their hut. "What are you doing, Mamush? It is late. You should sleep."

"Baba Yonah—"

"Josephus Prester—"

"Baba, I think we should leave."

"And go where, child?"

"Someplace better? Someplace with food and people who don't hate us for being different. I don't know where, but anyplace is better than here."

"Here is all we have. All we have ever had."

The child scowled in response, turning to the meager fire.

Yonah buried his fist in the red dirt where he sat and held it out to Josephus. "What is this?"

"Ethiopia."

"And what is Ethiopia?"

"My home. My family. My destiny."

"Good. Now which story would you like to hear?"

1

"I'm too tired, Baba."

Yonah sighed. He'd given Josephus all he could over the last ten years. He was a sad replacement for a mother and father, but he did his best. He'd made sure Josephus knew every story, every legend. The prophecy was in safe hands. Soon he would be the only one. Yonah's body was tired, his soul insubstantial. He could hear his heart sometimes, beating the erratic rhythms of the mourner's call. Yonah was ready to return to God. To be with his family again. The relatives in England knew Josephus had need, and they would be here soon. It had taken two days to find a working phone, but thankfully they were home and welcoming. More important, they had money and space for a growing boy.

Which was good, for Yonah could not hold on for much longer.

"Perhaps you will tell me a story then. The night is long and dark." And there was little to cut down the hours and the fear of the predators' cries drawing ever closer.

"Once this land was protected by angelic mighty beings called the guardians. The Presters, our clan, worked with the guardians. When they died out, the might of Ethiopia began to wane."

"No, Mamush. Not that one."

"Did you wish to hear of the prophecy? The gift our ancestor received to guide us in finding the guardians and the marked child again?"

"You know them all, Mamush. Is this why you did not want to hear them from me?"

"No, Baba it's not that. Never that."

"Tell me, child."

"Villagers here, they refuse to speak to us during the day. They have no interest in helping you or me."

Yonah closed his eyes. He knew what his grandson would say. Josephus was smart, smarter than anyone he'd met. The boy could work with numbers before he could talk. He'd always been observant, absorbing all he could until it was of use. "They turn from us during the day but have no problem watching me at night." Yonah said the words to make it easier on the child. He would always do whatever he could to make things easier for his Mamush.

2

"They watch you from the dark. Sitting by the fire, talking about the guardians. During the day they'll make fun of the way you move your hands even. Saying you think you're drawing angels from the air. I hate them. I hate them all."

"No, Mamush. Never hate."

"Why not, Baba? They hate us."

"Josephus, they are part of Ethiopia, and you must always remember, that makes them your responsibility."

"I don't want it."

"Sometimes, what you don't want is all you have, so you must consider it precious."

Josephus shrugged at the censure. "Yes, Baba."

His eyes downcast, he folded his arms across his middle and leaned forward. Even from where he sat, Yonah could still hear the child's stomach add to the night's call of want. "What would make my Mamush happy?"

"Tell me of rain."

"Why are you so fascinated by it?"

"It seems like such a dream. Water? Falling from the skies?"

"Rain is as real as my love for you, child. And as eternal. Never forget that." Josephus yawned so wide his jaw cracked. Yonah felt as if he could see straight into the child's empty stomach. "Lay down, boy. I will tend the fire. The villagers will have no entertainment from us tonight."

Josephus settled into the blankets, his head rested on his folded arms. "But Baba—"

His words trailed off as he began to slip into slumber with the ease only the very young and innocent can.

"Sleep, Mamush. Your Baba and God will keep you safe."

"I only trust you, Baba. I know no other."

Yonah sighed as the boy's words became barbs in his heart. Turning his face to the night sky, he searched among the stars. "Will he be safe, mighty one? Tell me, God. Please, tell me. Give me some sign. He will leave soon for England. Tell me he will be safe, grow strong. I have been a faithful servant to you all my life, a loyal keeper of the Prester legends. Give me this one thing. Tell me this child, my child, will know the peace of a job, of a life well-lived.

"Please."

As Yonah settled back against the blanket, he continued to repeat his plea. "I taught Josephus to search for signs, and now, just this one time, I ask you to show me one, one clear one, so I will know." Yonah felt his heart stutter, and start. His chest grew tight as if a lion were sitting on him.

Then he felt it.

Drops of water, precious water, falling on his cheeks. Looking up he saw it: one cloud, visible in the light from the full moon. More drops, gentle and cleansing, washing some of the dust from his skin and the fear from his heart.

He closed his eyes in thanks.

"Ethiopia shall reach out her hand unto God." —*Psalm 68*

CHAPTER ONE

Ethiopia's night gave way to a new dawn, leaving the sky swollen and bruised, just as it did in his youth. It was an inescapable truth. His country was still beaten. Bleeding. Trying to shake free of decades of drought and hardship, they were limping along like an ancient invalid, desperate to reach some form of sanctuary. Not well, yet not sick enough to garner help from healthier countries. Tired and burdened, the fabled empire of Kush was a forgotten outpost of faded glory, held up against the prominent panorama of tragedy that most of Africa had become.

To Josephus, there was no greater or more beloved landscape than the one he now viewed.

He stood on the ramparts of the fortress of faith, precariously balanced between religion and the abyss. A lone priest on the verge of being asked to leave his church again; he was a man with no family, few friends, and fewer allies. With the tenacity of a crocodile who'd just bitten down on its prey, he screamed truths in a world clinging to illusion. No one wished to hear him. Fewer chose to believe him. It was the most solitary place to stand. He held the weight of his ideals and hope for an entire country as his only armor against the slings of others' fears.

Now those beliefs were causing him to stand at this precipice.

He was about to leap … he just wasn't landing where he always thought he would.

Though the Debre Damo Monastery was at the top of the highest peak, most days an undercurrent of noise came from people in the course of their work. His favorite time was the moments before the sun took possession of the sky and he could wrap himself in the solitude of his vigil.

It was then he felt closest to God.

He worshipped this land of origin. To him it was still the mythical garden of Eden, unchanged since Adam and Eve had walked the shores of the Gihon River, the cradle of mankind. He felt as if it were as much a part of him as any of his limbs or organs, a privilege his countrymen each gained through great trial. Famine. Endless war. Restrictive religious edicts. Great rulers. Greater despots. More famine. The scenery his eyes lovingly viewed was a harsh one, the air so dry it hurt to breathe. It felt rough and full of barbs going in and then scalded the lungs. His country demanded the best of all living things in order to survive, and the only thing that managed to succeed was the purest part of the human condition: faith.

Faith to him was Baba. Well, Baba's stories—memories predating Genesis, told with fanatical discipline to each generation of his father's line so they would survive history's relentless march. Josephus was sad he'd never had a chance to give his own child the gifts his grandfather had passed on. Baba had been gone thirty years, yet the pain was still fresh.

His family were meant to be navigators. Baba taught him to always search for the signs. After he had been expelled from Ethiopia, he had learned to rely on those lessons. Josephus had never been let down. Whenever the way was unclear, or he was feeling lost, a path would light up with the brightness of a winter's moon. His family legacy was his first, best, and most useful education.

Baba believed and treasured knowledge above all else. It had always set his family apart from others.

This holy place was no different. Josephus was welcomed. He just was not accepted.

Josephus often caught the monks watching him with a mixture of awe and envy. He knew the way he spoke, ate, and even walked declared him a mystery. The patriarch, their church leader, ensured his very clothing would mark him. His black henna robes set him far apart from his brethren. The monks knew he had been born in their land: he had the same bone structure and brown skin. They made it clear in their expressions and whispers they knew he had not always lived in this place.

He knew they feared it would make them obsolete. The rest feared his insanity was contagious. Unfortunately, it was nothing he had not dealt with before.

It had taken the men in the suits three days to reach the village after Baba died. Within a week, he had a new name, a new country, a new life. The relatives had done much to try to help him fit in, even changing his name from Josephus to John in hopes he wouldn't be treated like an outsider. It hadn't worked. His school had been filled with boys who did not understand or accept foreigners well. His new life was no better than the one he had left behind.

As soon as he could, he returned to Ethiopia, as Baba had wished, but then grew tiresome to the Church's administration and their shortsightedness. When he went back to England a second time, he expected a harsh reunion, but his talent with numbers was useful to the family business by that point. Mutual interests prevailed, and he settled into his work and life there. He turned his back on Baba, the Church, and every vow he ever made until one woman breezed into his life and opened his heart. When she sent him away, it had been the saddest day of his life yet the one that marked his liberty.

He finally understood he would never be able to move forward unless he put away his past. Baba and his vows would wait no longer.

Josephus jumped down from the wall when the sun cleared the horizon. He saw three men waiting for him at the end of the walkway. Brothers by vow and similarity of souls, they were dressed in the identical robes of the monastery's order. It was their spirits that made them different. It had been his plan to leave them behind.

Plans change.

"I must go soon," he formally announced.

"We wish to go with you." John always took the lead, but his jolly nature hid a will of iron. Though they once shared a name, Josephus hadn't been called John since he recommitted to the Church.

Josephus shook his head. "That's not necessary."

Peter, the skeptic, spoke. "It is to us." His jaw tensed with his concern that they would be denied.

"Do you realize what you're doing?" Josephus asked. "You're aligning yourselves with a priest on the verge of being asked to leave our Church. I am known as the breaker of vows. How could I allow you to come with me?"

Paul smiled. "We're the ones making the vows."

"You do not have to ask. This is our choice," Peter added.

John shook his head. "After all we've seen and done, how could we not?"

"Things we witnessed—thanks to you."

Josephus reeled as if Peter's words had struck him. "You do not know what you're doing, the danger you invite into your lives. You souls are in jeopardy if you walk this path with me. I have never had companions before. I do not see why I should change now."

Paul, the peacemaker, reached out to grasp his shoulder. "Our people cannot hold on for much longer. Your way could be the answer."

"Or make worse problems," Josephus snapped.

John sighed. "You will not convince us you are not a good man or that staying here is our destiny. We intend to go with you."

"This place is a haven for all of you. I know what each of you escaped when you came here. These walls gave you peace—a rare luxury in this day and age. How can I ask you to give all of that away? How could any man? If you leave, I cannot vouch for your safety."

"After all we've seen and experienced—" Paul's voice caught with the emotion swelling behind his kind eyes.

"Did you really think we would be left behind?" Peter finished for his friend.

"If not for you, I would not have found the proof of the prophecy—"

John interrupted Josephus. "See? We were there at the start."

Peter and Paul finished together. "We need to see it through to the end."

Josephus eyed them with suspicion, "Need or want?"

"Need," John softly answered.

Josephus stepped past the men and took brisk strides down the pathway. The three monks paused, and seeing he was not going to stop, hurried to follow.

Peter's impatient nature made him blurt out their most vital question, "Was that not the correct answer?"

Paul chewed on his lip, "Should we have said want?"

"Want can't be right," John denied.

Josephus could not resist chuckling at their passionate fierceness. It was a good sign for their success in the future. "You had it right the first time."

"So we can go with you." John hesitated to confirm the delivery of the answer they had prayed for.

"I wasn't aware I had been given a choice," Josephus muttered.

The abbé, hunched over with age and concern for the world, stepped out from the library doorway and gave them his most stern gaze. His face was as worn and lined as an old piece of crumpled parchment paper, his robe as immaculate as ever. The three brothers took difficult swallows, more like gulps, and looked to Josephus, hoping for direction.

"This won't be easy," Peter whispered.

Josephus approached the old father with respect, bowing his head. "Abbé."

Gesturing down the ramp, the older man indicated they should walk together. The others fell in behind. The abbé could not help but compare this newcomer to a movie actor from America he had seen years before. The movie had something to do with slaves fighting in their Revolutionary War, and Josephus reminded him of that actor. His face was young but always held in a stiff mien with the weight of his thoughts and his life's mission.

"We were just discussing my imminent departure."

"From the moment you came, we knew we would help you all we could."

"It is not my desire to take and leave."

"Yet you will do so."

"Abbé." Josephus shook his head. "I made the vow to see to my family's prophecy long before I made a commitment to God."

"No vow should come before your responsibility to the Almighty."

"A vow is a vow, Father."

"I was happy to allow you to search for proof of your clan's prophecy through our buildings. A gift I also granted your grandfather when he was a young man. I am grateful for all the work you did to restore our walls."

Josephus gave an eager smile. "The books I found in the hidden room will do a great deal to restore your finances."

"God will see to our finances. The codex you found was touched by God."

"I would still sell them and invest the money."

The abbé laughed at the priest's vehemence. "Your understanding and love of capitalism is one of the many reasons the Church fathers disapprove of you."

"You are second only to the patriarch, the highest office for our Church."

"This is not the old times. I am answerable to many," the abbé lectured with a stern look. "Josephus, you could stop. Decide you shall start your life over from this moment, and make one clear declaration to God and follow it. A fresh vow you choose not to abandon. Many others have done the same in the past."

"It is not my way," he confessed with tears in his eyes.

"What is?"

"I must start with my promises to my grandfather. I would follow the words of the prophecy and fulfill the mission given to us by Azarius's wife ..." Josephus threw his hands up, at a loss for words. "As soon as I understood the meaning of the word 'promise,' he had me swear to do all I could to deliver my family's legacy. I may have been five, six years old. When I reached my majority, I turned from that path and started to enter the priesthood. The promise burdened me, and I ended up leaving for a while, only to return eventually. Now I realize I will never be able to give myself to anyone, not even to God, until I release myself from my grandfather's vow."

"And so we are here."

Josephus's head fell forward. "I have tried everything else. I truly believe my way is the only path that will lead us from this crushing darkness."

"So you will do what you are doing."

"Will you not grant me your blessing?"

"I have far more than that," the abbé informed him, feeling smug at Josephus's surprise.

The assistant who shadowed the old man everywhere he went stepped forward. He handed a small wrapped bundle to abbé, and then once more took his place in a recess in the wall.

The abbé faced Josephus and his three disciples and smiled with the grin of a soul who had lived and loved well throughout his life. "Here is the papyrus the men of your family searched for since the start of time: physical proof of the oral history your people have carried for our country. It is a gift for you and all of our futures."

"I can't take this." Josephus refused, though his eyes filled with deep longing.

"You leave us treasure beyond our imagining with the new books."

"I really shouldn't."

"And yet," the abbé pronounced, pushing the package into the young priest's hands, "you will."

"I … I am so honored."

The abbé, who felt he was father, mentor, and friend to all of the men who came to the monastery eyed the three hopefuls standing behind Josephus. Each of these monks had his own story and legacy, though they shared an overwhelming eagerness to see to the fruition of the young priest's goals.

John was the first to fall under the spell of Josephus. Now called John of Heaven's Revelation, he had been born to South African parents in Yemen, who had decided to settle in Ethiopia when their son had hit his teens.

Next was Paul, who had escaped from the white man's rule in the south right before they beat the spirit out of him. He had left behind all his family and friends, following the call of God to these walls.

The last was his greatest triumph and tragedy: Peter of the Trinity. It was the name the abbé had given him when Peter was baptized, eighty days after entering their Church. Peter of the Trinity refused even to say his previous name out loud. The wounds from this brother's former life were so deep within his mind and soul, the abbé feared he would never see this young man healed of his pain.

Each of the monks in this place was here because he had followed God's call. It was these three, however, who had heard the call the loudest and with the clearest souls. They had walked away from blood ties. He was quite sure Peter had walked through battles of unimaginable magnitude to make it here. His love for him was unbound.

They were his sons, students, and prodigies.

He could love no child springing from his loins more.

And now he would be forced into letting them go.

Their anxious faces and shifting stances clearly displayed their wish. They had latched onto the newcomer as soon as he had arrived, like a newborn to its mother's teat, and it seemed preordained this choice be laid before him. "I take it these brothers plan to go with you as well."

"With your blessing."

"I guessed this would happen."

Josephus turned away from the expectant hope in the monks' eyes and the simmering amusement in the old man's gaze. "I cannot guarantee their safety."

"God will," the abbé reminded him, "in this life or the next."

"So we go," John proclaimed with glee.

"One thing." The abbé enjoyed it when all three took concerned gulps. "You were each given new names when you joined the Church. Eighty days after you joined us, I oversaw each of your baptisms and gave you a Coptic name. It is not acceptable in normal circumstances that you use them in public, though under these circumstances, some changes must be made."

13

Peter trembled. "You're taking our names?"

His brothers placed a hand on his shoulders. The abbé knew his nightmares had left deep impressions on the men during the long hours between prayers. Peter had confessed some of them to his two closest friends, Josephus and himself. They were the only ones who understood his abhorrence at returning to anything that reminded him of his previous life.

"I only plan to amend them," the abbé explained.

All three gave him tenuous nods.

"John, I believe you should return to the name Mtho. Paul, I would find it more comfortable if you returned to the name Kwai. And Peter of the Trinity ..."

Peter stiffened with concern.

His mentor chuckled and shook his head at the others' hesitation at his edict. It was good they loved their names and their lives with this Church so much. This was a sign to him for all of their tomorrows. "I believe Peter should continue to use the current name he has. You should naturally continue to shorten it for others."

As the three brothers exchanged smiles of anticipation, the abbé turned back to Josephus.

The young priest had fisted his hands on the wall, his spirit gaining courage and consolation from the mountains painted with browns and golds stretching out as far as the eye could see.

"I do not wish to make the wrong choice again. I have done it so often in the past."

"Your baba guides you, son. Never doubt that."

Josephus swallowed hard when he turned back to the abbé. The old man gave him a look with such twinkling mirth, he felt as if all his thoughts and prayers had been written on his face for his friend to read.

"And you have your assurance," the abbé teased.

"You know the Church is not pleased with me."

"They cling to what was, not what can be."

"I've been called a traitor."

"Not by your friends."

"The Church says I am a priest who has lost his faith."

"Anyone who would do so does not see what I see."

Josephus gazed at the small man with the immeasurable spirit and smiled. "Which is?"

"A man who loves. Deeply."

"I remember what it was like. Growing up here during the famine," Josephus said forlornly.

"We all do."

"I believe finding the answer to the prophecy is the only way to see this world come alive again."

"Do you believe, or do you know?" The old man's question was sharp. It needed to be.

"I know." Josephus was proud of his response, sure it was correct.

"This is why I send you with my gift. This is why I encouraged your friends to go with you."

"And here I thought you wanted me to stay. All of us to stay."

The abbé's heavy sigh showed the weight of the years bearing down on him. "I would have all of you stay here, safe in God's protection."

Mtho, as he would now be known, formerly John, stepped forward. "Does God not protect all who walk with his love?"

"He does." The abbé smiled. "And given our history, I believe God has a special place in his heart for us Ethiopians."

"Our history was written by angels." Josephus smiled at the memory.

"These men"—the abbé threw out his hands to encompass the three waiting brothers—"who are impatient to see some of the world and make a change, shall travel with you."

"Seeing other lands is not always a blessing."

"Not many here would agree with you. Why do you feel this is such a curse?"

"In the countries where I have walked, I have seen everything we could be and all we are not. It haunts me, Abbé, to know we have such wasted capacity and potential. It's like a thorn in my heart all the time."

"It is only through inspiration that change may come." He patted the priest's hands. "So what shall you do with your helpers?"

Josephus cautioned them, "I must go to the birthplace of the Ark first."

"It was my hope you would send these three out to find the guardians."

"Keeping us together, at first, seems prudent."

The three men's mouths dropped open at this news. They were not doing this to be treated like children. "We can do more," Mtho exclaimed.

"It is safer my way," Josephus stubbornly maintained.

Abbé chuckled. "If they wanted safety, they would never have asked to leave here. My son, you must recognize that time is tight for us all. Someone must set up the sanctuary to guard these children. Someone must find the guardians before the world changes or corrupts them into something they were not meant to be. You cannot do it all. Your grandfather would have appreciated the help these men represent."

"What would you have me do?"

"Trust them as I trust you," the abbé admonished. "I have also cleared some things for you with the Church. They know you will do what is right, and you will do nothing to destroy their control."

"Your support leaves me without words."

"I don't want to hear your words," the abbé teased. "I'd like to hear the words of the ancients."

Josephus opened the bundle to reveal a torn papyrus packed between two glass bricks, and he caressed its surface as if he were touching the words upon it. "In the days of the new era, a marked child shall be revealed. She will be joined with the reincarnated guardians of the land of the people with burnt face. She will be the key to the knowledge of the ancients. Through her blessings, the land will find its gifts once more."

The old man nodded, as if his final decision had been made. There was no turning back now, for any of them. He would not take any of the hope or enthusiasm from these youngsters. In truth, he suspected it was almost too late for his country.

But perhaps they could still help the world.

He gestured to the four of them. "Go. Find the children, return our blessings."

The men smiled and moved to stand together, for they soon would have to, before the entire world.

"Just remember to come back and tell an old man your tale," the abbé called out to them, before he physically lost the four to their mission.

He had lost them spiritually long ago.

CHAPTER TWO

"Peace is costly, but it is worth the expense."
—African Proverb

Mtho, Kwai and Peter stood together at the edge of the property line and looked at the map once more. The three of them resembled a comedy movie scene as they kept looking down at the map, back to the land, again to the map and then back to the parcel of land spread before them. Peter scowled as he chose to be the first to break their frozen stupor. "Are you sure we are reading this properly?"

"We must be," Kwai muttered.

The three of them returned to looking between the map and the verdant landscape they hesitated to breech. Mtho began to chuckle and was soon hunched over with the force of his guffaws.

"What is it?" his two friends asked at the same time.

"Don't you both get it," he asked while wiping his streaming eyes, "our friend Josephus is always the embodiment of understatement. He said his cousin had purchased a few acres outside of Axum."

"Instead we find enough space to put all of Debra Damo and a good portion of Eritrea," Kwai filled in, sharing the joke.

"Are we sure this space was obtained in a legal manner?"

Mtho shrugged. "Does it matter?"

Peter nodded his head. "I have to agree. We cannot house the Guardian children in a place not brought to us with God's grace."

"Exactly," Kwai nodded his head.

Mtho rolled his eyes. "You two are becoming sticks in the mud before my eyes."

"What do you mean?" Peter asked his voice sharp.

"Loosen up brothers. We have been let loose in the world. We are on a mission from God with the power of heaven to guide us. Smiling will not make either of your cheeks break, I promise."

Kwai and Peter both folded their arms over their chests. "We are monks. Try to remember your training, brother."

"I am," Mtho protested.

"So how can you be so blithe about our quest?"

Mtho shrugged in answer to Peter's question. "It is not my being blithe about the quest. I just think we should enjoy this journey as well as our goal. This is going to be a time of discovery for us, all of us, so we should do so with joy to lighten our souls and steps."

Peter looked at Kwai pointedly. "He's lost his mind."

"Bound to happen," Kwai agreed.

"Too much television when he was younger," Peter filled in.

Kwai shook his head, "I thought it was those things he called comic books."

"You two are funny," Mtho said with a deadpan voice. "So funny I am rocked with hysterics." He glared at them, as he considered that he had told them how much he had wanted those things as a youth, not that he had had them.

"This does not solve the problem over what we should do about … all this," Peter brought them back to reality with his usual force.

Before them was a rich and lush plot of land filled with an array of thriving vegetation. The problem was, most of it was weeds, and even more of it was growing over the few structures left standing. There was a large central house with foundations on either side, where smaller buildings must have once stood.

What they were realizing was: they had their work cut out for them.

Actually, several teams of men had their work cut out for them.

"What do we do," Mtho asked.

Kwai gave a heavy sigh. Here was where he might be able to help the most. "Perhaps I should take the lead. I was the one who worked the most with ordering and organizing the church supplies. I would still be with the Patriarch if he hadn't requested I escort Josephus to Debra Damo when he decided to look there for proof of the prophecy."

"Do you think we can accomplish this, and still go and find the children?"

"With the help of Axum we can do anything," Peter answered.

"You mean with the help of God we can do anything," Kwai counseled.

Mtho chuckled, "For some people here it is the same thing."

They began the long walk back to the city, the source for most of their food, building supplies, and educational materials. Axum was founded around five hundred years before Christ. It flourished in economic importance during the Egyptian Pharaoh Ptolemy's reign. The Roman Empire only helped it continue to rise. The Persian author Mani considered it one of the greatest empires at the time, comparing it to his country, China and to Rome. It housed different religions and tribes, in peace.

In history, this city could be called one of the best settlements in the world. It was the perfect place to house a school for rare children.

"We have a great deal of work to do," Mtho muttered.

Kwai nodded.

Peter chuckled, "And you thought he was being blithe."

CHAPTER THREE

"He who learns ... teaches."
—Ethiopian Proverb

Josephus stood before the gates to St. Catherine's Monastery and gazed at the mountain looming above it. He was always struck by a strange sense of irony here. It was not the highest or most beautiful peak in the area. There was still an indefinable quality of majesty to it; something more. The biggest and most precious gifts were often found in the smallest packages. It made sense it was called God's Mountain, long before historians came along to prove it.

Baba, he whispered in his mind, *do you see? See how far I have come? How far will I go until I deliver my promise?*

Distance did not matter for peace of mind, or for the future of his country. His sense of humor seemed to be revived with the excitement of his hunt. He chuckled low and long. "What is it with me and mountains and monasteries," he muttered to himself. "I can't believe I have to climb this one, too." Turning to the gates, he hummed under his breath as he quickened his step.

St. Catherine's is one of the oldest continuously occupied places of worship on the face of the Earth, for all religions. He could see the buildings for both the church and the mosque. Checking his watch, he released a deep sigh when he saw the man he was waiting for, approaching him. One of his oldest friends, some would say his only friend, Hector was one of the monastery docents, his stark black and white robes standing out against the sand of the landscape. Josephus shook his hand and gave him a warm smile, "Father Hector, thank you for this chance. I can't tell you how much I appreciate it."

"I was happy to hear from you friend, and happier to repay you for your kindness in school."

Josephus chuckled, "Who would have thought two lonely boys would both end up as priests. I was so happy when I was sent to boarding school to find a like-minded soul. I was the first in many generations to leave my country."

"As was I," Hector reminded him, "I think it was these differences which led us to the priesthood. I see from your robes you decided to stay with your order?"

"If they'll let me. I have come to a tentative truce with the Church."

"You are being protected by powerful forces," Hector guessed.

Josephus's mouth fell open, "How did you know?"

"Such has always been the way with you," Hector gave a light chuckle, as he savored his memories of a friend whose every day seemed to be shaped by a mystic force. "It is a good time to visit. We have few tourists here."

"I do not think I will be long," Josephus assured him.

"You are most welcome, my friend."

"I realize I cannot go up the holy mountain until late, but I thought to look through the gallery of icons until then."

Hector's sage nod made Josephus smile, "You know the way. I must wait here; we have some scholarly Americans coming. They are guests of the Archdiocese. A special request, they are bringing their child to see the burning bush."

"I thought you were open to visitors all the time, now."

"We are," Hector nodded eyeing a sedan pulling into the parking lot behind them, "it does not mean I like it."

Josephus glanced at the car and noted with interest, a young blonde couple helping a small girl wrapped from head to toe from the backseat. He did a double take when he realized the girl was as dark as her parents were fair. The toddler looked oddly familiar to him. "We all must make allowances for the new age," Josephus commented, "or at least make allowances for Americans with large pockets."

"Hence the family," Hector gestured to the group as they approached.

"I'll see you later," Josephus stepped past his friend and the gates he guarded.

Walking through the halls was half artistic experience and half spiritual pilgrimage for him. The mosaics seemed to call out with echoes from a time when faith ruled all. It was an age of pure love and burning hate. The people of the world seemed to find a way to bring hate forward; Josephus was determined to rediscover the love.

Entering the library, Josephus paused at the threshold. He smiled as he noted the chamber was still lined with the same ancient shelves stuffed with all kinds of books and reference papers. The small bit of available wall space was covered with images of saints and Bible scenes. It pleased Josephus that the scholar's retreat was almost empty. He could not help being hopeful that the man he had spoken to would step forward and identify himself.

A young docent broke away from his work and approached him with a welcoming smile. "You must be Father Josephus," the man shook his hand. "I'm Eric, the assistant Father Hector asked to help you."

"Have you had any luck?"

"I haven't found much," Eric admitted with reluctance.

"Nothing about my home, either by its ancient names or the current one?"

Eric shook his head, "No references to Ethiopia, Kush or Sheba."

"Thank you for looking," Josephus's heavy sigh said much to his state of mind.

"It was my pleasure." Eric gestured to the books, "Is there something else I can help you with? I have many texts on the Ark of the Covenant for you to see."

Josephus scowled at the pile of ancient tomes, "I think I'll take a walk first."

"You should visit the burning bush," the boy offered, trying to be of some help.

"The remnant?"

"Whatever you call it," Eric shrugged, "you still shouldn't miss it."

Josephus thanked him and began to wander unhindered about the warren of pathways and tunnels running throughout the complex. It was a beautiful day; the sun was shining with a gentleness rare to him, as the breeze caressed his skin. The three monks he had set loose on their own in Ethiopia concerned him. How were they doing? What were they doing? Let them be well, he prayed. Safe. Josephus could not stop his worrying over how shocked and fascinated the three brothers were when they went to their first big city hotel. They were defenseless sheep in a world run by slavering wolves.

Lost in his concerns, he turned the corner and spied Father Hector standing with the family at the end of the lane. Looking up he realized for the first time the sun had disappeared and the breeze that was blowing before had dried up. It was as if the Earth had come to a complete and utter standstill.

Turning back to Father Hector he was surprised to see his friend staring at the man and woman in rapt fascination. The two of them were taking the last few steps to stand beneath the burning bush remnant; a thick group of branches hung down from an ancient stone wall. He could see no evidence of their child.

Suddenly, a slight moaning started from the ground, rising until it sounded like the earth was bellowing a complaint.

The ground began to tremble. Josephus grabbed at the wall in fear, wedging himself into a nook. He could see Hector holding onto a corbel and he could only pray the arch would protect his Greek friend.

Josephus wished he could call out to the people who appeared frozen in fear, but his voice would not reach them over the cacophony.

A crack of thunder split the air.

Then three lightning bolts followed, hitting the bush itself. The healthy leaves began to smolder, the smell of spent electricity clawed at the back of his throat, making his nose itch. Josephus watched in horror as the embers turned to flames and transformed the bush into a bright red-hot torch that lit the sky.

A series of claps of thunder boomed through the air, making his ears ring.

Lightning pierced the scene. Three heavenly bolts struck at once and moved through the visitors, as if searching for something. All of the projectiles converged on something in front of the couple.

It was their child.

The lightning wrapped it silver arms around the small girl and drew her up into the air. Josephus prayed as he watched the child disappear into the branches of the bush, the lightning still moving around her like some kind of obscene caress.

A thunderclap sounded once more, so loud it sent Josephus to his knees.

One more lightning strike cleaved the air. It drew the girl down from the bush and laid her down at her parents' feet as if in her own crib.

When the sun shone once more and the breeze returned, Josephus realized the storm must have passed. He watched with horror as the blonde couple crumpled to the ground, like marionettes whose strings had been cut.

Josephus began to run, hoping, even praying, that somehow his eyes deceived him.

Surely he had not just witnessed three people killed in a Divine act.

There was no way he could call the meteorological event anything else.

Baba, what did I just witness?

Hector flew to the side of the adults to feel for a pulse. Josephus moved to the child's body, his heart in his throat. His soul ached as he saw what resembled a broken and discarded doll. The dark banana curls were a riotous tangle around her tiny angelic face. Her chubby cheeks and glowing skin showed her good health and her parents' care. It was the fineness of her features beneath childhood's mask that gave a small hint of the great beauty the girl was destined to be when she came of age - if she grew up.

Looking over her face, he was stunned to see the lightning had left

25

the mark of the cross between her eyebrows, in the spot some people called 'the third eye.' Other than that, she appeared to be fine to him, with a strong healthy pulse beating in her neck. "The marked child," Josephus murmured. "She looks asleep." His palms itched as if they were meant to be holding her, and somewhere, deep within his soul, he felt a piece long missing click back into place.

Hector moved to the child's head, and smoothed some of her curls from her forehead with a shaking hand. "God in heaven."

"Who are these people?"

"They are," he looked back at the parent's bodies with a wince and coughed. "They were, visitors from America. Dear Lord, the archbishop will be livid."

"He can hardly blame you for this," Josephus pointed out calmly.

"I cannot tell him the truth."

"Why not?"

"He would never believe me," Hector confessed.

Josephus bit back a comment about organized religion having the most disorganized faith. He tried to reason with his friend, "If it is a scandal you are concerned about …"

"Of course I am worried about scandal," Hector swore. "We just started to gain the funds we need to renovate the eastern buildings. We have an excellent on-line presence. Any kind of notoriety will gain us exactly the type of reputation we don't need."

"My friend, what is it you wish me to do?"

"I do not know. This child obviously requires help."

Josephus found it impossible to tear his eyes from the girl's face. He couldn't stop thinking about the prophecy, and how every moment seemed to lead him to this. Touching her cheek, he was surprised at how warm she felt.

"The archbishop will be so mad," Hector muttered. "These people don't have any family as far as I know, but they are still prominent American scholars. You know how these English are. She's obviously adopted, but still, the problems this will cause."

"I'll take her." Josephus felt surprised by his blurted interruption, almost as astounded as his friend looked.

Hector shook his head, "I don't know if that's a good idea."

"We'll go to Jerusalem." Josephus suspected the smile he gave the docent was grim. "If she needs medical attention she can get it there, and then I'll take her to the American Embassy. I can promise you she'll have the best of care."

"But what will your Church say?"

"If she is the child I seek, they will not be given a chance to say anything."

"Are you sure you know what you are doing?"

"What I am doing?" Josephus's bitterness seeped into his soul at the question that had separated him all his life from everyone else he knew. Baba always said the prophecy was a blessing on his family, but it always seemed more of a curse. The responsibility of an entire country's future, possibly an entire continent, was a heavy burden for one man to carry. "I am saving my country."

"I'm just worried about your future, my friend."

"This girl may be exactly who I have been searching for. If she is, the Church will have nothing to say about it."

"Why?"

Josephus smiled and ran the back of his hand down the side of her face. "If she is the one I seek, this little lass will be the future for us all. Nothing and no one will stand in the way of that, Hector. Ever." He swallowed back the thought, if she were not the one he sought, he did not know what would happen to her. Josephus forced away the realization that he didn't know what he could do for anyone.

Baba, he offered up from the safety of his mind, *I am in the dark; it has been night for so long, with not one watch fire to help me find my way.*

The girl might be the light though.

She must be.

Looking down into her sweet face he could not help but hope she was exactly what he sought. It was hard to be alone in the dark after so many years. Faith in God helped you see the necessity for vigil.

It didn't mean you liked it any.

Baba, please bring me some warmth; something to light up the gloom where I have been trapped for so many years. Let this light be the hope for me, for I can no longer find it within my heart. I need some sign, some proof, that this is indeed the correct path. What embers were left within my soul are cold and dead.

It was time for a new day.

CHAPTER FOUR

"It takes a village to raise a child."
—African Proverb

The sound of hammers and saws rang out over the school grounds, as progress moved forward with merry abandon. Mtho had been proud to find Axum had lived up to its reputation. They had found an abundance of resources as well as people looking for work. Kwai and Peter were both shocked to the point of apoplexy over how many men had rushed to assist them in setting up the buildings to house the future Guardians of Africa.

One comment over the need for laborers had provided a legion of eager men who were not shy about breaking their backs.

If the men murmured among themselves over the purpose for the many structures, they tried to ignore it. The townspeople were not sure about the need for this mark of civilization so near their sacred borders. They were pious; it was true. They just did not like to see the marks of change when the confines of their world were so firmly entrenched in their minds.

Coming up beside the supervising Mtho, Kwai clapped him on the back. "It is going well."

"Yes it is."

Kwai peered at Mtho with rising eyebrows. "You are not pleased?"

"I am," Mtho admitted, while shifting back and forth on his feet. "I am just eager to go out and find the children we are building this place for."

"That is what I feared," Kwai admitted.

"What is it?"

"Peter is suffering from a similar affliction."

Mtho shrugged, "That should no more shock you than my own eagerness."

"No," Kwai examining the progress they had made thus far, "I don't suppose it does."

"You are not eager to go as well?"

Kwai shook his head. "No. I'm best used here."

"What? I never meant to make you stay."

His brother had to narrow his eyes against the glare of the sun, while he watched the other men hard at work. Before he left on his path, Josephus had taken them all to the bank in the capital. As he explained the ins and outs over the budgets the priest had allocated for the school's establishment and maintenance, only Kwai had understood it. The numbers seemed to make beautiful patterns in his mind. Even Josephus's brief explanations had come together into a mosaic of percentages and annual yields.

Added to his love of lists and organization, Kwai had a strong feeling he would not be traveling with the other brothers to find the children.

It was clear his purpose was right here.

"You should leave soon," Kwai directed him. "There is one thing though: I think you need to speak with Peter."

"Why?" Mtho looked sharp at him, "What has he done?"

Kwai rocked his head side to side while he tried to explain his misgivings. "I have seen him in the town with the children. Most of the time he is fine. It's rare, but there are flashes in his eyes, Mtho. Flashes no monk should have when near small ones."

Mtho shook his head, "I do not understand."

"You and I both know Peter had it rough as a child. He had it even harder from other kids as he grew up. I know he wishes to cling to his education and faith. It is just sometimes, all his hate ... all his pain ... comes bleeding through the mask of the monk, and it poisons him."

Mtho sighed with resignation. Josephus never said this path would be simple, or easy; only that they would be given signs to direct them along the way.

"I have noticed the same things," Mtho confessed to his friend. "I will watch him with a close eye when we are searching."

Kwai put a hand on his shoulder. "A very close eye."

"He will not do anything."

"I know," Kwai nodded his head with an eager smile, "I do not ask you to watch him to protect the children. I am asking you to keep watch over him so he doesn't do anything to hurt his soul."

Mtho smiled, reassured in the confidence his brother had for their choice. "Agreed, my friend."

They turned back to the men busy creating a campus for angels in the middle of the most beautiful landscape either had ever seen. Everywhere you looked there was wealth, under their feet even. In the hills surrounding the town there was such a long history of ancient soldiers and traders abandoning their cargo, you would often find treasure coming out of the ground after a harsh storm.

You could literally and figuratively trip your way into a fortune.

"There is something I have noticed," Peter announced as he drew near.

Mtho and Kwai both turned with budding smiles. Peter had made his thoughts plain to them all about the townspeople's nervousness. "What now?"

"We need to let the workers go."

"No," Mtho announced at the same time Kwai said, "yes."

Peter turned to stand with Kwai against Mtho's refusal. "We can do the rest on our own."

"Are you sure?" Mtho asked with an arch look. "We'll be leaving soon."

Kwai nodded, "You should leave tomorrow, but we can finish the rest on our own. The schoolroom is cleared; the boys' and girls' dormitories have both been operational for a while. The kitchen works great. The only thing remaining is cells for us and visitor's quarters."

"Sounds like we have all we need," Mtho joked.

"Not yet," Kwai snapped, "but we have enough for now."

Peter could not help smiling. "At least enough for him to do the rest on his own."

CHAPTER FIVE

"However long the night ... the dawn will break."
—African Proverb

The world looked so much brighter to him. *Baba,* he thought, *look what I have found. See what your grandson has discovered. The one we hoped for, prayed for so long is here. The delivery of Azarius' prophecy is in my hands, right now. She is a breathing, solid piece of proof that no one will ever take away from him or his people again.* Josephus pushed away the intense feeling of guilt that his exultation inspired. The marked child. He was holding the marked child. The joy of receiving an actual sign eclipsed even the excitement of finding the prophecy in writing. This was an indication the time was right.

His country would be reborn.

Resurrection was about to occur. The time for glory is now.

Josephus froze when the child sighed.

He thought the debate was over, but apparently his soul was once more tossed into the storm of indecision. Faith. Science. Right. Wrong. Vows to family. His vow to God. The parking lot seemed to recede from his vision as if his mind were moving, though he knew his body was rooted with a surprising firmness to the ground. He could see the path to the mountain lit by millions of small glowing embers. Hope. The way up the mountain was hope. It was the one thing he could not resist. No Ethiopian could.

He turned to the mountain.

As he approached the base of Moses' greatest accomplishment, Josephus saw the camp maintained by the Bedouin guides. There were two small fires, one for them and one for the visitors. A ramshackle hut held onto existence with courage matched only by the unsteady corral next to it. The two camels chewing grain from a bucket looked to be the most well tended living things in the vicinity. The cleanliness of the area impressed him. It was impossible to smell anything bad, even the animal dung. The scent of the fire was tinged with a slight musty odor that gave him a hint as to where some of the excrement was discarded.

It reminded him so much of home it was impossible not to smile.

Josephus paused by the fire as he tried to determine what the exact procedure to gain assistance might be. He'd never had time before to go up Jabal Musa. But he knew things in this part of the world always had a protocol attached to them; one just had to determine what it was.

A small boy, thin to the point of emaciation from poor nutrition and great amounts of exercise, appeared in the door to the hut just as Josephus was going to give up. "I am Mohammed."

"I'm called Father Josephus," he introduced himself with a kind smile.

"The monastery is that way," the lad pointed to Saint Catherine's gates.

"I need to go up the mountain," Josephus informed him.

Mohammad gestured to the empty clearing with a discouraging look and a regretful shake of his head. "I am here alone with Uncle Abdul. My Papa and his brothers will not return until tomorrow, Father."

"I need to go today," Josephus insisted. He juggled the child in his arms, "the little one does not have much time."

An older man appeared in the hut's doorway and began to make his way over to them. Josephus noted his twisted limbs and the halting gait he took, as if each step cost him both pain and dignity. Mohammed glanced at the man, and quickly turned away, as if he knew any attempt to help the older one would be rebuffed, even possibly … scolded. "You need a guide for the Sikket Saydna Musa. You must wait until tomorrow, Father."

He released a deep sigh; his impatience at any delay chafed at his decision to leap. "May I sit?" he asked the old man, juggling the girl once more.

"Yes, of course." The older man gestured to a log by the fire, with an open smile. "The child is ill?"

"She has had great sorrow." Josephus arranged his charge's body across his lap. Something about this girl made his entire being resonate with understanding. It was as if some invisible bands that only he could see and feel, connected them. He touched her forehead and his face twisted with concern. Her features were relaxed in gentle repose; her sleep seemed to be deep. The mark didn't appear to give her much pain. His worrying was due to the level of heat he felt coming from her skin. "Unfortunately, she also seems to have a fever."

"I shall get you a blanket," the youth offered, before dashing into the shack.

Abdul lowered himself gingerly to the log, regretting the walk to the strange priest and the female child. His joints let out loud popping noises as he settled himself, a groan escaping his lips before he could bite it back. "I must insist, Father. Please wait for my brothers to return from their trip. It is rare for them to be absent. The path of Moses is a long and difficult one. The animals help with the climb, but it is never enough."

"Why don't you take me?"

Mohammed returned with a homespun blanket and handed it to him. As Josephus arranged the cloth around the little one, he kept an eye on the two males who were pointedly glancing at each other. "Thank you, child," he smiled at the attendant for his generosity. Turning once more to the older man, he waited with expectation. "I don't see why you don't just guide us. I am quite sure you know the way."

"I thought the reason was obvious, priest." Abdul swore at him.

"Uncle Abdul stays with the fire, Father, and me."

Father Josephus gave them both his kindest smile, trying to show them he meant neither disrespect nor disapproval. "I think your Uncle Abdul is capable of doing more than he knows."

"He never goes up the mountain," the kid stated, almost struck dumb with shock.

Looking down at the small patch of the girl's face showing from the folds of the blanket, Josephus frowned. "Perhaps today should be the end of never."

He felt the priest's words deep within his heart. Of late, Abdul had felt that his burdening himself on his family was a heavy load. He was of no use to anyone. He was a shame on the family honor. Here was a shot, finally, to be something more than the cripple. Abdul drew himself up with newfound pride, "I will go."

"But you never go."

Abdul rose with great difficulty. Once he drew to his feet, he found the strength to stand straight; and gazed at the priest with an enigmatic smile. "The end of never is a good thing indeed," he acknowledged softly.

"I agree," Josephus nodded.

"Father will not like this."

"Your father treats me like a child," Abdul reproached the boy. "Don't you start."

"I would like to leave now."

"We must wait until it is the middle of the night," Abdul informed his first client.

"Very well," Josephus acquiesced. He ignored Mohammed's continued and growing astonishment. "Allow me to pay your family for your trouble, and for the blanket."

"But priests never have any money," the kid sputtered.

"Perhaps never is not a good word for you to use today, nephew."

"Yes uncle," he complied, with the same meekness he showed to any elder.

"A cousin recently passed and left me a large amount of money, boy. He is the reason this journey is possible."

"We shall leave after midnight." Abdul's stride was far greater, as he moved to the paddock to check the animals. He had a purpose now.

He had importance.

It would be Abdul who walked up the mountain today as a man, rather than wait behind as a child.

CHAPTER SIX

G azing from the top of the beast carrying them up the path with nimble grace, Josephus considered the area around him. God's mountain was not the highest peak. It was not some awe-inspiring feature of the landscape that would stop one in their tracks with its beauty. Just the opposite - it was a rather humble and modest mound of earth. This place was elevated on the surging wave of people's faith. It had enriched the molecules themselves. The strength of the remarkable aspect of the vista surrounding him was empowered by the millions of people who believed in it.

There was something even more indefinable about it, though.

As they made their way up the long trek taking them to the famous summit where God gave man his own laws, Josephus felt a different quality to the air. It was as if the absolute stillness of it seemed to push him. This was a test. A test he must not fail. To do so would destroy his country's future. The mountain made you work to reach the summit. It was only in the complete surrender to the movement of the animal, in the concentrated slow breathing of the air that you could complete the climb.

To him it was a mirror to accepting God into your life.

He glanced down and was not surprised to see the child was still.

"Sweet girl, I do not know how to wake you from this living death. I swear to tend you as any faithful parent would," he murmured to her precious face. Brushing an errant curl from her cheek, Josephus tightened the blanket around her.

The swinging lantern the guide carried gave Josephus enough illumination to make out the man's shadow. Even though all he could see was an outline, the changes wrought in Abdul were clear. The crippled and hunched Abdul stood straighter. He walked with a new purpose to his step, and an easy stride. No matter what else happened after this trip, the difference in this man, laboring with such difficulty to lead the animal, was a miracle in itself. *Thank you, Baba. This is something that shall help keep the fire bright within me.* Josephus noticed the guide walked with pride, though he was still in a great deal of pain. "Perhaps you should hold the girl and I should lead the animal."

"You paid me to be your guide," Abdul protested.

"But that does not mean we cannot share the work."

"I can do it," the man gasped.

"Very well," Josephus deferred.

Abdul paused to wipe his perspiring forehead with a cloth and took a long drink of water. Neither of them commented on the fact that his hand shook as it tried to hold the canteen. He studied his charge and the child. Facing away from them again, he informed the priest with stiff formality of some facts, in the interest of complete honesty. "I will not be able to get you to the summit with any speed. I do not know how this will affect the child."

"Have you ever heard we are exactly where we are meant to be when we are supposed to be there?"

"Now you sound like a priest."

"I am what I am."

Abdul swore to himself. Turning to the priest he gestured to his mangled body. "It would mean the accident which crippled me was meant to happen. I would prefer to believe there is more mercy to Allah than that."

Josephus chuckled, "As would I. Perhaps there is a reason we do not understand."

"You believe in Allah?"

"I believe in one true God." Josephus knew he was not masking the care he took in choosing his words for the other man. "I do not care what name you use to call on him."

Abdul smiled, "I think I could like you, priest."

"I know I like you, guide."

"Guide ..." Abdul's smile was brighter than the moon's beams. "I know I like that."

CHAPTER SEVEN

"Wisdom does not come overnight."
—African Proverb

They had shuttered the windows to their souls. It had taken Mtho a while to figure out what was wrong with the scene in front of him. The kids looked fine. They were in a clean environment, their clothing was threadbare, but tidy; he couldn't even detect any signs of malnutrition. There was still something off, however, in the pageant of the lost and unwanted. Forget that he heard little laughter. Or thought their smiles were wavering and weak, like the sun trying to break through on a cloudy winter's day. It went far deeper.

Mtho felt as if a light bulb must have gone off above his head when he understood.

It was the children's eyes.

Their eyes had the closed-down look of people whose hope had died.

For the first time, he was glad they wore robes in his order. His hands were concealed by the drape of the garment so the director could not see his fists. He wanted to strike out at something. Someone. Anyone. Just to make it stop.

Orphanages were not known for a great deal of space. The chamber they were in was used as a playroom, cafeteria and schoolroom. Mtho noticed the smell most of all. The cleanser, created from boiling down certain indigenous plants and then mixing them with sand, was unique to their world. The power of the cleanser's smell told him it had been used recently, most probably this morning. It reminded him of his mother saying: when you have too much time and too little food, cleaning is always affordable. This was a legacy he hoped they had all escaped. Homes should be filled with children's laughter and the odor of food from the kitchen. This place just smelled clean.

When Father Josephus had sent the brothers out to find the reincarnated guardians of the land, he could only direct them to start in the orphanages in this city. Thus far, this facility was the least objectionable they had visited, though it was the first place where he understood the source of his discomfort.

They were not here to return hope, though. It was not their mission. They were here to find the forerunner - a child who would be a beacon to bring the other souls to their notice.

Both the brothers wished they had some kind of map or plan to follow.

Josephus' only assurance to them was that they would receive signs as they proceeded.

He and Peter had set out in the morning. When they arrived in Gondar an old man had pointed them to a recently opened inn. The proprietor had an uncle who was a monk at Debre Damo. He was grateful for the paying customers, as well as the fact they could assure him of the old man's health. In his exuberance to be of assistance, the innkeeper had provided them with a guide who had contacts at every home in a twenty-mile radius.

It was just as Josephus promised.

Every time they needed a sign, the way was lit for them.

Mtho controlled his breathing and kept his gaze directed down so no one would see his rage. It was a good facility, the director who ran it was a man who was both respected and liked. Mr. Hods had run the place for years and was well known in the community of Gondar. There was no way these kids were being sexually or physically abused. The fact the director was able to feed so many, was a miracle.

"You see it, don't you?"

"What," he barked at the man, surprised out of his musing by the Director's question.

"Our residents," the Director gestured to the crowd of kids, "you see their eyes. It is sad. We try our best, but there is little we can do."

"Why not?"

Mr. Hods gave the monk a long look. He was surprised at how the once jolly-looking man had turned into someone who was clearly seething with anger. "They know they will not have homes. They know they will not have family. You cannot succeed in this country without a connection to your tribe, or without an understanding of your ancestry. The despair is with them all of the time. It is why you see what you do."

Peter and Mtho shared an understanding look. The director was correct. Africa had always been made up of a wide variety of tribes. Each country had its own clan warfare to address before dealing with the rest of the world. Few people outside of the continent understood the deep history or reliance on understanding from what side of the tribal lines you were born. Skin color had little to do with the true battles being fought in mankind's birthland.

He shuddered at his anger and helplessness. "It isn't right," he muttered.

"It is all there is," Peter interjected. "We're here on a quest."

"Yes," Mr. Hods spoke with hesitation, concerned about offending the powerful Church. "You are here to take one of our pupils away."

Peter scoffed, "Only if the child we seek is here."

The diplomat in Mtho came out in force at the older man's discomfort. "We are to take one of your students away to a school where they will be given a full education and support. The one in question will go far in life due to our guidance."

Mr. Hods crossed his arms over his chest and shook his head, "If you had not received support from the archbishop I would not be pleased about this."

"We will take excellent care of the one chosen," Peter assured him with a gentle tone.

The older man nodded his head as if settling an argument with himself. "Very well," his sigh was deep and portrayed his resignation. "This is what you wish, yes? Most of the kids playing here are under seven years old."

Peter surveyed the array of souls with deep satisfaction, "Exactly what we need."

"I have not heard of this school you have opened in Axum. We do not just give our residents away. We do our best to protect them."

The old man's protest was a surprise to Mtho; he had thought they had settled it. He wondered if the man was seeking reassurance any way he could find it. Resistance from the director was not something they had the time or patience for. "Our brother, Kwai, is there right now handling the final arrangements."

"We spent years at Debra Damo, and came direct from Axum; you should have no fear of our motives Mr. Hods."

"You must understand good brothers, I have cared for this ..."

Mtho interrupted the man before they were subjected to another long lecture about his responsibility to the kids. "You have done an admirable job with this place. I would think, considering how little these young ones have, a chance to give one of them the keys to a better life would be irresistible."

"We rarely have enough to feed everyone," the old man admitted.

"Food is just the start to the resources we can provide," Peter added.

"So why not just donate the money we need?"

Mtho smiled, "We will donate to your facility, but we still must have the one we seek."

"For what," he questioned, deeply concerned.

"Salvation," Peter's answer was soft and assured.

"Whose?"

"Our entire country."

"I am not sure if this is wise." Mr. Hods took a deep breath, released it with a rush of sound that seemed to blow his constraints away. There was no honor here. He hated that it felt as if he were sacrificing one for the good of the many. "Which of the souls I protect do you feel is the one you seek?"

The three men turn to watch the youngsters at play. It was Mtho who felt the connection to the kids the deepest. They were so much easier to understand than adults.

Most of the children were playing with others, creating small groups throughout the large room. He was attracted to the isolated ones first. They were all quite sure these kids' differences would set them apart from others. Mtho noticed one girl sitting in the corner at the far side, on top of a table. She had what appeared to be a moth-eaten tennis ball she was bouncing with great concentration against the wall. Why would this one ball work, when nothing else in the room did?

He felt his heart beating with a desperate rhythm against his chest. After everything they had gone through in Debra Damo, this was what he had been waiting for. This moment was the one that made his entire life worthwhile; each sacrifice would make sense. He closed his eyes and said a quick prayer. This was what he had dreamt of since he first saw Josephus climbing up the rope at the monastery. This girl would be his most important step.

If he was proved right, the real work could begin.

With a quick glance to check the others were not watching her, she tossed her toy once more. It bounced again, but this time it paused, hanging in mid air, before it returned to her hand. Mtho rushed back to the side of the Director and his best friend. "We need to speak with the lass in the corner."

"Her?" Mr. Hods pointed to their quarry with abundant shock. The student with the tennis ball was one of his greatest triumphs and burdens. Meggani had been found by the side of the road; hiding in bushes covered in thorns. The girl preferred to sleep in the middle of the briars to keep anyone else from getting close.

It had taken him many days to convince her to come to the orphanage.

Only fear of discovery by the authorities had convinced her to leave her haven. Meggani had recoiled from the other adults at the orphanage. She had tried to be with the students, but they in turn fled from her. After the first day she spent with them, he could understand. Things tended to happen around Meggani.

Magical wondrous things that terrified rational adults.

The problem was when she tried to sleep Meggani remembered all of the bad things that had happened to her.

Her nightmares had taken months to fade. She was thrown into the horror of her ordeal, from which there was no escape, each time she closed her eyes. Life had shown her little mercy and less kindness. The little he had overheard had left scars on his soul, and all he had had to do was listen. He could not imagine what it had been like for a young female to have lived through it.

The truth was, his heart was just as repelled by the girl as it was called to protect her.

Meggani had an ability to take any adult down; she used words as skilled as a surgeon's blade. The rest of the staff was constantly asking him to have her beaten, but Mr. Hods had always refused. It was his responsibility to watch over the infirmary where he had kept Meggani during her months of night terrors, so he actually knew far more about her history than she suspected. He had ordered that not one of them was to ever raise a hand to the girl.

As the director of this haven he was the first to recognize some children had been beaten enough.

He shifted nervously as he considered how to both guard the child and his possible future donation. "Meggani ... you do not want her. She is much older than seven."

Peter trusted his friend's impulse. "Yes, we do."

"She is precisely who we are looking for," Mtho added.

CHAPTER EIGHT

"Unless you call out, who will open the door?"
—Ethiopian Proverb

They paused at one of the many small shrines the faithful had built around the path. It was notable that reliquaries for Christian, Muslim and Jew existed side-by-side here. Without violence, hate or resentment. The devout saw no crime in the three faiths living together in harmony on this mountain's side. It was the greatest crime against God that they could not seem to achieve it elsewhere on the planet.

His only other example of peace and tranquility he knew of within the Christian world was his home. Well ... most of the time, anyway. Even they had their moments of tyranny. They were a small handful though, in comparison with most places.

Another sign of their gift of divine grace.

Josephus had laid the child on a small patch of grass next to him. The dawning was near, so close he could smell the wakening world in the air. It buzzed like pepper in his nose, making him itch to proceed to the next mount. Abdul brought the canteen from the saddlebag and handed it to him.

"We will rest for a few moments." Abdul could not keep a groan from escaping his lips as he lowered himself to the ground beside the priest's charge.

"I would like to walk the next part."

Abdul stiffened, "I can make it."

"You are not why." Josephus gazed at the older man and put all his earnestness into the look. "I wish to walk in Moses' footsteps. I need to tread this path." Josephus could not stop his eyes from straying back to the trail before him, over and over. This was the avenue. These were the stones Moses moved up. The great prophet was on a desperate journey to save his people, to find a safe course for a nation. They were the same in that respect. He was just as burdened and concerned for the future of his own country. Bless my mission, holy Musa, he prayed. Save my people.

Baba ... he called in his heart, *put in a good word for me with Moses.*

He had no question his grandfather was arguing his case to God.

The guide nodded and looked away from the heart shining in the priest's eyes. He recognized what the younger man was doing. His pride was fragile. His ability to identify someone trying to salvage it was easy. "Should we give your ward some water? It must be difficult with the fever riding so high."

Josephus felt his face flush when he realized in his musings he had neglected to see to her comfort. I wasn't as if she could ask for herself. He must always keep her as his first priority.

Baba, please make me worthy.

"Perhaps you can help me with her," the priest suggested with chagrin at his lapse. Together they lifted her to a reclining position, and dribbled a few drops of the liquid into her mouth. As the water cleared her lips she swallowed it down with ease; the two men shared a deep breath of relief. Abdul could not resist running his finger down the downy silk of her cheek. "It is sad to see a young one so still, so far away."

"At least she's drinking," Josephus pointed out, dabbing at the girl's mouth.

"What will you do with her?"

"Honestly," Josephus snuggled the blanket around her, "I do not know."

"My mosque would take her in," Abdul offered with formal civility. When the priest gazed at him with surprise, Abdul shrugged. "We take in more orphans than the Roman Catholics now."

"Yet, some of those efforts produce the most brutal serial killers in the world."

The two men faced off. Two faiths. Both human. Both proud. Both filled with conviction their way was the one of truth. Their eyes turned to the landscape, unwilling to pursue this battle on holy ground. They were both unable to get past hundreds of years of faith to step beyond the obstacles between them. They had found a tenuous peace; it was not one that could last. It never had in the past. For it to happen in the future, much of what had passed would need to be forgotten.

"We prefer the term martyr," the guide growled at him.

Josephus sighed, "I apologize. Your offer was most kind. It is not this child's place to become a martyr for your religion. I fear this little person has a more nebulous future for herself, one that only I can assist her in."

"What do you mean?"

The priest turned away from the guide and back to the one he protected. He must always remember her now. This small being would either be the life's beat of his dream or its death's toll. *She was the reason for all of this. Baba,* he called once more, *if she is not the right one I do not know if I can stand it.*

Abdul still stared at him, his eyes filled with a mutinous challenge.

"I don't know," the priest admitted to him. "I just hope God will show the way."

CHAPTER NINE

"It is better to be loved than feared."
—African Proverb

They were taken to one of the only private rooms in the complex, the director's office. Mr. Hods was nervous as he tried to make them comfortable, and then rushed off to find the girl. The chamber held a desk and three chairs, but it was certain to serve, under the circumstances. Peter kept grumbling to himself over the delay the interview was causing, but, unlike his brother, Mtho was adamant the girl should have her own say in her future. There would be no returning once she came with them.

Meggani was outside, standing beneath one of their few shade trees.

The director sat down next to the tree and waited for the girl to share with him. Pushing Meggani got you little. Waiting for her to share brought some of his fondest memories and greatest strides in helping the people he protected. "You know why they are here."

She nodded her head.

"If you do not wish to go I will not let them take you."

The look she gave him was teeming with so much doubt it was the first time he felt as if he had managed to pull one over on her.

"You'll be hurt if you do," she felt compelled to point out.

Mr. Hods laughed. "We will be no worse than we were before."

"Just no better," her bitterness turned her words into whips of despair.

One of his attendants took this moment to intrude and demand his assistance before the director could answer the girl's complaint. He was almost grateful for the reprieve. Mr. Hods and Meggani both knew he needed the time to come up with an answer.

When Meggani looked up and saw the attendant had stayed behind and eyed her maliciously, she knew she was in trouble.

The director was one of the only people she could call friend here.

As Mtho sat waiting, he noticed those flashes of unease passing over Peter's face like a coming storm. This had been the case in each orphanage they visited. Peter would be fine at first. As time would pass, something would build within him and sooner or later he would start to lash out. "What is it with you and kids?"

Peter sighed and looked to his brother with shining eyes. "My past is not an easy one to carry within my heart."

"Have you ever heard of the monk who was traveling with a postulant? They came to a river where a woman waited, trying to figure out how to cross. The monk offered to carry the young lady across the waters on his back. He did so with success, and he and the postulant went on their way. As they continued their journey, the postulant fumed. How dare his master break their vows and touch her, he thought to himself. It was against their order. How dare he decree to him, when the postulant knew better? After a few miles he could hold back his anger no longer. 'Master, how could you carry a female? It is against our way.' The monk chuckled as he turned to his student. 'I put her down three miles ago, by the river. Why haven't you?'"

"And your point," Peter asked with exasperation.

"You are a grown man, brother," Mtho's steady look made Peter feel ashamed, "let it go."

"It is not so easy to let go the memories of my sisters' broken and bleeding bodies. The faces of the young boys, their long dark rifles cradled in their arms. Some burdens are woven into your soul, brother, and are impossible to put aside."

The sound of approaching footsteps made them break off the conversation.

An annoyed attendant thrust Meggani through the door and shut it behind her.

"Please sit," Mtho suggested to her.

"What do you want?"

Peter mumbled underneath his breath about rude and undisciplined children. He took a deep breath and tried to be conciliatory. "We would like to get to know you."

"Why?"

The chosen student rubbed the back of her hand against her nose and narrowed her eyes with suspicion. She might have been charming if her eyes weren't filled with searing hatred. Her skin had the sheen of expensive dark chocolate, and her double braids kept falling forward. There was no mark or sign to indicate she was the one they searched for. It was rather something in the way her eyes seemed to be so old, while her body was so young. Mtho liked to think he detected some kind of grace in the way she held her head and moved her arms. He smiled at her, "It is our hope you will come to our school."

She folded her arms and leaned against the closed door, "No thanks."

"Don't you want to know more about it?"

"No." Meggani's refusal came out as a bark.

"We're not going to hurt you," Peter snapped at her.

The female's belligerence just seemed to rise. "What do you want?"

Mtho could see gentle direction was not going to get them far, or at least not far down the road they wanted to take. "We know, Meggani."

"Know what?"

"This one is hardly angelic," Peter muttered to Mtho.

"Give her a chance," Mtho entreated his friend.

"Look," Meggani's jaw tensed. "What do you want?"

"We're offering you a place in a school where you will get a great education and always have food to eat." Peter loftily informed her, and then barked a command. "So sit down and be polite, girl."

Meggani turned to the door and tried to leave. When she realized the attendant had locked it, she rested her head against the wood planks and bit back her tears. They could not do this to her. Life in the orphanage was hard, but it was safe. No one touched you. No one hit. She was still alone, but she could go to sleep at night and not fear what she might wake up to. She couldn't leave. She'd just gotten here. Once again two men were ready to take her away. Oh God, what have I done to deserve this?

"We know you can do things, Meggani," Mtho kept his voice gentle and soothing. He had a feeling she wouldn't forgive them for a long time if she cried in front of them. It was clear this was someone who prided herself on control. "We know you can do things other people don't understand."

The young woman froze and fisted her hands against her sides.

"I promise you, we will," Mtho vowed.

"You'll think it's bad." Her whisper was so tortured the two priests realized she must have pulled the confession from the deepest depths of her soul. Each of the men wiped at his eyes. What kind of world gave small children voices with pain? For the first time, Peter wondered if saving the world was a bad idea. Maybe it was just too late for them all.

"No, we won't." Mtho promised her.

"You're priests. You'll say its evil."

"No, we won't. I swear to you, we won't."

Meggani turned to them and her eyes glittered like ice shards. "My parents sold me to the circus because they saw what I could do. They said I was sent from the devil."

"We've seen some mighty strange and wonderful things," Peter confessed, begrudging her his break in confidence between him and Josephus. What happened at Debra Damo was supposed to be their secret.

"Do you know of others like me?"

53

"We were sent out to find others like you," Peter snapped at her.

"Yes, but you haven't found any have you?"

"No," Peter admitted. "Not yet."

Mtho wished he could reach out to her and give the child a hug. "Maybe that's why we had to find you."

"What do you mean?"

"Once upon a time, the land of Ethiopia was protected by an omnipotent group of evolved beings."

"They weren't omnipotent," Peter argued with him.

Mtho shrugged his shoulders, "They were close."

"Still, you should take more care with your words."

"Fine," Mtho gave a dramatic sigh more for their audience's benefit than his brother, "Once up a time, the land of Ethiopia was protected by a group of evolved beings that had many powers and great knowledge."

Peter took up his brother's story with the seamless aplomb of someone who'd known him for many years, "We call them angels."

"No one protects Ethiopia now. We're alone. Even the famous American movie stars don't come here."

"We believe you are a sign the alone-time is finally over."

Meggani gazed at Mtho's statement with surprise, "What do you mean?"

"Do you know what reincarnation is?" Mtho's question made his more conservative brother wince.

"How would she know?" Peter rolled his eyes with the question.

"You mean past lives?"

Mtho smiled in triumph at her question and shot a gloating look at Peter. "See," he chided him. "Very good, Meggani."

"I remember past lives," the child admitted with hesitation. She didn't trust them. They were adults. And men. And even worse – religious men. Still. They were offering her a chance to understand something about herself that terrified her. She could no sooner turn that down than she could the chance to eat three meals a day.

"We believe you are one of the reincarnated guardians," Mtho explained.

Meggani stuck her lower lip out with a pout, "Which one?"

"One of the guardians was called Meggani."

"So?" The child's eyebrow rose with the question.

"It is our belief Meggani was able to control the way things moved. She was known to make huge stones called stelae float on the air, like a leaf on a breeze."

Peter harrumphed Mtho's explanation, "She was also known for her sweet personality."

The girl stuck her tongue out at Peter, understanding his insult. "I don't like you."

"Ditto," the monk barked at her.

"You're not helping," Mtho admonished Peter. Ignoring his friend, he decided to continue with the test. He picked something up he'd hidden beneath the desk.

"I'm still not sure she's the right one."

Without another word, Mtho suddenly tossed a brick - directly at Meggani's head. She flung out her hand to stop the projectile in mid air and then floated it to the ground. The missile found a place on the floor with a gentle drop, the girl never once having to move from her space. When she caught sight of the two brothers astonishment she seemed to draw into herself as if a turtle retreating inside of its shell. Her shoulders went up, her head down, and her fists were buried in the folds of her patched, threadbare tunic.

"Still have doubts?" Mtho asked Peter, with smug satisfaction.

"Now I'm not sure I like you either," she stated to Mtho, before once more sticking out her tongue at Peter.

Mtho put his hand on Peter's arm. "Give us a moment alone." A begrudging nod was all he received before the older monk rose, knocked twice on the door to indicate he needed it unlocked, and left the room. Turning to Meggani, he was not surprised to see her stance had grown more wary. Muscles tensed, she vibrated between a fight or flight impulse. Her eyes glittered with passion, as if they were glowing stones. "Let's get a few things clear, shall we Meggani?"

"What?"

Mtho ignored the child's belligerence, recognizing it for the protective façade it was. "We will not hurt you."

"That's what men always say."

"I am a monk. I live with different rules."

"Fine," the child's head dropped as she studied her feet. Her dirty toes were clenching as if she were cold, though the day was steaming.

"You don't believe me." The look she shot him was filled with such smug superiority Mtho felt as if she had struck him. "I do not expect you to believe me. Here is what I do expect. Give me a chance. I recognized who and what you were from a room filled with children. If you listen to the voice inside of you, deep inside, you know something is different about me. I beg you to heed that voice."

She swallowed several times and began to blink her eyes, striving to keep tears at bay. "You frighten me."

"Why?"

"You are offering me hope," the girl confessed.

"This is a bad thing?" Mtho asked.

"If you let me down," she swallowed reflexively, "it will kill me."

"This I believe. It is time to show your true self, child. All I wish to do is help."

Peter re-entered the room and passed out ceramic cups of cold water. Mtho and he sipped while Meggani glared. "Are we ready to go yet? We have much traveling to do," Peter tapped his foot against the floor in a discordant rhythm.

"You are going to have to tell me something a lot more interesting to get me to go."

"I hope you have some ideas," Peter asked Mtho, clearly exasperated.

Mtho placed his hands on the table so she could see he was no longer a danger to her. The brick stunt might have been a mistake he realized. He needed her to trust him. How was he to foster it if he were lobbing projectiles at her head without warning to prove his point. "Meggani, we believe in you. We aren't going to hurt you. Brother Peter and I would do anything to protect you. It is our mission to go and find other children who can do things like you."

"Why are you telling me all of this? You're going to take me whether I want to go or not."

Peter could not stand to see the girl standing by the door, looking so forlorn. "Sit down, child."

"We will not rise from behind the desk," Mtho assured her. He had determined Meggani's discomfort with men. There were wounds on this youth he and Peter might not ever be able to heal. This was not something any of them had prepared for. Crimes against children had become a greater epidemic in Africa than Aids. It made him feel ashamed of men, especially of the ones who shared his skin color. "You are safe."

She sat down and once more he noticed the strange fluidity of her movements. "I know."

They were at a standoff. The reincarnated angel, both rebellious and skeptical—fighting against two monks inexperienced in handling the effects of abuse, fear and neglect. Mtho prayed in his heart that somehow they could find a solution to resolve this, for they could not continue without her.

"What are we going to do?" Peter felt frustrated they were throwing themselves against the bulwark of this young female's defenses.

Mtho patted his friend's hand. "Meggani, I believe our friend Father Josephus will not mind if we tell you a story." Peter shot him a look that stated with transparent abundance that he minded. He minded a great deal. Mtho ignored him. "Brother Peter and I spent the last few years living and working at Debra Damo, a monastery on the top of a mountain in the wilderness; one surrounded by desert sands, predators and dangerous river beds, where you can be washed away in a blink of an eye during our rainy season. We had never seen any miracles, until a young priest came to our home one morning."

"What kind of miracles," she could not help but ask.

"The kind that changes you for all time," Peter admitted.

"It began at dawn," Mtho's voice took a far away tone as he shared the sights they had witnessed with the young girl. They were in desperate need of her trust.

Her help.

Even more important ... her faith.

The three things, based on what they guessed of her history, they had no right to ask of her. They could only pray for inspiration, for without them, there was little doubt they would fail in their mission.

And somehow, that seemed the greatest tragedy of all.

CHAPTER TEN

"Where ever man goes to dwell, his character goes with him."
—African Proverb

J osephus managed to convince the guide to replace him on top of the beast, holding the child. He didn't mind pulling the camel up the steep path. It seemed to him everywhere he looked was one more joyous dish for the feast of his senses. The smell of the breeze was tinted with a honey scent that made his mouth water. His muscles burned from the arduous climb, but he felt joy in the fact his body was up to the task. The feel of the stones beneath his feet sent a pleasing heat through his sandals to radiate up his calves. His eyes moved over each new sight they came across with the love and care of a lost son who was returning to his home after years of travel. It was almost like arriving in Ethiopia for the first time after his eternity in foreign boarding schools.

Climbing was an arduous undertaking, but he felt like it was a fitting test for anyone seeking to stand for a moment at the summit of God's own mountain. Josephus was surprised at the number of times he considered giving up and returning the three of his party to the camp. The pressing need of the answers he sought gave him the strength to keep going.

As he cleared a bend on the way, he sent a brief prayer of thanks he had continued. He was almost there.

It was time to rest so he could face what he believed might occur.

The area where they stopped was a large amphitheater that looked like it had been carved out of the stone of the mountain by the winds themselves. Cool air caressed his cheeks, drying the beads of sweat. Josephus fell to his knees with deep reverence and lowered his head to thank God. Abdul was clumsy as he dismounted from the animal and stood nearby with his charge in his arms.

"This is the place of the wise men," Josephus murmured with awe.

"Yes," Abdul looked around with a mild interest confounding the priest. "Where the seventy wise men waited for the prophet Musa to return from speaking with Allah."

Josephus smiled, "You must know about each shrine we passed along the trail."

"Most," Abdul shrugged. "It was the one way I could help the others."

"You can wait here for us, if you like," Josephus was uncomfortable at the thought of the man following him, and how he would react to whatever might happen next.

Abdul looked down with concern. "The girl ... she moves."

"She doesn't seem awake," Josephus whispered as he took her from the other man's arms.

"It felt as if she was twitching."

Josephus gazed at the little face once more, but not seeing anything new, he shrugged. "We'll see when we get closer."

Without another word to him, Josephus started up the path with his ward held close to his chest. Abdul watched the priest enviously as he began to make his way up the last bit of the path with sure-footed ease, and was shocked to realize the last thing he wanted was to be left behind. Securing the animal in a comfortable position, he made his way after his clients. His steps were not as true as the father's but his stubbornness kept him moving with confidence. "I am coming with you anyway," Abdul called and was grateful when the other man paused for him to catch up. It was more than his brothers would have done.

It did not take them long to reach the top of the summit and the place where God gave the world the Ten Commandments. Josephus paused when he reached the plateau, allowing Abdul to join them. He knew what to expect, but it was far beyond his imagination.

There were few structures standing, from what he could see. It was not his intention to worry about the cave where Moses hid; the story seemed unreliable in its provenance. The Jews had long ago decided they needed no set building on the mountain to pray to God. Christians and the followers of Mohammed were not so restrained. The church and the mosque appeared to be made from the same materials, their simple brick construction blending with the landscape.

Father Josephus strode with the child in his arms to the center of the clearing, an equal distance between the two small buildings. He looked around with interest. Abdul tried to follow him but collapsed near a group of rocks at the edge.

"It seems like she's waking up," Josephus observed to the guide.

The child's limbs were wriggling, and Father Josephus gingerly put her feet on the ground. Her face lit with an angelic smile, and she slowly raised her hands to the heavens, her palms facing upward.

She lowered herself to her knees and fell forward in a prone position.

His guide moved forward to help him pick the girl up, but Father Josephus waved the man away. The child was speaking, yet she wasn't using any language heard in modern times.

Moving his robe aside to free his limbs, Father Josephus knelt beside her. In amazement, he realized the child was speaking a form of ancient Hebrew. His years of study were paying off, as he could understand most of her words. Father Josephus quickly pulled out his notebook and began to take frantic notes.

"This is the mountain of love. The true summit of God."

She turned to him and shook her head with a weary sigh. *"This is not the Mountain of Musa. The place you thought to take me is now called Jibhal Hasehm el Tarif. The prophet Musa did not wish to make the people*

61

travel back to this holy place. He knew there were two paths; two mountains where he could seek the Lord.

"Musa took the easy road; the one his children knew best. He would pay the consequences, as have the chosen throughout time."

"No argument here," Josephus muttered. His heart kept skipping as the child told the story he had longed to comprehend since he was no older than she.

"Can you see them? Their hearts were weary and sore. Their friends had returned to the mountain of fire, far away in the country known as Greece. The remnant was on its own, and they knew it well. The mantle of fear they had worn as slaves was hard to put aside. They embraced negativity, turning from the blessings they'd been given."

The girl rose and began slowly to walk over the mountaintop. She was still speaking in the foreign tongue that Father Josephus desperately tried to translate as she continued her story.

"Musa had been trained in the old arts. The most ancient knowledge and ability were gifted to him: the lost way of the forefathers. He climbed the summit to make sure the chosen ones would follow; obey. He used his gifts to create the one thing they would not deny—could not deny, upon penalty of death. He descended from the mountaintop to find he had failed, and wearily he returned. He had been warned that his decision could never be unmade, and he proceeded anyway. The Covenant was made, and with it, endless torment.

"He did not know how to control that which he had wrought." The gaze she turned to him was filled with a desolate agony. *"He wrought a portal to destruction and pain."*

Father Josephus looked at his notes with awe and trepidation. This wasn't what he had expected, but the child had spoken so forcefully and with such sorrow he had no cause to doubt her.

She turned and stared quizzically at the guide. The girl then shook her head sadly. *"Musa had a chance to choose the way of healing, and he chose destruction. This was why he came to the mountaintop twice; we had hoped he would go the way of resurrection.*

"Musa went the wrong way." She turned to Josephus. Her turbulent emotion-filled eyes were older than time itself. They flashed with all the colors of the rainbow, independent of one another, each showing

different hues. She did not speak until they returned to their regular colors, one bright blue, the other brown. *"You don't have to make the same error. You can right the wrongs of the chosen one's mistakes. End the curse of Musa. The tools have always been here."*

Josephus made the sign of the cross over his chest, deeply disturbed that after thousands of years so many could have passed over this ground and missed something. The child dropped to the ground and began to dig in the soil, her concentration so intense that speaking seemed like sacrilege. He smiled when the guide moved to help her, retrieving a flat rock to aid in the moving of the earth. Whatever the child knew, he wished to know as well.

It might be the only thing that could aid them in their quest.

He had never before been so empowered to deliver on his vow to Baba.

The fact that he still prayed he was doing the right thing was an issue for another time.

Right now, right this moment, all he could do was help this child.

Nothing in his life had ever felt so right and true.

CHAPTER ELEVEN

"For everyone who asketh, receiveth."
—Luke 11:10

The room was shrouded in the heavy mystery that the cardinal liked to imagine still filled people when they took Mass. Thick brocade and velvet drapes were pulled tight to keep all outside light from entering. It was this perpetual darkness that kept the walnut and mahogany furniture-looking showroom new. Incense scented the air with sandalwood and myrrh. The music was classical, though at the moment it was the recorded bells of a carillon. It made the room feel ornate and impressive. A few scattered Tiffany lamps were left on to create small pools of illumination. It created havoc with most visitors' senses. This was the Prince of the Church's intention.

One large round table was set in the middle of the chamber with three chairs spaced around the circle at equal degrees. This illusion of equality usually impressed his guests. If they thought he believed in it, they were bigger fools than he imagined.

He sat in a large cushioned chair surveying the room to ensure every detail had been addressed. His blood red robes were tailored and pressed, he changed them three times a day to assure his presentation was one of perfected elegance. As the great and mighty Cardinal Robeson, he knew the impression he must make.

I am a Prince. One day – Pope.

Nothing will stop me from this sacred goal.

The whole world will kneel at my feet.

A single knock on the door sounded before the portal opened and a man walked in without permission.

The cardinal gazed at the rabbi with mild annoyance. His gray and white beard made him look unkempt in comparison to the standards of the Roman Catholic Church. The Jew's eyes glittered with intelligence and cunning, the two attributes that frightened Robeson the most.

Both men wore their ceremonial robes, an uncommon event for the city. Formality didn't have a place in modern Israel. The Jewish state was in a perpetual tug-of-war between the religious and secular communities. Lately, even the most devout had attempted to bridge the line between them. Eliezer had once come for their conference dressed in a pair of American blue jeans. The rabbi had admitted he only wore his religious dress when he was fighting for something.

Well, something big had to be brewing now for him to put on his armor.

Rabbi Eliezer scowled at his counterpart in a rival religion, though they had developed a type of friendship over the years. Well, maybe he should call it acquaintanceship. Or at least, they would help if they saw each other bleeding in the streets.

Or at least he would notice.

Maybe.

"I thought we were to have a meeting in a few days."

"Something has come to my attention."

"What is it?"

"Sit down, my impatient friend." The cardinal hid his amusement at Eliezer's clear astonishment over his use of the word friend. What did it matter what language he chose? If it put the old man at ease and helped him get what he needed, his purpose was served.

The older man sat down at the table in his customary place and released a weary sigh. "I was not sure how wise these meetings were at first, but I have grown to appreciate them. Changing the schedule is an unneeded disruption."

"Our little summits have cut down on the violence in the holy city between most of the people," Cardinal Robeson reminded him.

"That is not much in this world," Eliezer snapped.

"I thought it would be better if we spoke alone."

"So ... speak."

Robeson took a deep breath, enjoying the outrage his next announcement was going to cause. "Did you know there is an Ethiopian priest who is searching for the lost Ark of the Covenant?"

"Shouldn't a priest be your concern?" Eliezer shot at him.

Robeson sat back in his chair, his eyebrows rising. "So you do not care if the Ark is found?"

"Of course I care. It would be a disaster."

"Precisely my point," Robeson pointed out with a smug look.

Eliezer eyed the cardinal with a rising concern. At first he had thought this was some kind of odd joke the man was playing; now he was feeling a growing concern that he was serious. "Scholars from both our faiths agree that seeing the Ark would be hazardous to even the most devout Jew's health."

This was a surprise to the Catholic. For the Jews, he thought the Ark was everything. At least followers of Christ had the grail to dream of and pursue. The Ark was the remnant that anyone wrote about from the Old Testament with any kind of consistency. Of course, it wasn't often used in modern popular culture. Still, he had never thought the rabbi would prefer it not be found.

"Precisely," Robeson threw his hands up in triumph.

"What is it you wish of me?"

"In truth, I was curious ... do you know where the Ark is?" Robeson tried to mask his actual feelings, pretending a casual indifference he did not feel.

Eliezer shrugged, "I like to think the Americans have it." The rabbi chuckled, not caring at the annoyed look the cardinal gave him; Eliezer always did enjoy his own sense of humor the most. "After all … they seem to have everything else."

"Well, since we are not in an Indiana Jones movie," Robeson drawled, "perhaps we can be serious."

The room grew quiet, as each considered the importance of these events.

"You said he is a priest." Eliezer drummed his fingers against his folded arms. "Make him stop."

"He's an Ethiopian priest."

Eliezer waited for an explanation, and then realized he was going to have to force the man into a fuller discussion of the conversation. "Which means, what?"

"The Ethiopian Church has always been a force to be reckoned with. I can't just tell them to stop him." Robeson's eyes narrowed with his frustration and annoyance at his lack of authority with the second oldest Christian country in the world. They came close to ruling their own country, a fact that annoyed him almost as much as it made him feel jealous. The Ethiopians were a people who defied his understanding of the universe.

He despised them even more, because he had no control over their Church.

After the Council of Chalcedon, the Coptic Church split from the Catholic dynasty. The Ethiopians then separated themselves from the Alexandrian headquarters of the Coptic faith. They had never obeyed the rest of the followers of Christ; even today, their churches venerated their holy tabot, or individual replicas of the Ark of the Covenant. It goaded the cardinal's sense of decorum, just thinking about it.

"I certainly cannot order him to stop by my own authority."

"Why not?" The rabbi could not resist needling the priest.

"They wouldn't listen." His jaw tensed, as he admitted the one fact he had wished to conceal.

"What can you do?"

"I do not know," Robeson confessed. "I will have to think of something."

"Let me know what I can do to help. The last thing either of us needs is to lose more followers."

"True." The cardinal considered the burden and complications one rogue Ethiopian might cause him. This was not a good time. He had just begun to cement his future on his rise within the Church. He was not meant to languish in this great city for much longer. "You really don't have any ideas where the Ark is?"

"I always figured it's either in Ethiopia or underneath the Temple Mount."

Robeson sat back in his chair, uneasy with what he was going to be forced to do. "That was what I was afraid of."

CHAPTER TWELVE

"Quarrels end, but words once spoken never die."
—African Proverb

Several hours had passed of the girl digging with steady concentration into the soil on a mission neither witness could begin to understand. The rim of the opening was over her head, but she continued to shift the dirt out of her way. She refused to discuss what she was doing with them. It was impossible for them to get her to speak at all. Josephus and Abdul altered filling a small offering plate they had found in the church to keep the trench large enough so the child could work within it with more freedom.

It was the only way they could be of use.

More time passed before she stopped.

She looked up at the two of them with a beaming smile and held her hands up to be lifted out of the chasm.

Josephus was grateful she had found what she was looking for. If she had kept going he feared they were going to tunnel a path to the base of the mountain, plus the guide was giving him more penetrating looks by the minute.

When she was set on the ground between her two bewildered witnesses, she held out her palm so they could see a crystal lying with a deceptive sense of inactivity. The silver sheen was unlike anything either man had seen before, casting back the light as if it were transforming it. The color gleamed in the afternoon sun like a newly minted coin.

"Musa did not trust the way of healing."

Abdul collapsed to the ground, weak, his body sprawled as if broken once more. Josephus felt horrible that the exertions had caused this kind soul so much additional pain. It was not his intention to hurt anyone.

The child turned to the guide and held the stone over his twisted limbs. *"Musa could not see the way of love."* The power inside the stone grew until it was like she was carrying a small sun.

As she moved the rock over the guide's legs they began to shimmer.

Josephus was aghast to realize he could see each of the man's bones, as if looking at a living x-ray. If this remnant was radioactive he was jeopardizing Abdul's health, and the baby's future.

"God's way is one of love," the girl murmured to them both. *"It is straight and true. Fear makes you think it is twisted and full of obstacles."* She pointed to Josephus, *"Pull his limbs so they are as the path, the true path of love."*

He knelt beside the guide and did as she ordered. The man's legs felt finely made, as if they were fragile pieces of porcelain that might break with the wrong pressure. He tried to be as gentle as he could, but when he glanced at the man's face, he was surprised to realize he seemed to be frozen. His weathered-looking wooden skin had an odd tinge to it, as if someone had cast a blue cloud over him. Josephus prayed out loud when he felt Abdul's legs respond to his manipulations.

It took only a few moves to straighten them into anyone's normal and healthy appendages.

"Dear sweet merciful God," he whispered his voice hoarse with the emotion of the moment, "we offer humble thanks to you for this blessing."

The guide began to mutter Islamic prayers as he touched his new legs with awe. He was shaking like the lone leaf in the storm as he made a slow progress to his feet.

Josephus watched with a smile as the child held the glittering rock above her head. *"The way of healing is now our choice,"* her harsh voice resonated with the command of hundreds.

Her voice echoed across the mountaintop and to the clouds above them.

Baba, Josephus called inside his heart, *look at her work.* The baby had been transformed before his eyes into the mythical prophet he had been raised to look for in each child's face that he met. Her being had expanded to eclipse all of the mountains around him. It was clear this was the spirit he had waited for.

A lucent beam embraced her body, turning the crystal into a perpetual explosive flash.

His nose was filled with the scent of millions of flowers, and the temperature felt as if it had dropped by twenty degrees in the moment it took to exhale. A rumble of thunder shook the skies. The ground beneath him began to buck, as the earth did when she was recognized beneath the burning bush remnant.

The child yelled something else to the skies.

It felt as if the world froze as her request was considered.

She was heard.

The answer was yes.

A bright light flashed from the rock sending out a shock wave, knocking all three of them unconscious.

Once more, the summit was quiet.

All you could hear was the mournful wail of the wind as it blew over the three still forms, as if seeking some remnant of what it had just witnessed.

CHAPTER THIRTEEN

"When there is no enemy within, the enemies outside cannot hurt
you."
—African Proverb

M eggani stood close to Father Mtho as she watched Peter finish
arranging her exodus from the orphanage with Mr. Hods. She
would not miss the constant pain of an empty stomach, the long spells
of cleaning the buildings, or the suspicion of the other children.
Meggani knew she would miss the long nights when the little ones
would ignore their elders' fear and turn to her for comfort. This place
was the closest she had ever had to a family; she regretted leaving it,
no matter what the circumstances.

The first thing she hoped was someone would take her shopping.
Her recent growth spurt had happened faster than Mr. Hods could
address. Her clothing was a patchwork of different outfits better called
rags. She felt dirty and ill kempt when compared with the pristine
robes and sandaled feet of the monks.

Looking down, she grimaced. Her feet were so dirty it would take the pounding of a rock to knock some of the dust from her toes.

Walking to their destination was not going to be fun.

Feeling Mtho's eyes on her, she decided to blurt out a fact she felt compelled to share. "He should not help find the others."

"Why do you say this, child," Mtho asked while kneeling next to her.

"Never mind," she muttered, glancing away.

Mtho ached at the anxiety he caught in her eyes, "I won't pass judgment on you."

"I know."

"So why will you not say?"

Meggani sighed, her shoulders slumping with defeat. "It is not time for you to know."

"Okay," Mtho acquiesced. As he stood up, he hid his grin when Meggani stared at him with open-mouthed astonishment. "I told you we were different."

The two of them lapsed into silence, each burdened by private concerns.

"How did you get the name Meggani?"

She looked up into his eyes and squinted. "It is mine."

"Yes," Mtho tried to explain, "but how did it come to be yours?"

Meggani shrugged, "I heard it in my dreams."

"Do you do that often?"

"What? Dream?"

He laughed at her joking. "No, my little comedienne. I was wondering if you dream of other lives often."

"Usually about the first Meggani," she confessed to him in a whisper.

Mtho could not help but look eager. "This might be a good thing for us."

"I'm glad you think so." She grimaced, "it is not always true for me."

"Was it always your name?"

"No," she admitted. "My parents called me something else."

"Will you tell me?"

Meggani's jaw clenched at the idea of sharing the name that had only brought her sorrow and pain. "I would rather not."

He could not help laughing. Another soul who suffered over her childhood was going to travel with him. You would think he would be used to these rules people made to prevent them from putting aside the luggage of their growing up traumas. "I think you and my friend Brother Peter have far more in common than you realize."

Peter interrupted any remark the girl could make by approaching them with a triumphant gloat. "Mr. Hods now has enough money to pay for food for a year."

"I was thinking it might be wise if we split up," Mtho suggested, studiously avoiding Meggani's flummoxed stare.

"What do you mean?"

"Kwai could use your help at the school," Mtho pointed out.

Peter glowered at Meggani, "This is sudden," he stated to his brother.

Mtho ignored the subtext, having been hit by another one of his light bulb moments. It had to be easier to find what he sought with her to assist him. Having one child to help find the others was brilliant. "Let Meggani and me see who we can find on our own."

"Fine," Peter snapped.

As the two of them watched Peter stomp away without an additional word, Meggani turned a surprised look to Mtho. "I can't believe you listened to me."

"I told you," Mtho squeezed her shoulder with his gentle reminder. "We're different."

Meggani noticed Mtho had turned back to watch Peter's fuming retreat with a great deal of regret. He's trying, she counseled herself.

Give him a chance.

"This really is for the best," she tried to console him, "he's safer this way."

"What do you mean?"

"He'll be safer at the school," she repeated for him.

Mtho suddenly realized he must be different from the other adults the girl had known in her life. It meant his time with her would not be like anything he himself had experienced before, and he only hoped he was prepared.

He could only pray he was worthy.

CHAPTER FOURTEEN

"When the heart overflows, it comes out through the mouth."
—Ethiopian Proverb

J osephus came to, reluctantly. Somehow his subconscious mind
expected to be greeted with pain, or at least discomfort. Nothing
could have been further from the truth. He felt invigorated.
Alive. His body pulsed with excitement. He was filled with a thrilling
energy he could neither understand nor trace. As he sat up in the dirt
where he lay, he gasped out loud when he saw the child. Rushing over
to her, he released a deep sigh of relief when he saw her sweet face was
the same as before. The only indication of any kind of problem was the
mark between her eyes.

After checking that her pulse was the same steady rhythm,
Josephus retrieved the blanket and wrapped her safely in its folds. It
was after he had settled her under a shady tree that he realized the
guide was gone.

Josephus decided he could search for the man in the two buildings
while the child continued to sleep. Heading to the church, he paused

before entering and moved to the mosque, recalling the guide's religion. He removed his simple sandals at the entrance and paused, stunned by the stark elegance of the room. It reminded him of the buried stone churches of Rohan.

He could see him by the altar.

Josephus approached Abdul with caution. For all he knew the guide thought the girl and he were wizards and he was planning their deaths. Abdul was kneeling on the floor, and Josephus could not resist a wince of sympathy for the pain the position had to be causing him.

"I am sorry to intrude on your prayers." Not willing to leave the girl alone much longer, and since Abdul seemed resistant to stopping his vigil anytime soon, Josephus hesitated to touch his back. "My friend, I just wish to know you are well."

The guide's only response was to increase his frantic mumbled prayers.

"Abdul," Josephus knelt beside him trying not to be seen as threatening. "I realize some would call what the girl did a bad thing but it really is not. She is a beautiful soul. This is a blessing."

When Abdul lifted his head to answer him, Josephus's breath froze in his lungs. The guide's visage was illuminated with the same silver phosphorescent glow the girl's crystal possessed. "Mother of God," he whispered, crossing himself several times with the force of his awe at the change in the man.

"The child showed me the face of Allah." Abdul smiled at him and chastised the priest. "I do not believe this was a bad thing."

Abdul's prayers took up a cadence reminding Josephus of heaven's music. He could not resist looking up for the guide's angelic choir.

"Come," Josephus tried to drag the man up to his feet, "we must show your nephew."

"No," Abdul leaned away from him to avoid his grasp.

"You should share your blessing with others."

Abdul shook his head, saddened at the stranger's misunderstanding and turned back to the East, "I will never leave this mountain again, priest."

"You must reconsider."

"It is already done. I have made my vow."

Josephus considered grappling with the man to force him to return. Abdul seemed to sense his dilemma though, and turned to him with a smile of such absolute peace and acceptance, he decided it was out of his hands. The guide's family could drag him from this place of joy if they so chose. It was not his job to judge or condemn. Abdul had been set upon his path, Josephus had his own to follow. "I wish you well, my friend."

"Allah." Abdul muttered, "I have seen the face of Allah."

Josephus didn't know if his joy at the miracles he witnessed was the reason the trip down the mountain passed so swiftly - or just because it was all downhill - but he found himself and the child back at the Bedouin camp before nightfall. He had managed to secure her on top of the beast so he could lead the animal with his arms free. As soon as he got within sight of the small fire, Mohammed came running over to take the reins, greeting the animal with a soft word and a pat on the side.

"Where is my Uncle Abdul?"

"He chose to stay on top." Josephus released the baby from the ties and laid her on the ground for a moment to check that the sling had not marked her. When it appeared she was still just resting peacefully, he wrapped her back up.

"But he has no supplies," the boy pointed out. He gave a forlorn look up the path.

"Will your father bring him some?"

"Of course. We take care of our own."

Josephus smiled at Mohammed to diminish what he feared the child took as criticism, "This is good."

"He probably just wants to pray for a while."

The priest wished to warn the boy he might have lost his companion for all time. "He is doing much more than that, child."

"What do you know?"

"Tell your family I said, thank you," he requested with stiff formality.

"For what?"

"They will learn when they see him."

He moved with speed to avoid any more of Mohammed's

questions. Or worse, his own concern and guilt over Abdul's new affliction made him feel burdened.

Baba, he called in his heart, *watch over him, please. Send someone to help Abdul understand his life. I will not pass judgment on his choice. I just don't wish to think of how alone he might feel.*

Josephus caught sight of a large viewing bus near the gates to Saint Catherine's, loading tourists to return to some kind of resort. He hurried over and stood near the vehicle's corpulent driver who was checking off names on a clipboard with impatient slashes of his pen. "We shall go direct. No stops. Straight back to Jerusalem," the man announced to his charges in broken English.

"Excuse me; I could use a ride."

The dispassionate man gazed at the priest, though his eyes softened considerably when he discerned the child Josephus was holding. "What's wrong with her?"

"She needs medical care. I need to get her to Jerusalem as soon as possible."

The driver pulled him to the front of the vehicle so his paying passengers wouldn't overhear their conversation. "I will let you on," the driver gave another sympathetic look at the baby in his arms. "You must not tell the others you do not pay. I will get an earful from them all if you do."

"I thank you for your kindness."

"You're not stealing her, are you?" The man gave a suspicious glare at Josephus and his charge. He backed a few steps away from them looking around for help. This was not a travesty he would be an accessory to.

Josephus shut his open-mouth with force that made his teeth snap like a gunshot. "I swear I am not," he spat out at the driver for the mere hint of something so sordid.

"We must all look out for the little ones "

"That is all I am doing."

"Get on," the driver touched his charge's cheek with a gentle finger. "I'll get you there as fast as possible. We'll be passing a hospital, so I can even drop you off."

"Thank you," Josephus offered.

As he settled in the seat, the child still in his arms, Josephus looked at her closed face; searching for more answers, when his questions overwhelmed his mind. It is just the beginning, he reminded himself, trying to calm his racing heart.

She made a small mewling sound.

He smiled at her and his tension eased.

"We must all take care of the little ones," he whispered to her. "For one day, it shall be the little ones who shall take care of us."

CHAPTER FIFTEEN

"Anticipate the good so you may enjoy it."
—Ethiopian Proverb

"How could one man do so many miracles," Meggani asked Mtho with awe.

"Father Josephus is a rather extraordinary man, Meggani. Almost as special as you," Mtho teased her. As they wandered through the town, the monk was struck by the colors, or the lack of them. It was as if the area had been painted in shades of brown that made the place look like it was carved from dirt. There was no sign of life he could see; even the mud brick houses appeared to be dying.

The smell was one of decay.

It clawed at the back of his throat. The oppressive taste must make the people wonder if they would always be stuck in a perpetual sea of despair.

Meggani was looking around with curiosity. Mtho didn't know if the child was struck by the lack of color, the people, or was just enjoying a look at a different type of location than the city where her orphanage was located.

"But Brother Mtho, if Father Josephus could do so many things … teach so many things … shouldn't he share the information with everybody else?"

Mtho smiled, once again struck by his enjoyment of the facile capacity of the child's mind. "He is. In his own way. Father Josephus is using his understanding of the world and history to obtain proof to help people believe. He is also seeing to all of our futures by creating this school for you children to grow and become more powerful."

"He's got a long way to go," she muttered.

"True," Mtho nodded, "but the hopelessness of the drought and our governmental inadequacies forced earth's people to leave us behind."

"So," the girl's lilting voice was a relief from the oppressive silence of the gasping town, "if the drought is over, why is there still so much death here?"

"Our drought is better. Not over. The earth is still healing from the bad times." Mtho hid his smile, the child's mind never failed to entertain him. She seemed to enjoy the new clothes they had purchased for her in a store in the city. He had allowed her free rein to choose and was happy to see she had stuck with serviceable cotton shorts, shirts and pants.

It was in the shoe store where he found her real weakness.

She had hedged as she stared at the serviceable brown shoes the saleswoman had suggested. Her eyes kept straying to a pair of white running shoes with bright pink laces. Because of his strict training, Mtho had managed to keep his chuckles to himself when she had quivered as he had insisted they purchase them.

Two days had passed since she had gotten them, yet he caught her walking again with her head down, to peer in rapture at her shining feet. Each time they sat, she would brush off the dust and dirt.

"Look around you Father; the people are still healing too."

"I had hoped we would find more of you by now."

"Surely you did not think this would be easy," the girl chided.

"How is it for one so young, you speak so old?" Mtho enjoyed teasing her.

"My parents kicked me out when I was three. I am not young. I have never been young, Brother Mtho."

His wince was so pronounced, he had no doubt he looked like someone had struck him. Mtho searched for some trite explanation for the stupidity of people, but he decided this girl would only accept truth. "They should have seen your goodness, child."

"All they saw was an easy paycheck when they sold me to the freak show." Meggani caught the pity in his eyes, and reacted with a scathing tone. "Besides, what you call goodness - most call brat."

"You cannot make me dislike you Meggani."

"I don't know why not. I try hard enough."

"Why?"

"People liking you are dangerous. It means you can get hurt."

"True. With great joy comes a risk for great pain."

Meggani stopped. Her eyes glittered at him as if they were lava rocks. "So why do it?"

"Because the joy can be so sweet."

She snorted. "Not so far."

"Cynical is unattractive in a child."

"Probably as much as naïve is in a priest," Meggani quipped.

Deciding he was a fool to try to match wits with the girl, Mtho attempted to turn them back to the problem at hand. "Well, this is definitely the town. The only issue is where do we go now?"

"What ... no orphanage here?"

"Nope, just an email from a frightened teacher."

"I told you we are cursed," she muttered.

His reaction was instantaneous, for it was this doubt that could be the greatest obstacle they faced. Mtho turned and knelt before her, he started to grasp her shoulders with his hands but she sidestepped away from his reach. "You are not cursed."

"Why is it so important to you that I believe ?" The girl's question came out as a whisper.

"For it is the truth."

"Okay Brother Mtho. I will try to remember."

"I am beginning to think you do these things on purpose." Mtho stood, his joints protesting the position with loud pops. He brushed off the dirt from his robe, hoping to restore his respectable image. *Another obstacle cleared with the grace of the Lord.*

"Such a thing would make me manipulative," she quipped with impish glee.

"Well no one would call you that," he added.

Meggani turned and cocked her head as if hearing a call beyond his ability to discern. He could see a tremor move through her body. A smile filled her face and her eyes lit with joy. There was no way for him to provide a scientific measurement of proof of what he was seeing, but his soul screamed this was a sign of the girl's proximity to the Holy Spirit.

The weighty feel of hopelessness was lifted, as the corners of her mouth turned up into an almost smile. "We need to go down the street on the left."

"How do you know?"

"Why else did you bring me?"

"You did not think I would like your company?"

Her gaze was suspicious, and glittered with her concern. "You're a monk."

Mtho shrugged, "I am."

"I would not go around advertising you like the company of little girls."

"How old are you again?" His question was uttered under his breath, yet she still heard him.

"Older than you realize," she answered with a pained whisper. "I believe if you thought about it, you would realize I am far older than you."

CHAPTER SIXTEEN

"The cattle are as good as the pasture in which they graze."
—Ethiopian Proverb

The Church of the Holy Sepulchre never made it into popular iconography like the other major locations recognized as being from Jesus Christ's life. Josephus had always thought it was due to the Ethiopian Church's hold over the building. Over the centuries they had lost some of their dominion, and were currently regulated to just the monastery on the top of the roof. Their hold on even this prime piece of real estate was a point of contention with many orthodox followers of Christ.

It was also true they had maintained their hold since the crusades.

Father Josephus ignored the studied attempts that the occupants of the building made to treat him as if he were invisible as he moved through the hallways. Apparently, word had already been passed around that he was no longer welcome. They thought he was disloyal for following his own quest. Traitor. Disbeliever. Unwanted. He made himself square his shoulders to show he did not care. He was on the right path. God's path. This was all that mattered.

A silent cleric led him into the archbishop's office with an ominous glower.

His room was decorated with a sedated elegance the handmade dark wood furniture evoked. It was not done in the most expensive materials, but everything in the chamber was old, and well tended. The desk and chairs were waxed and oiled to a high shine, the paintings and icons were beautiful, yet faded with the onslaught of time. The lighting was an immediate relief to the senses from the harsh sun outside. The incense was from home, the sweet scent bringing forth a feeling of love and safety. He felt his chest loosen and his soul ease. The archbishop stood up and shook Josephus's hand with a warm smile. "I was surprised to hear from you so soon."

"My journey was more successful than I thought."

The old man cowed with glee. "First I shall order us tea. I feel we will appreciate the refreshment, and I have no wish to see you interrupted."

"I thank you, archbishop."

"Come," the archbishop gestured to the large comfortable leather couch beside the wall. "Sit down with me. I must hear each detail."

Josephus knew he was being paid a great compliment. Most audiences were limited to the large ebony desk with wild animals of their home carved across the facade. The two chairs in front of it were straight backed and he remembered they were two of the most uncomfortable pieces of furniture in the world. "I believe," he paused and took a deep breath. There was no longer any turning back. It was time to finish making his leap. "I know I found the child I sought."

"You did? It was quick."

"It seems when all the factors are right, God answers prayers with a blink."

The archbishop sat forward with his eagerness. "Who is the blessed one?"

Josephus sat back as the memories of his momentous progress over the last few days danced behind his eyes. Thousands of years of waiting, and he was the one man in the family to find the proof. He had never expected to be the person to uncover the child. His family's inheritance was a great and mighty burden; and to be chosen to know the truth was an honor, one that left him breathless with awe.

"I watched her with her parents beneath the burning bush remnant. It was a perfect summer day until a storm came out of nowhere and struck them down. The lightning carried her into the bush and left the mark of the cross between her eyes."

Josephus waited to see if the archbishop had some response.

When the older man said nothing, he felt compelled to explain. "It is a Crusader Cross, just as our home."

The archbishop fell back against the cushions at the picture the young man was painting for him. His heart beat an erratic rhythm with the news of the progress made. "So your family's prophecy is true."

Josephus eyed his mentor, uneasy with his sense of awe. "There is more."

"Really?"

"I took her to the top of Moses' mountain." Josephus handed him a folder with a number of handwritten pages inside. "Here is my report."

The archbishop put the paperwork aside, wanting to hear it from his former star pupil in person. "What did she do?"

"She told the truth of Moses' work on the top of Mt. Sinai. The way he failed in his first attempt, returned, and finally succeeded. She stated there were two paths and he chose destruction. The girl spoke as if she knew the great prophet, archbishop. She might have been his friend, a relative, or even a student of the great father. It made me feel - so small - in the scheme of things."

"What was the other path for Musa?" The archbishop asked with unfeigned eagerness.

"One for which she had ample proof," Josephus professed with a smug smile.

CHAPTER SEVENTEEN

"A fool will pair an ox with an elephant."
—Ethiopian Proverb

Meggani led him with an unerring sense of purpose to the village's small school. It was located on a main street with a number of other tiny houses and shops. They paused to examine the front of the building, finding what they saw comfortable, even routine. There were over a dozen children playing in the dirt yard in front of the one-room structure. Mtho winced as he realized the kids were clothed in little more than rags. His petite companion looked at the group and frowned, "Where are all of the girls?"

"They do not go to school."

She looked at him, to the kids, and back to the monk. "Why don't girls go to school here? They do in the city." Mtho knelt at her feet; his robes spreading out around him like wings. When he reached out to catch her arms, she stepped away from him. Vibrating with unease, her eyes glazed over with the fear of being questioned, Meggani held up a hand to stop him from making contact with her body. "Please, Brother Mtho. No touching. No touching me ever." Her head fell forward as if she had carried something heavy for a long time and was no longer able to bear its weight. "I cannot take it."

Mtho hid his fists in the folds of his garment, as he considered how a girl of her years would find the slightest touch so abhorrent. The answer made him wince. Returning to the question, he tried to smile. "The girls take care of the home from the time they can walk. It is one of the first things we hope to influence. To change."

"It's not fair," she choked out.

"No, it's not." The swiftness of his agreement made her feel secure that he had made no effort to prevaricate. "Most girls of your age are married."

"That's disgusting," she whispered, "and should be your first priority."

"Yes Ma'am." As he stood up, Mtho watched uneasily as a woman, dressed in a faded colorful robe, came rushing out of the building toward them. Her eyes were narrowed with suspicion and he could see a faint tremor in her hands. "Think she's the teacher?"

Meggani shrugged. "She's bigger than I am by just a few inches. How is it even possible?"

"A side effect of the girls working so hard at such a young age. They do not get enough nutrients; so they never grow to full size."

"Serves them right," the girl muttered.

"You do not find it wrong?"

Meggani looked away from him. "Women must fight. Band together. Be strong. If they are content to accept this lot, I have no pity for them. Only judgment."

The woman came to an abrupt halt in front of them, and glanced around. She was uneasy, her body shifting in a nervous cadence with her concern. "May I help you?"

Brother Mtho tried his most sincere smile to put her at ease, "Are you Mrs. Adjani?"

"I am," she whispered, looking around once more.

He held out his hand to shake, but when she refused to take it, he withdrew the offer with an embarrassing amount of speed. "I am

Brother Mtho and this is Meggani. You sent an e-mail to the Church about a student."

Mrs. Adjani cast a concerned glance at the nearby children and moved her visitors farther from the playing school kids. "I did," she whispered.

"We came to help," Meggani interrupted loudly to try to assure her.

"Please. I do not want any trouble."

Mtho leaned back at a slight angle at the teacher's quick plea to Meggani's statement. "We just wish to help, Mrs. Adjani."

"You do not understand. The events ... they have stopped."

He bit back his retort. It was clear to him she had just told a lie. He tried his reassuring smile once more, and decided on a different tack than confrontation. "What were these events?"

"I do not think it is a problem." The teacher gave a slight forced laugh.

"Why don't you show us anyway?"

The teacher seemed to be grinding her teeth, "Well ..."

"You don't have to worry," Meggani inserted. "He's a good guy."

Mtho's eyes fell on Meggani, shocked at her compliment. He cleared his throat, unsure how to respond to the child's first sign of trust. "Thank you, Meggani." He grimaced at how unsubstantial his words seemed under the circumstances.

"I will show you," the teacher conceded. "But you must promise not to tell anyone."

"We won't." Meggani noticed Mtho's irritated expression and gave him an impish smile. "What?" she asked with false innocence.

"I could answer for myself," he commented.

"She trusts me more than you," Meggani informed him with a calm and adult look, which made him uncomfortable on a profound level.

Mtho looked at the teacher for confirmation, who nodded with a pained though amused smile. He shrugged, submitting himself to the forces surrounding him. It looked like his training as a monk was going to come in more handy than he had thought it would. First off, being his one year-long vow of silence. "Okay then."

"Why don't you follow me?" Mrs. Adjani asked, before casting a nervous look around her. It was clear she was being watched and that terrified her. Mtho hoped their answer to her request would not end up causing her more hurt than she had already experienced.

Silently, the teacher led the two of them into the single-room building. As soon as they entered it, Mtho could see what had caused so much doubt.

Problems.

Even ... fear.

It surprised him that the stark, unadorned chamber was so dismal and drab, with little to break the monotony of the brick walls and dirt floor. The back was filled with the vibrant colors of a flowering vine, heavy with ripe melons. They glowed with health and vitality. The leaves were a deep emerald, the flowers a royal purple and the melons a light amber. Its effect was of a sensual feast: soothing your eyes, nose, and making your palms itch to touch. Its light perfume made Mtho's stomach grumble at the mere thought of tasting the succulent fruit.

"Not sure I understand," Mtho stuttered.

"This is why I wrote."

"I think it's wonderful. I have never seen anything like it," Meggani observed. Her eyes had widened to saucers, as a faint smile seemed to be tugging at her lips. She moved forward to investigate the plant, and noticed something about the stalks almost right off. "Hey, it's not even growing out of the ground!" She fell to her knees to crawl around the base looking to see where it might begin and end.

"When did this start?" Mtho asked the teacher, longing to follow the girl through the dirt.

"It appeared a few weeks ago." The teacher seemed to be gaining confidence at their clear astonishment at the bounty. "Basically, a few days before I sent the email."

"You must have gone far to send it."

"I used the Internet café at the market in a nearby town."

"Do you know which child is doing it?" Mtho found himself moving closer to the foliage, the smell pulling him in like a siren to a passing sailor.

"None of my children had anything to do with it," Mrs. Adjani's mouth fell open at the thought. "All of our children are good. They would not do anything to upset things. They would not bring attention to themselves. This area has not recovered from the drought yet. Little grows here."

"Why or how did you think it started?" He tried to be as patient as possible, but inside he knew he was rolling his eyes at the woman's obtuseness.

"Most of the children here have never had much food. I told the boys to pray to God for a good crop."

"It showed up over night, didn't it?"

Adjani gazed at the girl's query with surprise, and then scowled at her. She had forgotten Meggani was even in the room. "I closed the school one day, and the next it was here. I could not understand how anyone could have brought it inside, without someone seeing."

Mtho could no longer resist the pull. He began to walk around the vine and inspect it, without daring to touch the fruit or leaves. "What does it taste like?"

"Oh, no." Mrs. Adjani's hand covered her throat. "We couldn't disturb it."

Their heads whipped around to stare at the teacher, mouths agape as their brains fluttered with shock.

"Your people are starving." His voice bit with the edge of his scorn.

"Her fear made everyone frightened of it." Meggani stood and folded her arms over her chest, in a fighting stance.

"It is a vine, growing out of nothing. It has fruit on it I have never seen," the teacher backed away from them and from their suggestion, horror on her face. She had thought they might be able to help. What she had not told them was, no matter how hard she attempted to eradicate the vine, it always returned come the new dawn.

This thing had to be evil. It was far too good to be true.

Meggani yelled, "It is food." Her eyes were wide and she bit her lip to keep her tears back. This woman's fear was keeping the other children hungry and afraid. She reminded her of everything Meggani had been fighting against for years. *This is why I am alone*, she thought. *This is why I have been shunned all my life. For all of the people who cling to misery and pain, no matter how much love was offered. She showed them the easier way to do things and they ran away from her for it.*

"She is not your parents, Meggani."

"No," the girl stared at him, blinking back her tears. "She's worse."

Meggani turned away and looked out the window, in silence.

"I told you I don't want any problems." The teacher held up her hands, her eyes beseeching the monk.

"You'll want to bring us the boys so we can talk to them."

"Why?" She teacher asked, the word sharp, her breath coming in slight pants.

Brother Mtho took a deep breath, as he tried in desperation to reason with the woman. "Whoever did this will eventually do something else. Obviously one of your students needs to consider coming with us. The next time, you might not be able to hide their abilities from the rest of the town as you did with this."

Mrs. Adjani shook her head in denial, "Who are you?"

"We are from a new school affiliated with the Church."

"Oh. Well I am afraid none of our student's parents' would be able to afford-"

"There is no cost."

"I'm hungry."

Meggani bellowed the two-word statement; making both adults stop and stare at her. She strutted over to the vine and plucked one of the melons from the plant. Sprawling on the ground, she pulled a knife out of her pocket and cut the thin-skinned fruit into slices. She bit into the piece with gusto, the juice turned her chin shiny, and enjoyed the revulsion crossing the teacher's face. Her satiated sigh made both adults' stomachs growl in protest at being left out. "Want some?" she offered them, not bothering to hide her smirk.

The brother recognized the challenge when he saw one, and he refused to let the girl down when it was clear he had been making considerable progress with her. No small feat with this soul. "I could take a taste."

As he moved to take the segment from Meggani's fingers, Mrs. Adjani backed her way out of the room, her eyes glassy with terror. Mtho doubted she even knew she was shaking her head, as if to convince herself not to succumb to the lure of the succulent fruit. "I'll send the children in, one at a time," she whispered, before fleeing.

"Her loss," Meggani shrugged.

Mtho laughed at the way the juice was staining her chin. The food was delicious; he would have to work hard to make sure he ate with more care than his companion. This was a difficult task. The magical melon brought to mind all the tastes of childhood: joy, freedom, and unlimited amounts of unconditional love. "It is her loss. Let's make sure we do not lose the child we seek this day."

CHAPTER EIGHTEEN

"Restless feet may walk into a snake pit."
—Ethiopian Proverb

The tea had gone cold, and the small sandwiches and cakes were nothing more than crumbs by the time Josephus had finished his tale. He was careful as he set his cup and saucer on the table, hoping to avoid damaging the fragile porcelain. Josephus loved and respected his mentor. He just didn't wish to think about the disparity between how the archbishop lived and how the rest of his Church eked out an existence. Preaching in Ethiopia did not bring riches. Starvation, while you ministered to the masses, was quite a common occurrence. He knew of brothers who could not imagine this setting, much less experience it. No, wealth and privilege were not evident being Church leader in their homeland. Josephus knew it had always been Church policy that priests who dwelled outside their country generated their own income and saw to their own comfort. At home, there were no funds.

Apparently, this was not true in Jerusalem.

"So you left the guide on the mountain?" The archbishop stirred his tea, his face vague with supposition of Josephus's story.

"I would not interrupt his prayers."

"You realize, the chances are he will never leave his vigil."

Josephus's gaze narrowed with suspicion, "I felt it was the right thing to do."

"It was," he assured the younger man with haste. "We do not pass judgment on others' paths."

"This was why I left him."

"It is a pity," the archbishop muttered. "He would make excellent evidence."

"Why would I need evidence?" Josephus asked, his gaze sharp as he stared at his mentor.

"If we are to prove to the world the girl is all we believe her to be, we will need much more than evidence. Irrefutable proof comes to mind."

Josephus shuddered inside at the archbishop's words. How could he think such a thing, much less say it? *Baba*, he pleaded in his heart, *why doesn't he understand? We mean nothing now. Our way is gone. Respect and deference for the males of the species must be put aside to venerate those with the talent to help us.*

Help me, Baba.

Make me wise enough. Strong enough.

Good enough.

Do not allow me to be swayed from this course. I may be the breaker of vows. I will not be the one to break my Baba's heart.

"The girl's abilities will help our country, archbishop. She is not a sideshow to be paraded about. She is a person. I have taken her care as a personal crusade. I will not have her exploited in any shape or form."

"Of course not, Josephus." The archbishop patted his arm, trying to console him.

"I will protect this girl."

"We both will," the archbishop touched his arm once more, while looking off into the future.

Josephus shifted with unease. His movements made the archbishop turn levelly to meet his eyes. "I warn you, archbishop." Josephus's tone was filled with a quiet resolve. "I took the child to the embassy, and she begged me to keep her close. I checked with the hospital and they feel she needs care and safety. I feel a deep need to see to this child's welfare … a need that easily eclipses any and all of my previous promises."

"Duly noted." The archbishop's instant acquiescing seemed to calm Josephus' misgivings. The priest would not have been so content had he been able to see the older man's eyes and the continued scheming in their depths. The archbishop might have acknowledged Josephus's right to protect the girl, but he was still determined to use the child as he saw fit.

A child who could save a country could do much more, though, for his personal ambitions. And that was something to consider, carefully, indeed.

CHAPTER NINETEEN

"The fool speaks; the wise man listens."
—Ethiopian Proverb

As the still-nervous teacher ushered the last child out, Brother Mtho could not help sharing Meggani's deep sigh of frustration. The bad news was they were getting nowhere with undue speed. The good news was the fruit was everything they could have dreamed of. His aching knees no longer hurt. Their stomachs were crammed with the succulent melon. Mtho was surprised to realize a few pieces filled him. In fact – he was stuffed. He felt as if he had just eaten a ten-course meal. It meant the harvest of a small portion of the vine would feed the entire village, even providing them some leftovers. This word amused him. It was an American invention. No other country had such providence and abundance.

"Well, what a waste."

Mtho chuckled at Meggani's muttered statement. "The children denying it ... I suppose it should not surprise us."

"Especially after the teacher's narrow-mindedness."

"Have compassion, child."

"Why?"

"Because it is the right thing to do," Mtho lectured.

Meggani snorted at his admonishment. "I'll try to remember."

"Speaking of which," Mtho began with a delicacy he found uncomfortable. He was groping his way, blind and inept. What did he know about females of the species? He didn't even have sisters. He wished to provide her with succor, but any physical overtures would be misread. The ideal of jeopardizing the new trust they were building terrified him. "We should discuss the knife."

"Father Mtho, why don't you just forget about the blade? I find it comes in handy."

"I will keep you safe," he snapped.

"Seems to me I'm more capable of protecting you."

Mtho released a heavy sigh, not willing to admit she was right, but just as much unwilling to patronize. The sound of the students playing outside drew Mtho to the window. "What shall we do?"

"You know what they say, when you can't interrogate them … " Meggani's voice was soft with her musing. "Join them."

It only took a few minutes of watching the students playing before Meggani was invited to join in. Mtho was surprised at how easily she was accepted into their midst, but he supposed that was normal. Kids are most comfortable with others of their kind. Meggani seemed to have the ability to fit in no matter what the situation. He guessed from their activity they were playing some form of dodge ball, with a much-repaired ball he was positive was older than he was.

Joining them outside, Mtho stayed back from the throng. He was determined not to hinder Meggani's progress in any way. It was much too beautiful a day to stay shut indoors. The breeze blew and lessened the oppressive smell of decay. He found it easier to find joy in the moment with his stomach full.

As Mrs. Adjani moved to confer with him, Mtho noticed two of the smaller boys take Meggani aside and begin to speak with her.

When she cast a triumphant glance at him, he knew she found

what they needed. Meggani had far more magic in her than she realized. It was a good thing. As her new friends gestured down a nearby street, Meggani nodded her head with eager understanding; Mtho laughed out loud as his charge began to glow.

Meggani's magic was a very good thing indeed.

CHAPTER TWENTY

"God conceals himself from man's mind, but reveals all to his heart."
—African Proverb

J erusalem is roughly the size of Paris, with three times the amount of people crammed into its borders. The number of hotels, motels, inns, plus rooming houses and bed and breakfasts filled books. If it had not been for the archbishop's direction, Josephus was sure he would have despaired of ever finding a proper place for him and the girl to live. That said, it did not mean arriving at the address passed to him did not have its own set of surprises.

A woman opened the door.

Mrs. Shapiro had been a shock to him. She came up to his armpit; her body was slender as a young tree. The first thing he learned was, it's impossible not to smile in her presence. The second thing he understood was it was even more impossible not to eat when she was near. She was always putting something into the oven, taking something out ... or planning on shopping to make more. Her house was small, even by Jerusalem's standards, but it smelled of apple strudel: a tantalizing combination of apples, spice, and warmth. The Jewish widow had opened her home, hearth, and heart to the two of them.

It was a much better situation than any he could have imagined.

Returning from his audience with the archbishop, Josephus gave the widow a warm smile as he entered the kitchen. As ever, Mrs. Shapiro was meticulous in her cleaning, the metal counters shining with the love the old lady put into everything she did. He watched her for a moment as she mixed her stew and hummed a lullaby.

"How is the girl?" he kept his voice soft, concerned he might startle her.

"Your child's fine, Father." The woman flitted around him like the small bird she resembled. Before he could say a word, she had poured him a cup of tea and served a piece of pound cake. "Just fine," she continued. "I put her down in front of the television just a little while ago."

"Why the television?"

"She seems to like soccer games."

Josephus nodded his head, "We noticed this, yesterday."

Mrs. Shapiro chuckled at his disgruntled tone. "Why not ask me, Father, what is on your mind."

"Has she changed?"

"Still the same. Poor little mite." Mrs. Shapiro poured herself a cup of tea and sat at the table, pausing to drink when she saw Josephus was still standing.

He sat, at her pointed look.

Mrs. Shapiro had the ability to make him feel like a young child. "I did get her to eat, though." When the priest began to nibble at the cake she'd served, she smiled with triumph. He was much too skinny. She was determined to put some more meat on his bones.

"She eats when food is put before her. Drinks when liquids are given her. Her body works fine … it just seems to be on autopilot. I was hoping she'd given you some other sign of life."

"I still think she smiles at the soccer."

"Are you sure," Josephus pressed. "Not one other sign?"

The woman shook her head, saddened at the child's

unresponsiveness. "Not a one. I am surprised the doctors at the hospital couldn't do more to help."

"Her psychologist advised me, when a child suffers a trauma it is best to keep her safe and fed. Let her mind fix itself on its own time. In its own way."

"Nice Jewish doctor," Mrs. Shapiro reminded him, "she would know."

Josephus sighed and sipped his tea. "She assured me the mind has a wonderful ability to heal itself. The woman kept saying children are marvelously resilient in the repair of their bodies and minds. I couldn't help wondering if this were true ... why are there so many broken adults?"

"Have faith, Father." When he gazed at her with raised eyebrows, Mrs. Shapiro chuckled. "Look at what I am saying, 'have faith,' to a priest. You are supposed to remind me of this. She's a good girl, the little one. Give her some more time. I am sure she will return to you, sooner or later."

"At least the burn mark is healing."

"The salve they gave you is working well. I should suggest it to my daughter-in-law for her stretch marks."

Josephus pushed his tea and plate away. "I appreciate you watching her."

"Of course," she patted his hand. "You two are the easiest boarders I have ever had."

"It must be strange to you to have a priest here."

Mrs. Shapiro laughed. "Not in the slightest. Anything I can do to help, you just let me know."

"Well, actually ..." Josephus took a deep breath. He silently wished Kwai were with him. He tended to have a better way of charming people. "I was hoping you would be interested in taking a little drive."

The old woman laughed at the sparkle in his eyes. "How little?"

"Not far," he hedged.

"So said Moses to the Israelites, on the way out of Egypt."

"You have no idea," he muttered.

CHAPTER TWENTY-ONE

I t took three security checkpoints and over an hour of steady driving for them to clear the stifling confines of Jerusalem. Josephus had been thrilled when he had managed to convince Mrs. Shapiro to go out with him and the girl on the sunny day. It had also meant he did not need to rent an automobile, for she had insisted they use her little compact hybrid. He had not been sure how difficult it would be to travel to the vineyard on the far reaches of the Israeli border. Josephus was sure it would go faster with an Israeli resident with the appropriate papers by his side. The old woman turned out to be a gift from heaven when dealing with the nervous guards.

She rejoiced in mothering everyone she met.

They pulled up to the front of the house on a slight hill. He thought it was promising that the architecture appeared as old as time itself. For this to work, he had to find the right home where the Ark was kept while King David tried to decide if it was safe to bring it to Jerusalem. Josephus stretched as he exited the vehicle. The view, as far as he could see, was of emerald fields of vines covered with ripe jewel-like grapes. They glistened in the sun, swaying in the slight breeze. The thick sweet scent of the fruit filled his nose and made his stomach grumble.

Mrs. Shapiro was busy clucking over the girl strapped into a car seat in back. "I don't understand Father. Why are we here?" She pulled out a wet nap and used it to cool the child's perspiring face.

He leaned against the door as he waited for her to finish. "It is my job to go to each of the sites where the Ark of the Covenant was held." He gestured to the ancient house that showed little work had been done on it to bring up to modern standards. Whoever lived here obviously had an appreciation for architectural integrity, or no available money for the little modern conveniences most took for granted. "I believe this is one of them."

"When did this start?"

Seeing she was done, he waited for her to step away. "I began at Mount Sinai."

"I still don't understand why we are here."

Josephus leaned in and unbuckled the girl. "When the Temple was built, King David hesitated to bring the Ark into his new city. He kept it for a while in a house belonging to a man named Obed-edom."

"This house is here?"

"I believe it is." He lifted the girl in his arms and extracted her from the vehicle, taking care not to bump her head. Since she could not talk, it was always foremost in his mind how she could not communicate any pain or hurt she suffered. They were careful to the extreme not to inflict any on her through inattention.

"Why am I here?"

He gazed at her, unsure if he was about to offend. "I thought, since the owners are Jewish ..."

Mrs. Shapiro's walk was buoyant as they moved to the front door. "And we all stick together ..."

"Not what I meant."

She gave a girlish giggle belying her age, but made clear her amusement at his discomfort. "I am not offended, Father." Without another word she knocked on the plain wooden planks of the portal with bold confidence. "After all, it's usually true."

A tiny woman wrenched open the door. She could have been related to Mrs. Shapiro, based on size, though not on mien. Her frown was so fierce, Josephus and the widow gulped. She had short, white curly hair, and wore a sheepskin vest. The combination made her look like a lamb to Josephus, and he resisted the urge to glance around for her shepherd. Mrs. Shapiro spoke to her in a few short sentences he guessed was Yiddish.

She gave him a sorrowful shake of her head. "I do not think this will be easy," Mrs. Shapiro confessed.

"I can't believe she won't let us in."

Mrs. Shapiro snorted. "She won't even offer us a drink or a nosh."

"What is it with your people and food?"

"About the same thing it is with your people and guilt."

"Here I thought your people enjoyed their guilt as well," Josephus quipped.

"Only to our sons."

Josephus, considering, looked at the owner. "Would the fact we are helping the girl lend authority to your argument?"

"Not likely," Mrs. Shapiro turned back to the house tyrant, as she now thought of her. *The nerve*, she thought to herself, *to show such a lack of hospitality. What kind of Jew was this woman? Not a good one.*

They exchanged a series of sentences in one of the few languages Josephus did not know. He could detect a few German-based words, but the majority went over his head. When she was done, the door was shut on them, without the merest smile crossing the homeowner's face.

"What now?"

Mrs. Shapiro was surprised at the priest's defeated attitude. "Surely you didn't think every door would open right away for you?" When she clearly saw the guilt in Josephus's eyes, she laughed. "She won't let us in, but suggests we look at the next hill. There are ruins she believes are the original homestead."

"I guess we're not in the right place?"

"Since the door just shut on us, I would guess so."

The two of them took the brief walk to the ruins. Josephus tried to hide his disappointment that the child never responded to the place in any form.

He tried putting her down on the ground.

Nothing.

Josephus uncovered her feet and moved them in the rich loamy earth.

Still nothing.

He even managed to feed her some grapes fresh off of the vines.

No response.

Mrs. Shapiro kept silent as they returned to the car. The adults were as quiet as the child. She realized she wanted to say something to take the defeated look out of the kind father's face. It was such a sad contrast to the happy light she usually saw. How do you guide a man whose life is dedicated to helping others? "Well, a waste of time."

"Half the places I take her to she has no reaction." Josephus hid his expression by making sure his charge was buckled in tightly.

"What will you do next?" Mrs. Shapiro asked after they were both secured inside.

"The one thing I did not wish to. I fear we have no choice now." Josephus began to drive them back to the city.

"Is it dangerous?"

"Very."

"Do you have a choice?"

"I do not think I do." Josephus shook his head as he kept his eyes glued to the road. "It is why I left it for last. After we take this step we will need to leave the city right away. I hope you will not mind if we depart earlier than expected."

"Of course not. There is always someone else who needs a home."

He glanced at her to share his smile, "And you are more than willing to provide it. We will miss you when we go."

"I should hope so. I shall also miss you both." She checked on the girl and sighed, "I never did have any daughters, much to my husband's and my regret." Mrs. Shapiro moved in her seat so she could speak with him face-to-face. "How will you travel with her? She has no papers."

"Papers can be found, or, made."

"You jeopardize a great deal, Father."

"For my country, it is worth it." His voice came with the fierce reverence of a prayer.

"What of the girl?"

"I would gladly give my life to keep her safe."

Mrs. Shapiro nodded. "But then, who would protect her?"

"God protects us all," Josephus preached.

Mrs. Shapiro grunted. "Take it from an old Israeli; God appreciates it when his children protect each other. So what else can I do?"

"I noticed you have some boys' things in my room. I could use your assistance getting the child ready for something special.

"More special than today?"

He shifted around in his seat as he drove the car, uncomfortable with the question. "Special is a word I use loosely."

She was left speechless by his next words. The widow was a good woman who could see the kindness in the priest's gaze with the ken that age and experience brought. Earned wisdom was a blessing. She was not happy about this request. It was difficult to hide her unease, even horror. The priest did not know what he risked. He was jeopardizing the child and his own future. The father was not a resident of this chaotic city. Josephus could not conceive at how much danger he was dancing this small precious soul into.

How little help he would receive should they be caught.

Nothing she said could persuade him from this course.

It took a week to get ready. Mrs. Shapiro wanted to argue with him, but forced herself to hold back; a new experience for the old woman. Still, Father Josephus could feel her displeasure like a weighted cloak on his soul.

The chosen night, Mrs. Shapiro had Josephus waiting in the living room, when she carried the girl in with a triumphant grin. A job done was worth doing right, even if you did not approve. The little body she held close to her heart wore boy's clothes. The ripped jeans and denim shirt were remnants from her own sons childhood wardrobes; the faded cotton plaid shirt she put over the outfit was from her grown grandson.

Mrs. Shapiro had asked Father Josephus to say a special prayer, for the boy had just started in the army. He had managed to hide his shock that she would ask someone not Jewish, but she had just made a quip about every little bit helping.

"What do you think, Father? I was sure my boys' clothes would be perfect."

Josephus judged the girl in silence for a few moments, trying to see her from a stranger's point of view. "I have an idea," he brightened a great deal at his brainstorm. Turning to the fireplace, Josephus pulled the saucer from under one of the kind woman's houseplants and mixed a paste of dirt and ash. "This should be a perfect mask for her features." He smeared the concoction over her cheeks and chin with gentle fingers.

"Are you sure about this?" Mrs. Shapiro gave a nervous swallow over what he was doing to the girl. "She's not even conscious. What if she catches something?"

"From a little dirt? Not possible," Josephus scoffed.

"I don't know, Father," Mrs. Shapiro bit her lower lip with worry. "I wish we could be sure she isn't hurting."

"The archbishop warned me it would be easier if people assume the child is a boy."

Silence stretched between them, like a tightrope.

Mrs. Shapiro burst out first. "The Arabs take the place very seriously, Father." Mrs. Shapiro warned, "Be sure about what you are doing. They will never forgive you. It is a sacred thing."

"Yes," Josephus remembered the lectures the archbishop had given him before leaving his office. The message was clear: should he be caught, he was on his own. Again.

"Everyone seems to be as terrified as you are of them." Making a few additional swipes of the mixture on the little one's face, he nodded with satisfaction. Turning her to the widow he waited for a comment, and when none was forthcoming he decided to push for confirmation of what he suspected. "What do you think?"

Mrs. Shapiro released a pent up sigh, recognizing she wouldn't turn him from this path. "He looks fine," she offered.

"Exactly," Josephus glowed. When the woman looked at him her eyebrows raised for additional impact, he explained his triumph. "You said HE looks fine."

"You be careful, Father. This is a dangerous time to commit sacrilege."

"Any time is a bad time to commit sacrilege."

Mrs. Shapiro chuckled, "Yes, but right now you will not have to wait for God's revenge."

"God will protect us," he gave her his soft assurance with complete confidence.

"Sometimes God expects us to protect ourselves," her pragmatic tone made his smile grow.

"Yes," Josephus nodded. "But you forget I have the blessed one with me."

"This sweet child is many things, but blessed does not seem to be one of them," the widow observed with wry honesty, knowing the priest was no longer listening to a thing she said. Mrs. Shapiro added a small silent prayer of her own for this unusual duo.

After all, God liked to watch out for fools and children.

She just wasn't sure if the priest qualified for one or both of those categories.

CHAPTER TWENTY-TWO

"To one who does not know, a small garden is a forest."
—Ethiopian Proverb

The sun was starting to seek its own home when Meggani stopped playing with the children and returned to Mtho's side. He understood her instinct to avoid abandoning her new friends and returning to their quest. Mtho had liked watching her with the group of kids. It was the first time he had seen her interact with other people her own age; he was overjoyed that the shadows haunting her eyes had lightened.

Just a little bit, but it was a break in the stormy night that filled her gaze.

"Ok Sherlock, what did you find out?"

"Who?" Meggani frowned.

"At least I know where to start your education," Mtho muttered.

Meggani sighed, with the universal weariness that all children felt when adults spoke about things they didn't understand. "I don't think the boy who did it comprehends what he did or how he did it. I am guessing he is real little."

"How do you know it was a boy?"

"You said it was only boys who are educated. Besides, the teacher was easy to read."

"The boys aren't?"

Meggani gave a slight smile, "They all know the responsibility for the family will be theirs one day. They know their father's way is dying. Even the youngest ones are worried about what they will do."

"I can see how that would make things hard."

"The ridiculous teacher should make them embrace new possibilities." Her voice was bitter with the lessons of a far older soul as her eyes grew dark again.

"Meggani, if someone had tried to make your parents see your abilities as good … would it have worked?"

"It would have been nice had they tried."

Mtho faltered as he sought a way to ease her pain. She just stood there, kicking at the dirt with her precious shoes. He realized some things were beyond his capability.

He prayed time and the school would help.

"Enough talking about the past, we are here to find the future." Meggani stood up and tugged impatiently on Mtho's robe. "Let's go find him."

As they walked through the serpentine streets of the village, curving around in a pattern creating multiple dead ends and blind turns, Meggani didn't know what she wanted to do more. Watch Brother Mtho or look for the boy. Mtho seemed to be studying everything around them. Ground. Sky. Buildings. Walls and pathways. Even the meager straggling weeds dotting their path did not escape his intense scrutiny.

"I don't get it. You knew how to recognize me. Why is finding this boy so difficult for you? Shouldn't you just be able to know with one glance?"

"We were instructed the first child would be found in the city. Peter and I visited many orphanages before we found you at Mr. Hods."

"Don't you know how to uncover the others?"

"The prophecy just said there would be signs."

Meggani chuckled, a sound she was only beginning to grow accustomed to. "The prophecy didn't know Ethiopia well. Or at least not the way the country is now. There are barely any roads, much less signs."

A few houses down, Meggani spotted a child about her age, leaning against a rock fence and watching them with a wary despair. "I don't see signs," she mock whispered to him, "but I do see a boy." She rushed over to him with Mtho trailing behind. Meggani tried to hide how determined she was to prove her usefulness, but she guessed she had already tipped her hand. "You're Rohan aren't you?"

"Yeah. You've got a great hook for the game." Rohan scuffed at the ground.

She beamed with pride, "You should see me play cricket."

"What's cricket?"

Mtho moved to stand beside Meggani and smile at the youth. He hid his shock at the boy's age. He had been told they were looking for children under seven. This child was closer to ten. "Hello Rohan. I'm Brother Mtho."

"Are you here for me?"

"What do you mean?"

"I heard the other kids saying you are here because of the vine in the schoolroom."

"Whoever did it may like to go to a special school we are starting. It would not cost their parents anything and the child would be able to explore his abilities without fear."

"The more I hang with him, the more I can do." Meggani smiled at the boy trying to prove her helpfulness.

Mtho whirled toward her. "I didn't know this."

"No offense, Father," Meggani muttered, "but what you don't know, is a lot."

"When do I need to leave?" Rohan interrupted.

Meggani turned to Rohan a dawning look on her face, and then her eyes narrowed with suspicion. She masked her reaction before the males in the room noticed her. Something didn't feel right.

She just didn't know what it was.

"Rohan, why don't you show me what it is you can do?" Mtho's gentle question was phrased so he wouldn't scare the boy.

The lad led them into his house. They each paused and took off their shoes. Meggani grimaced as she did, though. She hated even getting her socks dirty now. They had shining stones in the cuffs that twinkled like the stars.

Rohan's house was what she expected. It was one room, similar in style and structure to the schoolroom. Meggani noticed the chamber was small with a low loft above the living area. There was a simple hearth, a large bed in the corner, a table with several chairs set around it, and a dirt floor. In one corner she saw a curtained alcove where Rohan took Mtho and Meggani. Pulling back the fabric, dust blew into the sunbeams dancing like whirling dervishes. Rohan revealed a small plot of growing plants. "Does this count?"

Meggani looked up, and through the slats of the loft she could see a small face peering down at them.

"Would you like to go to the school?" Mtho walked over to the indoor Eden as he cradled one of the fruits from the plants.

Meggani clenched her jaw as she stared at the boy.

"No," the boy answered honestly. He shrugged, "but if you are going to make me, anyway ..."

Mtho sputtered, protesting, "I would never make you do anything."

Looking up at the small face still smiling at her through the gaps in the wood, Meggani began to connect what was going on. She smiled at the little one above her. Focusing on the argument happening in front of her, she noticed Mtho's face resembled a thundercloud over the mountains in the rainy season.

"The teacher said you would take us away, one way or another," Rohan cried.

Mtho whispered to Meggani, "I should have listened to you about her being trouble."

"Our parents are good people. They work hard." Rohan crossed his arms over his chest and clenched his jaw.

The girl felt her blood began to boil. Even she knew you shouldn't lie to a religious man.

"I am sure they do, child." Mtho spoke in a soothing tone to placate the boy.

Rohan turned away.

"Stop it," she bellowed, at the one she was now sure was an imposter.

"Meggani?" Mtho reached out to her and, remembering her dislike of contact, retracted it and stepped away from her.

"Stop lying to us."

Brother Mtho was stuck looking between them, trying to understand what exactly he had missed.

"What do you know?" Rohan asked her.

"I know you're not the one we seek," she spat.

"No you don't."

"You think you're protecting him."

Rohan ground out through his teeth, "He's my little brother. I'm supposed to."

"We won't hurt him." Meggani released a deep breath, as she tried reason. "Staying here will."

"Explain. What do you mean?"

Meggani pulled a handful of colored marbles from her pocket and tossed them into the air. She closed her eyes and focused to make the stones freeze in the air and then circle her in a kind of dance.

They made several passes before she recalled them to her hand. "How do you think I can hook the ball when I throw it?"

He scowled at the stones. "That's cheating."

A small boy's voice pierced the silence, building as Rohan and Meggani continued their standoff. "No more, Ro."

Scratching sounds of a toddler scrambling down a ladder were easy for them to hear. When the hiding child came forward, neither Mtho nor Meggani could conceal their smiles. He was dressed in what they guessed was his father's shirt, hanging straight to the floor, hiding his hands. "They good," the child exclaimed, standing proudly in front of Mtho and Meggani, to peer up at his older sibling.

Rohan tried to push the boy behind him, "I told you," he spoke under his voice. "They're gonna take you away."

"To a good place, not a bad one."

Brother Mtho squatted down so he wouldn't tower over the children anymore. "Hello. We didn't get to meet at school. My name is Brother Mtho, and this is my friend Meggani."

"Me, Jake." The child beamed as he pointed at himself with his thumb.

"Jake? What kind of name is Jake?"

"It's not the name our parents gave him." Rohan answered Meggani, scowling over the entire situation. "It's the name he calls himself."

"I'm betting it stands for Jakaranti." Mtho explained, smiling at the lad.

"That's me!" the child crowed.

Rohan grabbed Jake and shoved him behind his quaking body. "Ignore him. He doesn't know what he's saying."

Mtho's eyes shone with empathy for Rohan's fear. "I think we need to speak with your parents."

"They won't be back until late. They are looking for work."

Jake evaded Rohan's grasp and moved to Meggani with an entreating smile. "Show more," he demanded, before poking at the pocket where Meggani had placed the marbles.

Mtho interrupted before Rohan objected. "Jake, why don't you show us more of what you can do?"

"Promised Ro not to."

Meggani jabbed Rohan in the shoulder. "Tell him it's okay."

"The reason my folks can't get work is because everyone is frightened of him."

She shrugged, "They're stupid."

"Doesn't change the problem, Meggani." Mtho eyed the three kids trying to find a solution. There hadn't been any classes in his seminary on how to resolve differences between two reincarnated angels and one protective boy.

"Jake, I liked your melon vine." Meggani informed him, ignoring the two others.

The boy beamed at the compliment, "Want more?"

"Jake … No." Rohan pleaded with his brother.

"Hungry."

Rohan fell to his knees to stare at Jake. "Me too, but you can't do it."

"Hungry," Jake repeated.

"I'm hungry too, Jake." Meggani added, ignoring Mtho's smirking at her blatant truth stretching.

"Rohan, what if I promise to give your folks work?"

"How can you do that?" Rohan asked suspiciously.

"The school we wish to invite Jake to attend is large, and in need of staff. I am sure we could find something both your parents would like to do. That way we could keep your family together." Mtho beamed at his ability to resolve the situation with such ease and equanimity.

Rohan scuffed at the floor with the big toe of his right foot. "It's important we stay together."

"You and Jake would get a great education."

Rohan turned to Meggani and studied her deeply. "Do you promise?"

"For a priest and a grown-up, he's not bad."

Jake returned to his brother's side and took his hand. There was no need for words. As Rohan looked down at him, it was clear to Mtho and Meggani just how the two were connected on a deep level. Mtho realized in the end, the two boys, and not the parents, would decide the course the family took.

The conversation continued in flashes between the boys' eyes.

Rohan gazed at the newcomers and gave them an unsure nod.

"Go ahead and show 'em, Jake."

Jake proudly led his brother, Mtho, and Meggani out of the house and to the family's small garden plot. There was no sign of life. The few bits of plant life they could see were withered and brown. What should have been a parcel of soil, a deep rich brown, was nothing more than a bit of sand.

The idea of anything growing here was absurd.

Rohan directed them each to sit on the small stone fence surrounding the garden. Once they were out of the way and safe, Jake lay down in the dirt.

"What is he doing?" Meggani's whisper earned her a glower from Rohan.

He pointed to his brother, who was smiling at the soil. "Watch."

Jake began to croon to the earth with a light song. They could only make out some of his words as the chanting reached them. "Come out. Come on. Come to me."

The patch of earth began to move as if there were thousands of bugs planning a sudden exodus. Shoots of fresh green plants began to grow, bursting from underneath, and into the air. They continued to move and increase, until the plot was filled with ripe and succulent fruits and vegetables.

"See?" Jake ran his hands over the leaves and buds as if welcoming them. "Friends."

"Do you children know the stories of Jakaranti? He was one of our country's most beloved protectors. It was said that as he walked, plants would grow in his footsteps, for his energy was pure goodness." Mtho reached out a hand to touch the leaves as Jake did. He was not welcoming friends. He needed to ensure his eyes were seeing something his hands could feel.

He needed to know it was real.

"Jakaranti … Me!" Jake pointed at himself with his thumb once more.

Mtho smiled. "I believe you Jake. More importantly, I believe in you."

"Now you've got to come to the school." Meggani could not resist gloating to Rohan. He deserved it. He was after all, a boy.

CHAPTER TWENTY-THREE

"If you offend, ask for pardon; if offended, forgive."
—Ethiopian Proverb

The golden gleam from the Dome of the Rock shone over the despair surrounding it, like the spring sun after a long hard winter. It did not matter if it were day or night, good weather or bad, war or peace. The Dome was a constant reminder of the power of faith. It was the hope of a better tomorrow, and a gift from a long gone cherished yesterday. Built by Caliph Abd al-Malik ibn Marwan, he had intended the structure to be used as a shrine for pilgrims. The narrow lane leading to the holy place was lined with lush and leafy trees, a present from a long ago king.

Between the gifts of the caliph and a king, were the armed guards and tanks that kept the peace - or maintained the war, depending on the side of the Jordan you were born into. It was a pitiful statement of the human race that one family could cause so much pain in the pursuit of glory for ostensibly the same God.

And that is what they are. Islam, Christian, and Jew … distant cousins all.

Father Josephus was standing by one of those trees, watching as the men returned from their final prayers for the day. He held the girl in his arms, in her disguise designed by Mrs. Shapiro. He hid his smile; he was a priest, holding a girl of unknown origins, disguised by a Jew, about to enter one of the holiest Islamic sites in the world.

Who said missions of faith were boring?

The archbishop had promised him he would be met by a contact at the end of the last call for the day. He noticed a small Muslim man in his late seventies coming toward him. The older man had zeroed in on him like a torpedo. So much for subterfuge, he thought to himself. Subtlety was not in this man's vocabulary.

His contact was a wizened, robed character, with the eyes of a rodent. He reeked of garlic and roasted lamb. Josephus pulled the girl closer to his heart, unwilling to let anything happen to her.

"I am Daoud," the man informed Josephus with a sibilant whisper. He watched the priest with clear unease, as he furtively glanced at the passing worshippers. It was obvious this man was nervous, both about being seen and seeing. "You are the one?"

Josephus juggled the child in his arms. "I am."

"We must wait until dark, so the Mosque is clear." He shifted away from the other worshippers, his eyes darting around in his head. "No one can see us entering the shrine so late."

"Understood."

Daoud glanced nervously at Josephus's bundle. "The boy. He is sick?"

"Yes. It is why I seek a healing at the holy site."

"It is odd … a priest turning to Islam."

Josephus juggled the girl a little, holding her closer. "This child deserves my seeking God wherever I must." The archbishop had provided the answer to give a plausible explanation for the subterfuge and nature of their late night visit.

"Yes." Daoud touched the little bit of the girl's hair lying across her forehead. "My son died in a bombing."

"I am sorry for your pain and your loss."

"A priest showing concern for a Muslim? This has never happened before."

Josephus smiled grimly. "I've never done well with the word never."

"How I wish this was true of us all." Daoud turned and began to lead the pair toward the Dome.

CHAPTER TWENTY-FOUR

"What is inflated too much will burst into fragments." –Ethiopian
Proverb

Cardinal Robeson's favorite time of day was sunset, when the city grew quiet with prayers. Peace; a pause in the pulsing life and hatred, baked into the stones and people that made up this spot on the map. It was as if the entire population held its breath at the same time to listen to the holy men of the city. Robeson even liked the calls of the muezzin, echoing over the rooftops. This was also when his office became deserted, most of his staff off seeing to their own needs. It was during these hours, he chose to meet with the people he was not comfortable being seen with.

He was sitting at his desk, tapping his fingers against a folder as he watched the amber glory of the ending day. A brief knock, and a man entered without waiting for permission. Michael Allen was in his early twenties, and known to him since the moment he had entered this world. He shut the door behind him, and knelt before the cardinal to kiss his ring with reverence. "Your grace."

"Rise, Michael. I do not require such formality."

"A pleasure, your grace."

"I have a job for you."

Michael hid his smile, which would betray his eagerness to be of use. "Of course."

"There is a priest from Ethiopia I wish you to watch."

Michael shrugged as he sat in the chair beside the desk. "Just to watch?"

"This priest is seeking something, something I cannot permit him to find." Robeson hid his anger. He could not get the Ethiopians to clean up their own mess. They would not face the truth or deal with the responsibility. He would have to do it for them.

"So, if he finds it, I should take it?"

"And make sure he never is able to tell anyone of his find again." The cardinal waited to make sure the supplicant understood exactly what he was asking of him.

In silence, they reached an understanding.

Michael sat forward. "What does he seek?"

The cardinal contemplated spelling out the details in the report he held. He had had another contact steal it from the Ethiopian Church office earlier. Robeson decided the intricate nuances involved with finding the Ark would be far beyond his personal henchman's capabilities. He decided to share the lighter points of the tale. "Have you ever heard of the Queen of Sheba?"

CHAPTER TWENTY-FIVE

"Move your neck according to the music."
—Oromo tribe of Ethiopia

The simple majesty of the location called the Dome of the Rock is moving in a way no cathedral or synagogue has ever achieved. This place was different from all of his other experiences. There was a palpable sense of holiness. *Baba*, he thought, *can you feel it? Are you here?* The most contested building in Christendom gives off an atmosphere of peace and tranquility. Its golden color seemed to represent hope to a world frozen in fear.

Josephus had been shocked at how easily the archbishop had set up this meeting. He must be wary of his former mentor's unchecked ambition.

Looking down at the girl in his arms, he swore again to protect her.

From everyone. And everything.

The guide had met him in the assigned place, taken his bribe with a hissing whisper, and had scurried off to make sure the way was clear.

Daoud carefully checked around the building to make sure it was deserted before leading Josephus and the child inside. He was always alert when he committed sacrilege. It was the irony of his sense of faith, and the only possible relief to his empty pocket. "I apologize for my caution," he informed the priest, "but it is for our security. Not many would understand."

"I would appreciate a moment alone." Josephus stood by the side of the room, clinging to the shadows, hesitant to meet Daoud's eyes and reveal his dishonesty.

Breaking someone else's religion's rules gave Josephus pause. He did not want to do this. He just saw no other choice. His gut roiled with his apprehension over this course. This break in a belief of Islam was not a sin to him, but it would be to others. He prayed he would not regret this. Josephus kept having to push away his concern.

And Mrs. Shapiro's dire projections.

"It is important I speak with the others who attend. I will be back, though."

Josephus moved to the center of the walkway ringing around the large room, looking at the high fence guarding the center stone with interest. "When you return, please do not interfere with what I am doing."

His stare was hard, tone threatening. "No matter what you may witness."

"I will not allow any defilement." Daoud clenched his jaw.

He felt the girl start to twitch, as she had on the summit. "I do not seek to do it."

Daoud grunted his approval before leaving through a side door.

"Let's begin." Josephus set the child down and unwrapped the blanket carefully. He marveled at the effect they had achieved; she had been so well disguised she appeared to be a delicate boy. One who was sick. After making sure her curls and the mark were still covered, he set her on her feet and knelt beside her. Josephus took out his pad and pen from his robe's pocket. "Go ahead little one."

The girl's face split with an angelic grin as she began a slow walk around the outskirts of the shrine in a clockwise direction. *"Long did it reside in the tabernacle, a simple tent, as inconsequential a housing as man's reign on the earth. The chosen king hesitated to bring it to his city, the new jewel of the world. Finally, a new ruler came, a son who would eclipse his father. This would be a worthy inheritor of its power: a man who embraced its many gifts. He was set on the course to build a home. A temple built around a stone, the foundation of this world, the only piece of Heaven remaining in this realm. Here the glory and pride of the chosen lived and breathed, casting its magnificence on all who dared to approach."*

The child finished her third route around the Dome and then walked over to the stairway set to the side of the room. Josephus vibrated with anticipation. This was the place he was most interested in seeing her reaction. She seemed to float downward, her feet never touching the ground.

His chosen one had found the Well of Souls.

The Well was the location where it was rumored that the faithful and true of heart could hear the sound of laughter of those living on Heaven's shores. Few people today had been able to witness this miracle, though he had read every bit of lore he could find on this forgotten wonder. Josephus knew some of the rarest legends claimed the Ark was housed at some point inside of the deep cavern, for its own protection.

Whatever the Ark and the spirit of God intended to tell him, it would be easiest to communicate in this place, where the veil between man and God was the thinnest.

Surely, here he would learn the most.

Josephus followed her down the steps to the Well of Souls with quick feet and a light heart.

"All came to see the place where God dwells, to sit before the throne of mercy and plead for their desire. Whenever it was taken, woe came to those who dared. Israel grew mighty with the ransom they demanded to take the return of their holy relic. Here the maidens of the Ark came to be taught by those who had come before. To understand what their job was. To take over their responsibilities with the knowledge of the ones who had walked their steps before them. Even Musa had trained the first chosen maiden in tending what he had wrought."

Josephus reflected upon the idea of standing in the place where women once came to be filled with the fire of Heaven.

The Ark Maidens. Carriers of the torch of God.

"Having to teach the maidens was the prophet's final punishment."

Mid-way down the stairwell the child stopped and tilted her head, as if listening in a deeper way than most mortals achieved. She had one hand on the rock walls, caressing the stone beneath her fingers. Her other was held out, as if calling something forward. Josephus could hear the sound of rushing water, as well as the faint sensation of hundreds of people laughing from a far off distance.

"Here the pious can hear the sounds of the dead as they rejoice in Paradise. Here the Ark rejoiced as well." The girl inhaled, her breath quavering, and Josephus caught the faintest trace of incense on the breeze. Soon the air was bursting with its heavy smell. One he had never experienced before, which surprised him, given his long association with all kinds of religious tools.

The child brushed past him as she scurried her way up the stairwell back to the main part of the shrine. The attendant, Daoud, had returned and waited impatiently by the doorway.

A slight humming melody began to resonate through the chamber.

Josephus, confused by the noise, looked to the attendant for explanation. "What is that sound?"

"I do not know."

Father Josephus turned from the attendant back to the girl. Her body was being drawn upwards by an invisible force. She flew over the protective barrier to land on the shetiyyah, the foundation stone of the universe. Once the floor of Solomon's temple, it was revered by Muslims as the place where Mohammed stepped when the chariot from Allah was sent to take the prophet to Heaven. As her feet made contact with the same depression where Mohammed was said to have stood, the noise grew louder. She strutted to the center; holding her palms to the ceiling, she fell forward. Her descent was slowed by an invisible force, so she landed gently on her face.

Both men lurched to assist her, but they staggered backwards when the noise swelled to a nauseating level.

The swift increase of volume was so intense it felt as if it were screaming in his head. It was a song of outrage. Defilement. It was made to punish whoever heard it. *Understand my displeasure at what you have wrought*; it pulsed into their souls with each brutal tone.

You shall pay.

You shall all pay.

Josephus clasped his hands to his ears to try to lessen the resonance. It felt as if it were being beaten into his mind. Somehow, he was still able to hear the attendant when he shouted.

"Merciful Allah, what have you done?" Daoud was terrified, gazing at the girl with wide-eyed horror. "I think it comes from the shetiyyah."

With his acknowledgement of its origin the tune changed. The overwhelming cacophony leveled off into a gentle crooning. A song. It was a melody caressing the senses with the caring touch of a mother, a blanket encompassing love's tender embrace. This was about healing. Rebuilding. Resurrection.

It was about hope.

"A lullaby," Josephus gasped. His voice sounded as hoarse as his ears had felt tortured.

Daoud knelt on the floor, "we must pray," he lowered his forehead to the ground.

The song continued to build; the walls, floor and ceiling joining in the welcoming tune. He could see the vibration life the girl's body a few inches off the granite face. Josephus knelt to touch the stone and was surprised he could not feel anything. He was allowed only to hear, and he realized even this privilege was given begrudgingly. Being a witness to this miracle did not mean it was meant for his eyes. This celebration was not for him.

"Dear God," he whispered. "It is singing … singing for her."

As the tune died away to a slow pulse, Josephus noticed the attendant was frozen in his hunched-over prayer position. He hurdled over the barrier, wrapped his charge in the blanket, picked her up, and rushed from the chamber. They did not have much time. He didn't know how the attendant would ultimately respond to the audio miracle they had just experienced, but he had no intention of waiting to find out.

When he was done with his prayers, and he was sure the song had stopped, Daoud rose. His thoughts were tentative with the fear that something worse would happen.

This black night would haunt him for the rest of his life.

Once he stood up, the sound began once more. This time it was a melody of sorrow. The stone structure was weeping. A lamentation, filled with such remorse it wrenched his heart and soul. It reminded Daoud of his wife's crying when they had found the broken body of their only son.

It was a noise of such loss and desolation, no joy would ever reverse.

Daoud looked around him with alarm. "What have I done? Merciful Allah, what is it I have done?" He blanched and fled from the room, as if the hounds of Hell were in pursuit.

As far as he was concerned … they were.

CHAPTER TWENTY-SIX

"When one is in love, a cliff becomes a meadow."
—Ethiopian Proverb

Addis Ababa is the capital city of Ethiopia. A place filled with possibilities of the future as well as tragic remains of the past. They could see examples of both everywhere they turned. Brother Mtho pointed out to Meggani the scars on the buildings from previous wars, as she marveled over the new construction. Healthy people of all colors zoomed by in expensive vehicles with diplomatic plates, never once stopping to help the people lining the street who had collapsed from hunger, left to die on the ground.

It was the embodiment of ironic dichotomy.

Father Mtho carefully guided Meggani around a beggar, while desperately attempting to avoid the poor penitent's eyes.

She stared at him over her shoulder as the monk pulled her along. "Someone should help him."

"This is what we hope you and the other children will do one day."

"What about now?"

He tried to quicken their pace down the sidewalk. "You are too young to understand."

"Don't get all stupid adult on me now, Mtho."

Brother Mtho gave her an indulgent smile. "Impudent child."

"My middle name, I believe."

Releasing a heavy sigh, Mtho tried to explain. "When you grew up or lived through the famine, you learned one thing: how to survive. Sometimes it is not possible to save everyone. Sometimes you must decide the right path and turn your mind and heart from anything not associated with your path."

"This is not my way," she informed him stiffly.

"My deepest fear is you will not stay at the school for long."

"I'll take what I need and then follow my own way, Mtho."

He stopped and pulled them to the side, so they would not be in other people's way. "I suspect you were the harbinger for the others. It explains why you are so much older. Whatever we can do for you is our pleasure. You will not be forced to do anything you do not wish."

"Darn straight."

Seeing the argument was settled, he prepared to cross the busy thoroughfare, overjoyed when she took his hand. Time and miles had made headway in her protective manner.

They could hear the sound of children laughing with innocent glee.

Looking across the street, they could see a row of ramshackle apartment complexes with façades pockmarked by shells and rifle bullets. It was not until they looked all the way up that they found the source of the voices calling to them, there was a group on one of the buildings' roofs.

One of the girls made a running jump to leap from one structure to another. Her arms and legs flailed with wild abandon. When the child hit the middle of the gap, she paused and floated in mid-air. Her body held in place as if invisible strings were attached to her limbs. The others cheered her feat exuberantly.

She completed the distance to the next location.

Turning to her friends, she waved them over.

Each child made the leap easily, but only the first girl had the flying experience. This differentiated her from everyone else. Mtho and Meggani smiled as they watched the children's antics.

"They are so free," Meggani whispered.

"It is the nature of childhood."

"Some of them," she muttered.

He grimaced. This was a sore subject, and he would be wise to start remembering it.

Meggani quivered, longing to try what they were doing.

Brother Mtho waited until the last of the children completed the jump. "Looks like we now know who else we need to speak with."

"I can't do that." Meggani looked between the roof and the monk with open-mouthed astonishment.

"You are able to manipulate things around you."

"But I can't make myself fly." She crossed her arms over her chest and tapped her foot against the sidewalk, with angry impatience. "It would have come in handy at the orphanage. It would have come in handy in a lot of places, especially the freak show."

"Perhaps at the school you will learn."

"I'd better—," she pronounced with another threatening glower. "It's just brilliant."

"You wish to be smart?"

"No," Meggani shook her head. "I need to be free."

He felt some of his tension ease. At least he no longer had to worry about her going to the school. It seemed the more powers she witnessed, the more eager she was to begin her training.

Mtho could only pray it would be so easy with all the children he encountered.

CHAPTER TWENTY-SEVEN

Mtho thought it would take them hours to track down the children from the roof. Meggani laughed at his worrying. She took out her ever present marbles and sent them whizzing through the air. Fifteen minutes later, the first leaping girl and the last boy who had jumped came skidding to a halt in the alley, following the returning floating orbs. "Can you use those to find anything you want?" Mtho asked, his eyes as wide as his gaping mouth.

"How do you," the flying child started.

"Do that?" The strange boy finished the question for her. Mtho realized if they weren't twins they were close to it. They had the same close-cropped hair, really just fuzz covering their skulls, and the same brown shining eyes. Facial features and builds were close as well. Their bond was easy for him, an outsider, to detect.

"I'm like you." Meggani looked uncomfortable at being vague with them as she tried to explain.

Mtho gave a slight chuckle. "In more ways than either of you might realize."

"What do you want," the female asked.

"I'm Mtho, and this is Meggani."

"Mani," the lad introduced himself. "This is my cousin Ani."

The girl moved forward and took Mtho's hand. She turned it over to examine his palm, calm and silent. "You are here to take us away. You wish to make us go to your school."

"I am here only for you, Ani." Mtho looked between the two children questioning him with matching unblinking, uncomprehending stares. "Why don't you take us to meet your families? We should discuss this with your guardians."

A walk up six flights of stairs brought them to the living quarters for the almost-twins. Ani led them into the place where the entire clan seemed to be gathered. The two-room apartment was packed with furniture and people. It was clean but hot. Though the day's temperature was mild it felt as if all the air had been sucked out of the dwelling. The faintest odor of vegetable stew laden with spices made his nose itch.

Mtho realized they must have arrived right after the family's noon meal.

Ani sat on the divan between two older women who closely resembled each other. They quickly introduced Mtho to the dual Mrs. Lalibelas, who were twins that had married twins. Mani and Ani were the only children born into the family that were not a part of a set.

Cousins, they acted closer than siblings.

The rest of the room's occupants varied in age and size. There were two grandmothers, three aunts, and a large collection of children, aged two to twelve.

"You understand why we are concerned ..." the first Mrs. Lalibela began.

"Our children are precious to us," the other Lalibela finished.

Mtho hid his exasperation when he realized he was going to have to get used to this disjointed conversation to speak with the protective parents.

"We have little to give them." Mrs. Lalibela glanced at one of the grandmothers, guiltily. "Our husbands don't know what to make of them. We took most of the others and put them in apprenticeship programs."

"Our husbands are good men." The second Mrs. Lalibela inserted.

"They had good prospects through the United Nations."

"I understand." Mtho answered the first Mrs. Lalibela. "I am just offering Ani a chance to go to a school which will allow her to be herself."

Meggani felt like Mtho wasn't getting anywhere.

She had to help him. "He is a good man." Her eyes met the stare of each female in the room. "I swear it."

"Why do you offer it to her?" The grandmother speaking seemed to approve of the transaction and Mtho let out his pent up breath. "What makes her so special to you, monk? We do not just give our blood away."

Meggani hid her smile beneath her fingers. Nice family, she thought.

Ani stood up and moved to put her hand on Mani's shoulder. "I cannot go without my cousin."

"Could you explain why?" Mtho did the calculations on how it would affect the integrity of the school's mission to have another non-chosen child admitted. They made room for Rohan; surely this one would find a place.

It was created to protect the kids from negative influences, not make them miserable.

Ani seemed incapable of being without her cousin. Who was he to argue with them? Perhaps she accessed her talents through the proximity of his soul.

"He is meant to come, too."

"I would feel better if her cousin went as well." The two Mrs. Lalibela's shared a tremulous smile.

Ani directed her appeal to Meggani, sensing a sympathetic soul. "He is meant to go."

The room grew still and silent as the two girls assessed each other. Meggani shrugged. "Invite the boy as well," she commanded.

"Meggani ..."

"Trust me." Meggani entreated him. When he did not seem ready to concede, she took in a quivering breath. "Please."

Brother Mtho nodded. If she was the forerunner he had to trust her. Perhaps this could make up for his mistake with the brick. He still winced when he thought about how he had pushed her.

She turned to Ani beaming her triumph. "Mani is invited as well."

"We would expect to see them." Mrs. Lalibela silently reached over to grasp her sister's hand.

"I am sure we can arrange something amenable."

"You will need to speak with our husbands." The second Mrs. Lalibela warned the monk. They were a close family. The men would not be overjoyed at losing their children to a place so far away.

Meggani scuffed at the floor with her sock, watching the monk closely, nervous he would refuse. It was easy to read how much she wanted another girl at her new home. The idea of being with someone of her own sex, who would understand her differences and empathize, was as tantalizing as food to a starving man.

She was still terrified, though.

Brother Mtho's smile was charming and relaxed. Here was an obstacle he understood. A wound in Meggani and a need he could fulfill for the school with disturbing ease. "I'd be happy to."

CHAPTER TWENTY-EIGHT

It took him the entire day to get Ani and Mani enrolled in the new school. Meggani was quiet and respectful to their fathers when they arrived. She sat in the corner with her hands folded on her lap and her head lowered. The family of doubles was so impressed with how well behaved she was, they tried to convince Mtho to take all of their kids.

He had promised to let Meggani pick out anything she wanted for their dinner, as a thank you.

The next day they set out, after Mtho had planned their itinerary.

Stopping at the side of a pretty river to have lunch, Mtho was pleased the weather had stayed so nice. It was the perfect conditions for his plan. None of the children had ever experienced a picnic, so Mtho was excited to introduce them to one. He had a feeling he and his brethren would be responsible to present many new events to the old ones. He had obtained a blanket from their hotel and a repast from the café across the street. It was mostly injera, a simple flatbread; niter kebbeh, a spiced butter; stewed lentils and fresh fruit. There were some roasted vegetables, but they were limp and faded so he didn't push the children into trying them when they refused.

He had saved his special surprise for last.

They would drink ej, a honey wine with their meal, and for dessert there were some dabo kolo, which were small fried cookies, his favorite treat.

"So this is pic-a-nic?"

"I thought you would enjoy it."

Mani scowled. "It is food with dirt. What is to enjoy?"

The cousins were sprawled on the blanket, each of them leaning against the small cloth bags their families had sent with them. Their fathers had beamed proudly when they gave Mtho some money to pay for whatever extras their progeny might require. He suspected he would return the cash to the Lalibela's soon. If they had any idea how well funded Josephus had made sure the school was, they would be asking him for money, rather than donating it to their unique cause.

Meggani decided to jump in to save Mtho from having to match wits with the cousins. He was outgunned. Again. You would think he would get accustomed to not fighting with re-born angels. "I don't get it. How come Ani is like me?"

"Perhaps you're like me," the little girl pointed out with an impish smile.

"You share souls," Mtho swiftly explained.

"So Ani can do things I can't?"

"Yes," Mtho nodded to Meggani. He saw all three children were seeking more of an answer. "In time you might teach each other your abilities. My friend Josephus is searching for someone who will guide you all on how to pool your resources."

"How come we share souls?" Meggani tilted her head, considering the possibilities. "Isn't it against God?"

"Yeah." Mani and Ani spoke as one, as always.

Meggani divided the food for the cousins, making sure they had a small taste of each dish. She was a great caretaker. The little ones received the best of the offerings on the blanket without complaint from her. It warmed Mtho's heart when he saw she had given away all of the cookies, leaving none for herself. He put his own dessert on her napkin when she wasn't looking. All children should get some kind of treat, and be able to enjoy some sugar. His widening waistband did not need any more help than it had already received.

"It may be against your religion," Mtho's voice was gentle as he introduced this concept to them, new to all three of them. Drawing the children away from things they had learned, from their parents or other adults, would be a sensitive maneuver. They needed to learn a new way of looking at things. The old way had certainly only brought them all pain. "It may be against your religion," he repeated, "but it is not against God."

"Okay," Ani shrugged her acceptance.

"So," Meggani questioned Ani. "How come Mani had to come?"

Ani faced Mani. "You should show them."

"How?"

The boy's unsure whisper sparked both Meggani and Mtho's interest. This was bound to be fascinating.

Without another word or question, Ani picked up a knife from the blanket and slashed her own hand. She held up her arm so they could see the blood dripping down, the thick fluid covering her fingers. Mani moved to cover the wound with his palm. When he took his hand away the cut was gone.

Meggani couldn't help gloating. Her instincts had been correct. She felt invigorated. "Good thing we brought him, huh?" She pushed Mtho's arm.

"Also, I doubt our moms would have let Ani come by herself.

"Is it all you can do?" Mtho asked Mani.

"What do you mean?"

"There are stories of Shemani healing other types of things as well."

Meggani leaned forward as she studied the five-year-old boy. "It's your name? Shemani?"

"No, it's Mani."

"We must assume not all the children would be named after their progenitor in a direct way. I took a guess based on his ability and his name being so similar." Mtho smiled, elated to know something the children did not.

"Like I'm Ani, but I'm connected to Meggani."

Meggani couldn't help snorting. "I guess it will be a good thing, otherwise this school could get real confusing."

"I fix animals."

The three of them regarded Mani, surprised at his blurted revelation. It was clear by Ani's irritated look she had not been aware of this.

Mtho nodded in deep contemplation. "Makes sense," he praised. "We shall have to find some pollution for you to try a hand on."

"Like a big garbage dump?" Meggani asked. "Eww."

"No," Mtho responded quickly before the cousins objected. "One of the most polluted rivers in the world is in Africa. I think Mani could do much good to heal the waters and give the area an entire new chance at life."

"Funny, I thought this was what you were doing for us." Meggani laughed at Mtho's expression, and the two of them shared an understanding look, shutting out the cousins. It felt good, Meggani realized. Having friends feels good. She had always thought it would be a burden or annoying. It wasn't though.

It felt good, even if he was a boy.

And an adult.

And a monk.

Who knew?

CHAPTER TWENTY-NINE

"A close friend can become a closer enemy."
— Ethiopian Proverb

The archbishop came into Cardinal Robeson's office with all the reverence and grandeur of the pope on parade. It disturbed the cardinal, because the archbishop had been able to do it since they were young men. Both had labored for weeks in Rome, and even went out on a missionary assignment together. Friends. Now acquaintances. Or enemies, depending on how you looked at it. The cardinal's scowl twisted his face at the intrusion, though he would have preferred not to have given the interloper any recognition of any kind. The Ethiopians, as a whole, were an unusual people.

Its Church was a constant thorn in his side.

Completely beyond his jurisdiction, they behaved as if they were able to blackmail the Roman Catholics into doing things.

Problem was, he suspected they just might be able to do it.

He had always suspected something subversive had freed them from the Alexandrian Coptic Church Patriarch in the nineteen fifties.

Silence gripped the room. The two of them were caught in each other's stare:

The white man in the black robes.

The black man in the white robes.

Polar opposites in visage, wardrobe, beliefs and technique.

Even in honor.

It was true, on the surface they shared the same religion. Generations ago their two organizations had splintered away from each other on different paths. Now they were light years apart. There had been an unseen simmering rivalry between the two groups ever since.

"Funny," the cardinal muttered, "I didn't hear you knock."

"I didn't see a need," the archbishop answered.

In normal circumstances, the cardinal would have set the scene for this type of audience with careful attention to detail. The well-lit office was not his normal choice. He did not bother to rise from his desk where he was making notations on a document. If his former friend wished to compel this meeting, he deserved little respect or formality for the dubiousness of the occasion.

"You wanted something?" The cardinal forced himself to return his attention to the paperwork.

The archbishop sat in one of the chairs and arranged his robes. "Not happy to see me?"

"I was expecting Michael."

"He is trailing my representative. He thought we should speak. Coordinate our efforts, as it were."

The cardinal slammed the folder into a drawer, not caring it clearly betrayed his mindset at the mention of what he felt was a rogue priest. The archbishop should have stopped this insanity. "The ending of your man and this foolish mission is vital."

"And why is this?" He spoke as he examined his fingernails, pretending mild disinterest.

"Finding the lost Ark of the Covenant will set off a round of violence to end the world. The Jews will want to rebuild their Temple, the Muslims will want to stop the Jews, and the followers of Christ will each present their debate as to why they should keep the relic."

The archbishop chuckled at the cardinal's dire prophecy. "Of course the use of the Ark as a weapon has nothing to do with your concern."

"I am only trying to protect the world."

"As am I," his voice threaded with steel.

"You don't give a damn about the rest of the world. You only think about your home, your lands … the blighted protectors of the Ark." The cardinal half stood in his seat, veins protruding from both sides of his temple. "You are trying to protect your country."

"To Ethiopians, our country is the world." The archbishop was secretly amused as the cardinal collapsed back into his seat.

Robeson recognized the expression from over many hands of bridge.

He was vanquished before he stepped foot on the battlefield.

"What is it you want from me, to stop your rogue priest?" The cardinal covered his eyes, to mask his defeat. "Whatever it is you want, is yours."

"Actually," the archbishop allowed himself a little gloating, "not a thing."

"You will stop him for nothing?" His hand fell from his face.

"I would never give up the Ark. No Ethiopian would allow such a travesty. We have a special relationship with it. I will however, be happy to bargain with you for how whatever my priest finds is distributed."

The cardinal shook his head and shuffled his papers, as if he were being efficient. "I have heard of this supposed miracle child …"

"And?"

"If you believe in this, you are a fool."

"Naturally, you would think so."

Robeson shook his head. "When did you become a demagogue?"

"Is that what I am?"

"Seems like it."

The archbishop gestured to their sumptuous surroundings. "Appearances can be deceiving."

Robeson rose, finished with this useless negotiation and the man who clung to beliefs few still maintained. "Consider with care what you will give to keep news of what we find to ourselves. I will not hesitate to take something dear."

"A warning. If my man sees a chance, he will take these matters into his own hands."

"If your conscience would permit this, then I pity you." The archbishop paused as he considered the other man, one who should have been a friend. And yet, he remained behind his large ornate desk as if it would protect him. He pitied him. It was clear the biggest thing he was hiding from was the truth. Miracles were for the world to rejoice in. They were never to be controlled by one organization. They were a gift to all. It was time he realized it. "Whatever happens is between you and your God."

"We worship the same God," he sputtered.

"Do we?" The archbishop looked saddened by his words. "I see no such evidence."

As the door closed behind him, the cardinal swiped the desk clean, sending files, papers, lamp and pens flying. He peered down at the chaos on the floor with a sneer of distaste. This is what the world will be like should the Ark be discovered. This is what he was fighting to prevent. He picked up the phone with a lightened heart. The choice was made. The priest would have to be ended. The cardinal would save the world.

It would be he who controls the access to the Almighty and all of its gifts, just as it was meant to be.

CHAPTER THIRTY

"Knowledge is like a garden; if it is not cultivated, it cannot be harvested."
—Ethiopian Proverb

S tanding on the hill path over Axum, Mtho breathed in all of the components of home. He could smell the flatbread cooking over the morning fires the women built behind their homes. Hear the sound of the bells on the camels and goats the Bedouin herded to their next campground. He imagined he could even feel the caress of the Almighty on his skin as the breeze danced past him from the ancient ruins bordering the holy site.

Home.

A single man traveling with three small children should be the definition of hell on earth. And he had grown up in a country beset by years of famine and drought.

Meggani, Ani and Mani tried to behave. It was just normal high jinks. Most youngsters seemed drawn to them as if under a magnetic force. They were unaccustomed to traveling or having to keep things to themselves. Ani and Meggani not using their levitation powers was one of the harder obstacles to navigate with them.

When they camped under the stars in the wilderness the rules were relaxed. He had often woken in the night to find all three children floating past him, shaking with their giggles over the prank.

One Meggani called practice.

Being so close to the end of the journey made him shake with relief.

After being on the road for weeks, they had not found any other reincarnated angels. Meggani had convinced him the cousins deserved to see a little more of their country than they had up until this time. She needed a chance to bond with Ani, but it turned out the little girl's ties to her cousin were exclusive.

His brothers had decided they would move around the country, mostly by foot. It ensured they would not miss a child in their wanderings. The kids were not enthusiastic about long hours of walking. They were also always looking for entertainment.

Parts of a stone wall lined the path. Under construction, it was one of the more ambitious projects they had planned. It made an impressive barrier. Mtho was pleased at how much progress Peter and Kwai had achieved already while he was haunting the roadways in search of the old ones.

Meggani paused as she waited for the cousins to catch up. "So why is the school here?"

"Axum has the Ark sanctuary." Mtho took out his canteen to take a long drink and passed it to the girl.

"No, it doesn't," Mani and Ani chorused.

Meggani drank from the canteen and handed it to Ani to take a sip. She noticed Mtho's confusion and shrugged. "Axum has the sanctuary, but not the Ark."

"But that's impossible," Mtho sputtered.

"If you think impossible is possible," Meggani gave him a steady answer, "you really shouldn't be working with us."

Deciding an argument was beyond his mental or physical capabilities, Mtho returned them to walking up the steep hill. They followed the fence. The children laughed as they ran beside it, their hands tracing over the stones. Mtho appreciated the way the rough gray and silver stones stood out, against the verdant landscape. When the kids reached the gate, they paused. Mtho felt as if he were unveiling some great holiday surprise as he pulled open the latch and ushered his charges past the threshold to their new home.

Stepping onto the grounds for the first time, the children looked around, fascinated. They could see a large plot of grassy land, with several different small buildings lining its perimeter. There were piles of building materials dotting the enclosure, including a small pile of boulders near the fence. The largest building had solar panels, glinting silver in the sun; they were the only source of power for the school. Meggani looked up, realizing for the first time there were no phone lines running to any part of the facility. She had been disconnected at the orphanage, but communication was available. Here it would be a different story.

Apparently, they were truly going to be out of the world's eyes.

Safe to grow and learn; far from other people's fear and negativity.

It gave her a newfound respect and liking for the man who stood grinning beside her, and a strange sense of peace.

This was the way it should be.

"Welcome home, children." Mtho threw his hands out to embrace all they were seeing.

Brothers Peter and Kwai both stepped out of one of the buildings to wave happily at the new arrivals. Jake came running from the far side of the buildings with Rohan chasing him; they released joyful laughs at the sight of Meggani and her friends. Peter stopped when he saw the new faces trying to hide behind Meggani. Ani and Mani were holding each other's hands, their fingers braided together, their knuckles turning white from gripping each other.

"So you found more," Peter observed.

Mtho hugged each of his brother's. "This is Ani and Mani. They are cousins." He pointed each of the kids out to them. "Their families prefer they return during the summer and at the holidays. They would also like the children to write to them on a regular basis."

"Of course. Already Jake and Rohan's parents have become true assets." Kwai smiled at the kids and gestured the two brothers over.

Peter stepped aside to let the boys get closer. "We would not be this far ahead without them."

"Excellent." Mtho beamed at Meggani, "I told you it would work out."

"Yes, because I had nothing to do with it," she said cheekily.

Peter shook his head. "I see you still have the rude one."

"I missed you, too." Meggani rolled her eyes.

Mtho moved to stand in front of Meggani to protect her from Peter's biting sarcasm. He winked at her. *This was impossible. They will pull me back and forth until I split down the middle. He is a monk*; he mentally scolded his brother. *He should know better.* "Do not fear, Peter. We will be leaving soon."

"I do not think it wise you keep traveling with her."

"He'd rather you travel with some boy?" Meggani asked with mock confusion.

"She has been most helpful," Mtho defended her to Peter.

"I have," Meggani declared vehemently. She had planned to continue needling the older monk, but turned to Mtho in wonder. "I have?"

"Of course you have," he reassured her. "You have been the key to our success."

She stiffened because she felt he was pitied her rather than giving her respect.

Taking deep breaths, she sent out her inner sense to determine why the monk was being so nice to her, so complimentary. She could feel no shame, or superiority or patronizing. Perhaps, Mtho was telling her the truth.

"It is your choice," Peter mumbled. He stalked away from them, ushering all the other children with him. The kids kept looking back at Meggani with longing, intimidated by Peter's foreboding attitude.

Meggani bit her lip as she resisted the urge to snatch them away from Peter. There was no harshness in him for the cousins. They would be safe.

She decided she should make sure to teach the two how to tell these things for themselves. It would be their defense against Peter's mercurial moods. This would help them feel more at home at the school.

Mtho despaired as his friend left. He felt as if the gap between them increased with each step. He was his brother; he did not wish bad will between them. Peter grew angrier with each additional piece of evidence that Meggani was meant to lead the search. There didn't seem to be anything he could do about it. He bit back all the things he wanted to say. Words just didn't cover it. At least, the way he used words didn't. Mtho felt Meggani's hand slip into his before he understood she had moved to stand beside him.

"You know he's jealous, right?"

"He is not jealous of you, Meggani."

"No, he's not." She released his hand and stepped away. "He's jealous of your faith."

Kwai witnessed the exchange and was happy at the inroads Mtho had made. Mtho's letters of Meggani's isolated character had broken his heart. His imagination had left him nauseous at the thought of the abuse she must have suffered. He stepped closer to speak to Mtho. "We have received other help from the good abbé at Debra Damo. He sent us a few of our brothers to assist with the teaching."

"Did he say why?"

Kwai shrugged. "He felt it was important we keep a one-to-one ratio between adult and child."

Meggani moved to stand before the two men. She knew they were not excluding her on purpose; they just thought she wouldn't be interested. She hadn't told them just how much she knew. Her dreams had changed since she started traveling with Brother Mtho. Once they were not much more than nightmare images from her past, sent to leave her trembling and alone. Now they were filled with knowledge and empowerment. They directed her and gave her the information they needed to accomplish this great quest. "To make sure we have maximum development," she provided.

Both men gazed were startled. "This was what he said."

"When do we leave to find the others?"

"Soon, child." Mtho patted her shoulder awkwardly, never sure if she would accept a physical act of compassion.

Kwai sighed. He didn't want them to leave.

They'd just gotten there.

"Must you?" He winced at his tone, no grown man should whine.

"As the children's powers grow, the chances they will be misunderstood or harmed, grow as well. We have to get them here before they withdraw."

"Very well," Kwai sighed again. He ushered them to the first building, the future schoolhouse. There was much to show them and experience. He didn't wish to waste a moment. "We shall have to see to it that you rest in the quickest and most efficient manner."

"Why do I think rest is the farthest thing from your mind?" Mtho narrowed his eyes as he studied Kwai's feigned innocence. They had traveled far enough, and spent enough time together, for him to recognize when he had some ulterior motive.

"Because it is," Meggani confirmed, looking at the young monk's aura.

Kwai resisted the urge to point out the two of them were a step away from completing each other's sentences. "Now, now. Just because I set aside a few chores for you both doesn't mean you should carry on so."

"Why do I think we were safer on the road with the cousins?"

Meggani laughed with Mtho. They were instant conspirators. "I'll grab Ani, you get Mani," she suggested.

Without another word, Kwai took hold of each of their hands and dragged them into the schoolroom. His look of mock fierceness meant little. Their laughter soon had him smiling as well. "The first thing we should discuss is this feud with Peter."

"Run Mtho, run," Meggani begged.

CHAPTER THIRTY-ONE

"As the wound inflames the finger, so thought inflames the mind."
—Oromo tribe of Ethiopia

It was a quiet day on the Nile. Father Josephus expertly piloted his felucca through the waters around the resort city of Aswan. The narrow craft was formed from native reeds done in a manner similar to the vessels of his home. Looking out at the other skiffs scattered along the shoreline, they reminded him of toys strewn across the water by some giant child.

The sun reflected off the water, glittering like a well-cut sapphire. All around him were modern pleasure vessels he had to circumvent. The effect was as if he were moving around clouds that were gliding across an earth-bound summer sky. His boat maneuvered with the speed and agility of a hawk among the larger craft. The shore featured a variety of greens and golds. He could see the life of the foliage from gardens and farms, the gold of the brick and stone buildings. In the distance he recognized the statues and ruins of a long-lost Egyptian empire. The port town had been a central trading post and vacation spot for thousands of years.

As he approached the island, he used the current to avoid the rocks guarding one side of his destination. The breeze kicked up a spray of water, stinging his eyes. Josephus learned how to manage the choppy waves easily from years of travel to his own Lake Tana. This place was more light-hearted. The boulders resembled elephants cavorting in the waves and brought a smile to his lips. He glanced at the child, secured in the front of the skiff, wishing she could experience this beauty with him. "It is such a magnificent world, little one. I look forward to sharing it with you when you wake."

He hoped that day would be soon.

Landing the ship in the protected cove, he secured it, and picked up the girl. He comforted himself that she looked healthier than she had in Israel, and the burn mark on her forehead had faded away. The archbishop had been kind enough to direct him to another housekeeper, one in Aswan's city proper, who helped him care for his charge. Josephus missed Mrs. Shapiro's sunny smile, the new woman walked around with a thundercloud for a face. She was helpful, so he was grateful. He had instructed the child be dressed in simple light clothing appropriate for the temperature.

Elephantine Island was once the location of multiple archeological digs. All he could see was the skeletal remnants of ancient temples dotting the landscape with unclaimed columns; flights of steps leading nowhere.

There was no question of his direction.

Josephus knew how important it was to be prepared.

He had done his research in the archives before setting out on this trip, so he knew precisely where he was heading. Time was slipping through his fingers. Josephus made a face when he realized, in his belief in caution, that he had been on the road with a semi-comatose child for weeks.

This was one of the first locations they visited together where he was worried.

When she began to speak, he was always transferred to the time and people the baby described with such intimate ease. Often he was so lost by the knowledge she shared he would forget where he was; what he was doing. How important the secrecy of his mission was. He might completely miss an entire army walking by, much less some stranger who might try to take the girl away.

Or report him to the press.

Either option terrified him.

Reaching the plateau, Josephus set the girl down in the center. She hadn't given him exact coordinates when she directed them here, he hoped this was close enough. He pulled out his pen and paper to be ready when she began.

Watch over us, Baba. Keep us safe when I cannot.

She didn't even give him a warning as she had in the previous episodes. The child quivered with eagerness to tell her tale. *"The children ran here from the evil king, taking the Covenant with them. They believed it would protect their way. They did not understand the truth of what they carried. It had grown too powerful, and harder to control, with time. It was no longer possible to harness its power. They tried to appease it. They built a temple that matched its far-away home, but it was not the same. It had given them each measurement, explained the placement of each block, and embedded the building techniques in their dreams. Still, it was not enough. It could never be enough."*

His charge walked in a circle around his trembling body and began to mutter her story in a foreign ancient tongue.

"English, my child. Please speak in English."

Returning to the words the father understood, she began again. "The torch had been lost. Once the flame of God was seen on the Ark, between the two cherubim on its top, and within the eyes of the maiden who tended. It was a fire that granted knowledge, blessings and protection in equal measure. How mighty they had been then. The torch could not tell the chosen of the blessings and curses they invited on their heads. It could not explain the materials needed for its home. It felt an inconsolable sorrow here. Everything was so wrong. It hated that no one could understand."

"Where did the torch go?" Josephus peered between his notes and her face, confused.

"The Covenant burned with an unquenchable fire. The torch was needed. Only a torch can bear such burning." Once more he ached, as she lifted

her arms and fell face forward into the dirt. Josephus thought surely such a position was uncomfortable, at the least, it must make her nose hurt a great deal. The problem was, touching her would break the spell. He lay on the ground so he could hear her more easily. *"The torch had followed its heart to the land of the people with the burnt face. Israel's children realized their only hope was to follow the torch, and pray the maiden knew how to control it; to save it; to save them all."*

She began to writhe on the ground as if having a seizure. Her body made swirl patterns in the dirt. Josephus felt the heat of her skin, even though he was a good foot away from her. He gasped when he saw her face was covered with tears flowing from her eyes. The mud it made with the dust covering her, masked the chocolate shine of her skin. To him she looked like a marble statue for a moment, a frozen tableau of pain.

"The Covenant's fire was burning their souls," she gasped.

"Why?" Josephus tried to wipe her face but the heat coming from her singed his fingers. "Why was it burning them?"

"The Covenant wept while here. The soil was unclean to it. This land made it weak, and made it sad. When it grew so sad, it became angry. Seething with rage, it would not be denied."

Josephus gasped at the power he was dealing with.

"Fear and negativity were turned onto its caretakers. So it finally manifested revenge."

Josephus eagerly noted this on his pad. "What happened next?"

"The children maddened their neighbors with their egos. The Covenant would not save them. They were forced to leave for Meroe. Onward in search of the torch, onward in search of salvation for all of the children, everywhere."

Her body stilled, and Josephus could feel the fire diminishing in her veins. He wiped the dirt from her face with his sleeve, his touch tender. Gentle.

"They searched for the memory of a legend in the hope that she could soothe the fire. They did not know how to find it. They did not know if they would live to discover her. They only knew she was their only hope of harnessing the power and glory of heaven. They knew, if they did not find an answer, the question of destruction would be for the entire world."

Her words reverted again into the earlier dead language she had used. Josephus shook his head. "How foolish with heaven's things we are."

"Excuse me, is she speaking ancient Hebrew?" The female voice made him look up in surprise. An African-American woman in her mid-forties, with the grace and beauty of an ancient queen, was standing near him. She had approached without his noticing. She wore a linen camp shirt, and a pair of khaki pants with multiple pockets, filled with different items required by an absent-minded researcher. "I'm Rhonda Sith, a professor of antiquities at American University."

He shook her hand when she smiled warmly. "Father Josephus." With considerable unease he realized there was a man in his late thirties standing close-by, holding a video camera. His black hair was long, and kept falling forward into his light blue eyes. His pale skin looked as if it were already burning under the mild Egyptian sun. Josephus didn't want to imagine this man ever visiting his country. He would melt in moments.

Then Josephus swallowed with fear. He had a video camera trained on them.

Baba, this is what I asked you to protect us from. A little warning would have been nice.

"Do you speak ancient Hebrew?" he asked conversationally.

"I am conversant in more ancient languages then modern ones," she joked. When the priest didn't laugh, she gestured with nervous hands to her camera-toting white friend. "This is Jack Kerr, he is a professor as well."

Jack came over and juggled the equipment so he could shake the priest's hand. The man's slight drawl told Josephus he was from the American South. He tilted his black baseball hat back to show a pair of laughing eyes with lines radiated from their corners. "Good to meet you. I got most of her performance down."

"I never thought of videotaping her."

Rhonda was unable to keep from interfering. There was a puzzle here. She loved solving puzzles, no matter how much it meant poking her nose in where it was not wanted. So, her late husband had been right: she was a busybody. "I realize this is odd, but what exactly are you doing with this little girl?"

He lifted the child and moved her to the shade of a nearby tree. It gave him time to decide if he was going to trust these Americans. How like them. Stepping in to get involved, no matter how little they might understand the situation. Fortunately, he liked people that tended to butt in. He usually did the same. Josephus lifted his head as he felt the wind pick up. It was a welcome relief from the heat. The breeze filled with the perfume of the flowers that grew around the bottom of the hill made him decide to go with the flow of the Lord. "It is a long story," he admitted.

Rhonda shrugged, "We have a long time on our hands."

"And we brought lunch," Jack added with a quick glance at the cooler sitting at the base of his tripod.

Josephus smiled at the man's enthusiasm. He didn't think Americans ate food anymore; certainly they didn't seem to be comfortable with showing their appreciation for it. "I am hungry."

"I never had kids of my own, but I do adore them." Rhonda ran her hand over the girl's cheek with a wistful expression on her face.

Deciding at that point was even easier. "How much do you know about the Ark of the Covenant?"

It took their entire lunch for Josephus to catch the others up on the scope of his mission and his travels. In the interest of complete disclosure, he began with the stories his grandfather used to tell him at the fire in the middle of the night. The Americans loved that his Baba had used the psychotropic effects of khat to distract him from the worst of the hungry time. He relied on the stories of the old ones and their miracles for all others.

Josephus was shocked at the end as he watched the two Americans sit back on their blanket and look up at the sky. They were both moved in a deep way, he could tell by the sheen in their eyes. Josephus looked between them and coughed. "So that's where I am. The girl is the closest my family has ever gotten to finding an answer to the prophecy."

"I wish you had some documentation." Rhonda rubbed at the bridge of her nose as her eyes squinted.

Jack nodded, "Some kind of proof."

"Only my word." Josephus pulled himself up.

"That's enough for us." Rhonda reached over to squeeze his hand. "The problems will come from others."

Josephus directed a nervous glance at Jack. "Others do not count."

"Your love of your country and God reminds me of my husband." She wiped her eyes with a trembling hand.

"Rhonda." Jack's voice held a tone of warning.

"I would like to help you." Rhonda held up her palm to Jack to stop the protest springing to his lips.

"You would?" Josephus managed to close his mouth only with a great deal of force.

Rhonda nodded her head with her determination. "Definitely."

Her friend sat forward as he stared at his companion. "Rhonda, this man intends on going into Sudan."

"I can help," she maintained, with a mutinous expression.

Jack threw up his hands with exasperation. "He hasn't needed much help up to now."

"But I can make a difference here."

"Great." Jack drawled, before covering his eyes with his palm.

Josephus's thoughts whirled with the decision before him. The way before him could be fraught with danger. Did he have any right to involve a stranger in these affairs? Worse: an American? Her knowledge, gender, and wealth would be convenient. Was this a support sent from God, or a test?

The prophecy was a sacred gift to his family. He should not need anyone else's help. *Baba, is this a test of my commitment to my vow?*

Could you be so cruel?

No. His smile deprecated at his fears with fond with memories of the old man. Baba would never be anything but good. How many times had he watched his grandfather offer to help the villagers who scorned them? Too many to count.

This was no test.

It had to be a gift.

Traveling and tending to a little girl was difficult for him. She had grown. It was harder to keep the food going into her mouth, to keep her body tended. He worked hard to make sure there was a kind woman who was willing to do some of the more intimate tasks she required. Bathing her was one of the more awkward chores on the list, as far as he was concerned. Looking between the woman and the child, he took a deep breath.

He could only follow his heart.

"God is merciful and just," he whispered to himself. "God would only send you forces to assist. He has no reason to test your faith. Your country's history is nothing but ..."

"I haven't said I would accept your help yet."

Jack snorted at Josephus's bemusement at Rhonda's faith and determination. He shook his head. "That will not make the slightest difference."

"So nice to see men trying to be reasonable."

"We're done for now, father," Jack quipped to the laughing priest. "You're stuck with us for the long haul. Not much keeps this one from a goal she's set her sights on."

Rhonda gifted the two of them with a smile. "Now we can make plans."

"Fasten your seat belt, friend. Welcome to the wonderful world of Rhonda Sith."

CHAPTER THIRTY-TWO

"Not to know is bad. Not to wish to know is worse."
— Amharic tribe of Ethiopia

Meggani grew to love the academic world, with all of its new wonders. Her days were easy to portion out. It had been decided the children would spend the morning learning of the current world, and the afternoon would be spent on the past. Brother Mtho made it clear to the monks that the students would be working with their new teachers, not under them. This was their first introduction to a democratic process. Most of the time before dinner was spent on personal projects, whether for the school's building, an academic pursuit, or a hobby.

The monks started to follow Mtho's lead in dealing with Meggani.

It was difficult for her. Meggani didn't like secrets. She refused to confess that she wasn't sure she was the true forerunner. It didn't seem to fit her. It felt wrong somehow. Still, there was no one else to do the job. She was learning to like it.

She was consulted constantly regarding many of the choices for the students. It was a new experience for Meggani to feel so much a part of something. She felt the pleasure of standing inside, for a change, rather than stuck spying through a window.

It made her want to laugh and cry at the same time. It made her feel free.

Watched Father Kwai finishing the fence from the shadow of the girl's dorm, Meggani felt bad as she noticed he was sweating profusely as he tried to position one of the stones into place to continue building their barrier. Meggani surreptitiously moved closer, her eyes glued on his back.

When it looked as if he was about to lose his grip, Meggani squinted her eyes to make the stone levitate into place.

After it was secure, Kwai turned to look at the girl he knew was close-by. "You did not need to do that."

"I know." Meggani shrugged and scuffed at the dirt with the toe of her sneaker.

"Why did you?"

Meggani shrugged and looked up into the deep mahogany of his eyes. "There is no shame in needing help."

He smiled at the girl; her tone was so gentle there was no way for him to take offense. "I know, child."

"If you can help someone, you should. There should be no shame in that, either."

Kwai nodded, "I agree."

"I wish Brother Peter did." When Kwai started to say something, Meggani waved her hand, denying him the opportunity.

She moved forward to lean against the part of the fence that was completed. The cool stone felt good against the heat of the day. "Ani and I could finish this in no time." When Kwai sat on the ground with his back to the stone, she slid down to join him. "It would probably be good practice for us, and if we joined our abilities we might be able to finish in a few days."

"Maybe I like doing it by myself."

"No, you don't." She snorted amused at the stretch of the truth he had just committed.

"Maybe I think this school is about helping you children. Not you children helping the school."

Meggani shook her head. "Maybe our helping the school is helping us."

Kwai's shoulders fell, his sigh loud enough to rival the wind. How could they teach a child that had such an intrinsic sense of wisdom? How could they keep her from growing angry and full of ego, so she was far beyond them? Teaching those you should follow seemed inherently hypocritical to him.

One thing he could address was her feud with his brother. "Peter does not mean to be antagonistic to you."

"I know. He wants to be the one to journey and see the world."

"Perhaps you should take him out, next." Kwai smiled at the thought of the pair traveling.

Meggani shook her head. "I won't go with him."

"Why not?"

"It's not safe."

He took a moment to digest her choked out confession. It had come from deep within her, and he felt as if he should offer some soothing words of comfort. Whatever antagonism she might have toward his brother, Meggani wished no harm to come to him. Kwai was stunned to see the infinite goodness of her heart. "Very well."

"You aren't going to question me?"

Kwai shrugged. "If you felt comfortable in telling me you would have volunteered the information. I trust you to tell us what we need to know; when we need to know it."

"I think your faith is deeper than Mtho's," Meggani shared, with awe.

"Faith has no measure, child." Kwai corrected her. "It is a fathomless force, if it is planted in an appropriate way."

"Very well," she nodded her head. "Now. How about I go get Ani and together we finish this fence?"

"In truth?"

"Definitely." Meggani chuckled. "It was you guys who taught me to appreciate truth."

"I would appreciate it with all of my heart."

His eager and grateful expression made her giggle. When he joined in with her, their mirth grew. The peals of her laughter resonated in the air and made the day just a bit brighter. Kwai realized the children seemed to be growing in the few days they had lived at the school. Not in size, but in spirit. He didn't know how it was affecting their powers, but it was clear their souls were taking a type of nourishment from this place that was beyond his ken.

It reassured him that they were indeed on the right path.

She hopped up. Leaning down, she patted his shoulder. "Don't worry, Brother Kwai. This will be fun. We'll make sure of it."

He felt his mouth drop open and knew it would only be by force that he could close it. The boulder near him had risen into the air and began to turn in large circles as if moving to music he could not see. Meggani not only lifted it with her mind, she made it dance for him. The smaller stones acting as filler between the two sides also rose to move in orbit around the greater stone. "I thought you were going to call Ani," he whispered, frightened at distracting her and possibly causing an avalanche.

"She'll feel me working and come on her own," Meggani informed him with a wave. "We can feel each other when we use our abilities now. She'll come running in a moment. This is not something she would be able to resist."

"Of course she wouldn't," he chuckled, as he sat back to better watch the show. He only regretted he didn't have a camera.

CHAPTER THIRTY-THREE

I t was very late when she heard the call. The school was deep in slumber, locked in their evening's dreams. A subtle sound drifted through the girl's dormitory, no more than an obscure note that floated on the intermittent wind. A melody that was carried on the night air made her quiver with expectation. Meggani sat up in her bed, pushing the light blanket to the floor. The odd, almost bittersweet song held her motionless, making her long to hear more.

She held her breath, listening with an intensity she had never felt before.

The tune curled around her body, tantalizing her at a threshold that defied memory of this life, curving through the night and extending her recollections to other times. This song was written into the fabric of her soul. Each sound was filled with magic, a rhythmic pulse that could not be denied, pushing past the defenses she had erected to protect her heart when just an infant.

Her head cocked as the song embraced her; slipping her feet into her sandals, she began to follow it.

The music.

It wrapped around her body, dancing through her mind, leaving a trail of joy and happiness in its wake.

The music.

She could not resist the music.

Meggani noticed Ani sitting up in the bed and she guided the little girl back to her pillow. "Sleep," she encouraged the child, "I'll see to it."

It called to her, and she turned from her charge to follow it once more. Walking outside, she noted the progress the school was making. There were several guest cottages going up on the far perimeter, for when the student's parents or relatives wished to visit. Other students were bound to have families who would show up. The extra space for the solar panels provided them with additional energy to run the computers that the brothers had managed to obtain for each of them. Meggani had not managed to hide her astonishment at being handed her first laptop, though her joy helped her ignore the brothers' laughter.

She had never imagined that her faith in the two monks would gain her access to more knowledge and power than she had ever dreamt possible.

Called back to her mission, she trembled with excitement.

Follow the music.

She could not see its source. Meggani searched around, confused. She could hear Rohan trying to calm Jake and Mani in the boys' dorm. She thought about helping him, but she had already been sufficiently delayed to resent anything that kept her from finding the composer enchanting her with such ease.

Going around the brothers' cabin, she kept moving until she had cleared even Jake and Rohan's parent's cottage. The mother had helped Ani acclimate to being so far from her close-knit family for the first time. They had been helpful to the school though she refused to get close.

Meggani tended to shy away from the kind woman's attempts to befriend her. She felt the wounds of her own mother's betrayal far too much to ever accept a substitute.

Continuing to move, Meggani left the school boundaries, slipping through a break in the fence. It would only take Ani and her a few more days to complete it, under the gentle guidance of Father Kwai.

She thought it funny that he was relying on two girls to do all the heavy lifting while he handled the placement and mortar.

The music continued its call.

Scrambling up one of the hills towering over her, it felt as if the notes were assisting her progress. Embracing her, renewing her depleted soul, they guided her through each step she took.

The music. Do not deny the music.

When she realized how far she had gone from the school, whose buildings were little more than a dark shadow in the distance, she became uneasy. What did it matter, the music compelled her. Do not turn from the call.

Shrugging, she turned back to the notes and continued to search for their creator.

Climbing up the hill, Meggani ignored the scrapes that the scrub and pebbles were causing to her skin.. She had left the school in her t-shirt and shorts that she liked to sleep in. She kept moving, her head cocked to the side, trying to understand what was driving her with such force.

Reaching the peak, she found that she was looking down at a large Bedouin encampment. There were multiple tents, three different animal enclosures, and six different warring fires. Meggani paused, hesitant to trespass on their territory. It might just look like a camping site to some, but she was fully cognizant of the fact that this was really their home. To breach their perimeter would be a gross act of incivility.

It would be a complete disregard of manners.

She would never be so rude.

Meggani turned on her heel realizing that the music was not coming from below, but from the top of the slope. She saw a small boy sitting under a tree, with a large audience spread before him.

An audience comprised of animals.

Slowly, with a last sigh, the song disappeared into silence. The final translucent notes of the tune were carried away on a chilled puff of wind.

Meggani stood at the edge of the hill, transfixed by the spell, aching as the silence reflected back the emptiness of her heart. She hesitated, feeling her cheeks chill from her flowing tears.

Then it began again.

She joined the others, as the boy resumed his tune. Sitting down, she wrinkled her nose as she settled closer to the animals. The heat they were putting out was nice, but it wasn't the only thing. Sheep were pretty in pictures, but they stank in real life. Meggani soaked in the vision around her as a sponge did water.

The boy's eyes were closed, as he worked his magic on the small wood flute he was playing with absolute concentration and dedication. His fingers moved over the holes, his body swaying with the notes.

She curled closer to the sheep beside her and rested her head against its side. The animals surrounding her ranged from large camels, their coats matted with sand, to small mice scampering between the others' swishing tails and stretched feet. Set apart from the others was a lion, his mane moving in the breeze, and giving his usual lunch a dispassionate look. The king of the jungle was just as hypnotized as the rest of them were.

Meggani enjoyed recognizing the many birds that were present. Some were a wattle ibis, an entire legion of black-winged lovebirds and white-collared pigeons. The ibis was a loud bird in normal circumstances. This was the first time she had witnessed one sitting quietly, just moving its head to the beat. The lovebirds and pigeons intermixed to make a chessboard pattern in the trees above them.

A camel turned to her with disinterest, as it chewed its cud.

She felt no fear that there were predators in their midst, for the other animals were placid in spite of the threat. A pack of thin hyenas were curled up around each other, their shaggy manes swaying to the song that embraced everyone present.

Meggani remembered the picture of the first Christmas with Jesus that Father Kwai had shown her. She wondered if this was what the stable looked like on that vital day.

Certainly, the miraculous feeling had to have been similar.

When the tune ended, Meggani stayed still, as each animal rose and made their steady way back to their lives. She held her breath as the lion left, hoping that the sense of enchantment would hold so its fellow audience members would not be taken as a snack. When it walked by her, she had to smile at the rumbling she heard, as if the creature were chastising her for even thinking it would be so rude. The birds took off into the sky, forming a colorful cloud that covered the full and pregnant moon.

The boy stowed his flute in a pocket of his robe before he noticed the first human to attend his evening exercise. "Hello," he whispered. "I am Tera."

"Meggani," she smiled. She watched the boy, trying to assess why he had brought her here. He was about her age, though she guessed he had just turned nine. She would have her natal day in a few weeks and be eleven years old. It had taken her a while to get used to being the oldest, and responsible for the younger children at the school, but now that she had, she did not wish to give it up. "I'm older than you," she boasted. "It's my job to take you to the school the Church set up for us."

The boy cocked his head to the side as the lion had, as he listened to her pronouncement of his future. He had copper colored skin with shining agate eyes. His head was shaved, and he was wrapped in the white and black robes of his tribe. She did not understand why his foreignness made her feel good. Meggani could see a series of tattoos marking his hands and neck. The swirling patterns made no sense to her. "Do this often?"

"Every night," Tera confirmed. "First time anyone ever came, though."

"It's only animals?" When he nodded, a tentative look of friendliness filled his eyes. Meggani gave him a broad smile. "I have a feeling that you are meant to go to our school. It's a special place, for kids that have abilities; kids who are special. Kids that can do things that other people might not understand."

Tera turned to look down on the encampment. "They do not understand me."

"I do," Meggani informed him. Her voice was soft but they both recognized the strength behind her words.

"How would I know that?"

She released a deep sigh as she turned to look at the camp as well. "I know how frustrating it is when you see adults doing things that hurt themselves and you can't make them stop. I know how mad it makes you that no one will listen. No one hears. I know how the power builds up within you until you know that if you don't use it, if you don't share your abilities, it will make your head explode. I know about the dreams. Dreams about different worlds and past times, dreams that leave you shaking with confusion and fear, dreams that remind you how miracles are within your ability - in your hands - your hands alone. It is a gift we share, a gift that comes with great price."

"A price," he cursed, a hoarse set of words that made Meggani look away. "A price of no parents. No friends. Being alone all the time, even when I am in a place filled with people, at a cost of living a life in isolation as no more than an isolated soul. That is not a price. That is a curse."

"Yeah, I guess. You say tomato … I say tomato."

"What's a tomato?"

Meggani laughed, and felt the mirth lighten her soul at the reminder of everything she had lost when she gained her ability. She had more in common with this foreign boy than she thought possible. "I think I am going to like you."

"A friend will be a new experience," Tera conceded.

She stood up and held out her hand, to assist him as well. "So will tomatoes."

The next morning Meggani watched as all the adults looked astonished when Tera arrived at the breakfast table. She handed him a dish and rejoiced inside at the interest they caused. Her finest moment was when Jake came over with a basket of fresh picked fruit from the school's garden. "This is a tomato," she handed it to the boy.

When he bit into it like an apple the adults all gasped. Chewing thoughtfully, the red juice changed the tone of his skin to that of a piece of antique jewelry. "It is good."

"Told ya so." Meggani took one of the fruits and bit into it like her new friend.

Mtho came over and pulled her to the side. "He belongs here?"

She smiled as she saw that the other kids surrounding Tera. Meggani nodded, as Kwai and Peter both joined them. Peter bristled at her affront of her bringing someone in that they had not approved, so when he spoke his voice was just short of a true roar. "How did you find him?"

"He called me last night."

Peter crossed his arms over his chest. "And how did he call? We still have no phones."

"Don't ask questions, brother," Mtho admonished. "There are some answers we will never understand."

"It is not right," he thundered.

Kwai stepped in, concerned at how fast Peter was escalating. "Brother, you must stop this. Meggani did not mean any harm. She has done what we asked of her. Found other students for our school. She should be commended, not chastised."

Mtho shook his head. He had hoped his brother had overcome this problem. "Some calls are beyond our ability, my friend."

"I did not mean to cause a problem," Meggani whispered.

Peter looked between the two men he had known most of his adult life and recognized that he would not win this confrontation.

The others stared back at him with blank looks, hoping he would diffuse his own anger.

Kwai shrugged. "I think it's wonderful that they share this connection."

"What do you know," Peter muttered, before returning to the buffet.

Mtho watched with a heavy heart as Kwai followed him. "Don't take it personally, child." He gave Meggani a reassuring grin.

"I don't," she shrugged with feigned indifference. "I just wish he could understand."

She wandered back to the other children, leaving Mtho behind staring after her. When she was alone with Tera, he motioned back at the monks. "That one," he whispered, pointing to Peter, "that one has very little aura left."

"I know," she glanced at the scowling man and turned her back to him before he noticed. Meggani was still conflicted about how to explain to the brothers what she and the others saw. Peter was an adult. Their word could mean little when held against his. If she tried to cause such a battle at this point, she could very well split apart the school that was still finding its foundation. It was not time yet.

Tera turned with her. "What will you do?"

Ani and Mani joined them, having caught what they were speaking about. "We can do nothing."

"Why not? Why not just heal him?"

Meggani shrugged. Their newcomer had much to learn. "He's not some animal that hasn't a right to free will."

The cousins shared a silent conversation while they watched. Jake joined them, staring at Ani with clear adoration. She nodded, resigned yet resolute. "We may not interfere. He is not to be healed. His illness is of the spirit."

"Father Peter must decide to accept himself as he is. He must release his jealousy."

"What is jealousy?" Tera asked.

Meggani snorted. "If there was any doubt before about whether you belong here, you just erased it."

"Good," he murmured to her. "I think I shall like friends."

As he bit into his second tomato exuberantly, she laughed. "Almost as much as you like tomatoes."

CHAPTER THIRTY-FOUR

"Mama Africa has so much love to share."
—Akon

The outside of the truck was encrusted with rust, the patches spread over the surface like great constellations of decay. Its owners had created this façade with wise intentions. No one would want to be near the vehicle, much less investigate it. The filth and grime on the outside was the complete opposite of the inside, which it was pristine, without a speck of dirt.

Nothing was present that would contaminate their cargo. The old army transport had been filled with sacks of seeds, grains, and boxes of medical supplies. The sacks made comfortable seats to endure the rutted and pitted roads that they bounced over at breakneck speeds. Rhonda had the girl clasped tight, safely in her arms, to make sure that she didn't get jolted from the sacks onto the metal flooring. The adults all braced one hand on one of the support struts for the tarp that covered them.

Each was covered with a light sheen of sweat from the close

confines. They never looked outside. Their companions had assured them that they did not want to see the wastelands they were passing through. After the first day they found a rhythm. Sleep most of the day under the truck or inside it. Travel at night when they were less likely to be seen. It was rare that they got to see the sun.

Josephus, Rhonda and Jack knew that there was something about them that the brigands chauffeuring them found entertaining. They just couldn't figure out what it was.

The bandits were unwilling to admit their secret to them. It was the strangers' expressions that were so funny. Their heads were bouncing around so much they looked like the bobble head dolls that people put in the rear windows of their cars.

Jack scrutinized the three mercenaries sitting at the entrance to the truck, holding automatic weapons cradled in their hands, much as Rhonda held the girl. "I don't like this," he muttered.

She glanced quickly at the three men who had used black makeup to make their dark skin no more than shadows in the afternoon sun. "This was the best way I could find into Sudan. We had to wait for months in Aswan to manage this ride. We couldn't afford any more delay."

"These men will be fine." Josephus said with such absolute confidence that Rhonda gave Jack a triumphant grin.

"I'm so comforted," Jack mumbled.

The leader handed his weapon to his companion, and holding onto the metal supports at their highest peak he made his way over to the four passengers. Jack looked up at him in absolute fear. The man was well over six feet tall with the build of a professional linebacker A scar ran from one temple to his jaw line. His eyes reminded Jack of a great white shark, flat and soulless. No light of God's love. This was a man that had seen the worst of human kind. How could he not give out what he had received in equal measure?

"You speak English, yes?" he asked the three adults with a broken clipped growl.

Josephus nodded, "We do."

"The others," the bandit informed them. "They call me Danger."

When his companions' faces froze in an almost comic spectrum of extreme fear, Josephus' sigh was heavy. He had not foreseen how his companions would react to the truth of African life. The line between right and wrong was not as concrete as it was in their home. To them, there were countrymen and then ethnicities. Here you were judged on the color of your skin, the religion you worshipped, the tribe you came from, and your political beliefs. "It is nice to meet you. I am Father Josephus; this is Rhonda Sith and Jack Kerr. They are Americans, but I try not to hold it against them."

He knelt beside Rhonda, and with a single fingertip he reached out to touch the dewy softness of the child's cheek. "The girl. She looks like my daughter."

"She is a very special lass."

Danger looked at Jack and shook his head. "We will not hurt you."

"I do not mean to insult you." Jack looked to his companions for some kind of direction or assistance. When he found neither of them, he turned back to the obsidian glare of the man he was certain had been a mass murderer at some time. "I just think ..."

"You are a white man surrounded by strong black men. I think it is normal that you are nervous."

Rhonda found her voice once more and thought to offer the only Caucasian member of their group some token show of assistance. "He's not like this. I do not believe in any other situation he would have a problem with the color of your skin. If I had thought this, I would not have travelled with him to the corner, much less to a different country."

"You see," Jack tried to explain before Rhonda's inane explanations got him shot, "You're bandits."

"We are bandits." Danger turned and spoke a series of words to his two friends. The men smiled and held up their weapons with a triumphant sweep.

Jack and Rhonda looked at Josephus for help, who gave them a simple shrug. "I speak a lot of languages but that one escaped me."

"We are proud to be bandits," Danger continued to boast.

Jack held up his hands, palms out, as if he were trying to surrender. "That's my point. I've never been around bandits before. It makes me nervous."

"Do you know what we do?"

The three of them each wagged their heads, keeping to the time of the bouncing vehicle.

"We bring food and medicine to people who would not otherwise get it. We protect those that have neither the skills nor the resources. We are the justice and the right in a world that has abandoned the poor and innocent. It is good to be a bandit. Our country is our honor, and our work is there for those that have nowhere else to turn."

Jack tried to hide his face so that the pontificating man would not see him roll his eyes. "For which you charge a great deal."

"This risk is great," Danger spat, "so too should be the reward."

"What would you do if there was a chance to make your country strong again? Make your country a place for right to be might, rather than the other way around." Josephus's question made the others grow silent and introspective, after Danger repeated it to his friends.

"You think I want my world to be torn apart by civil war?"

Rhonda saw Danger's stiffness and stilted question as a bad sign for their continued travel, not to mention drawing their next breaths. "It is how you make your living."

"The Americans ... so egotistical."

As soon as the other bandit translated his pronouncement to his friends they all nodded. It was clear now that Danger was the only one who spoke their language. Josephus sat forward to prove his earnestness, as much as to block Rhonda and Jack from interrupting. "I would just like to understand." His noble manner and the import he put behind the words easily broke through the men's reticence.

Danger's jaw stiffened. "I would give up this life in a heartbeat; we all would, if we knew that our children were guaranteed some kind of future."

"Some things are worth any risk," Josephus stated, looking pointedly at Jack.

CHAPTER THIRTY-FIVE

"Smooth seas do not make skillful sailors."
—Ethiopian Proverb

Tera proved himself both a new addition to the school and an excellent travel agent for the continued search for other reincarnated guardians. He arranged for Meggani and Father Mtho to get a ride with his former tribe. The Bedouin were happy to assist them. The camel train was a new experience that Mtho and Meggani both enjoyed with open-faced glee, much to the nomads' amusement.

Neither of them even noticed the smells of the animals or the heat.

From the tribe they were dropped off with another group who were moving produce from a farm to the big city. Riding in the bed of an old truck was bumpy on the back, but easy on the feet. Meggani was happy they wouldn't have to walk into the next country, Eritrea, which had been a part of Ethiopia before the last war.

That was the funny thing about war, she pointed out to Brother Mtho, there always seemed to be another one waiting on the horizon.

It was hard to ignore the heat and smell inside the truck. With the camel train there had been the hope of escape from the stench. While perched on top of crates of scraggly vegetables and fruit, it seemed to permeate the cells of their bodies.

Still, they found a way to laugh through the ride.

There had been many changes for her. Mtho had taken Meggani shopping at one of the outposts when the nomads stopped. Meggani felt like a princess with her new possessions. He had given her a free hand to pick out a book, and laughed when she trembled over the hair beads on one vendor's blanket.

It was the one thing she remembered from her parents that she missed.

Mtho insisted she purchase three sets of the multi-colored glass and carved wood adornments. He guessed from her grateful look that he had finally made up for the brick incident.

A backpack was bought to hold her clothing, shoes, and precious books. Mtho was uncomfortable forcing her to travel the same way that he did. It was a simple matter for him to wash out his robes when they stopped at a location. He felt no need for possessions, but he had made that choice as an adult.

No matter how old Meggani acted, she was still a little girl at heart.

It amused him at how gleeful Meggani was to be riding in a truck to the next location.

She was especially content that their assistance meant she wouldn't be wearing out her new shoes. Her shining white sneakers were a constant source of pride . Each night Meggani still cleaned off the tops with tender care. She didn't feel like seeing holes in the bottoms so soon. They were, after all, her first new shoes.

At the moment, their journey's biggest problem was that they had not yet discovered any additional children. Mtho had shared the brother's concern that if the kids were not found and secured soon, their powers would be corrupted. Even taken. If they saw their abilities as a bad thing, the reincarnated guardians had the power to wish them away. Or worse. They would use them to manipulate and control, rather than to support and guide. She couldn't imagine her life without her talents, even with all they had cost her.

The farmer's shipper had deposited them with a large lunch in a park in the country's small capital. Sitting on the bench swinging her feet, Meggani noticed that Father Mtho looked tired. "I don't think we should give up yet."

"Nor do I child. I am just waiting for a sign." He went back to chewing his bread and honey while gazing at their chaotic surroundings with weary eyes. They were facing a busy thoroughfare swollen with cars of all sizes, trucks, animal-drawn vehicles, and zipping motorcycles that made his eyes cross with their grating whirr.

He knew Meggani liked to eat with grass under her feet, but Mtho longed for the safety of four walls. Not to mention the comfort of a table and chairs.

This place was such a contrast to his country. There was trade here. Commerce. He could see rebuilding and growth with every vehicle that blew by their seat. The people were well fed, and their eyes shone with hope of knowing without a doubt that they would have an even better tomorrow.

Exactly what he wanted for Ethiopia.

Mtho watched apprehensively as a five year-old boy darted into the traffic to cross the street in the middle of the block. "That cannot be safe," he muttered to his charge. She looked where he was staring and understood his fear.

The traffic light released a torrent of vehicles bearing down on and the child froze in terror at his coming death.

Meggani and Mtho rose with their hearts in their throats. Mtho leapt forward knowing he could not reach him in time. He still felt a deep compulsion to try. He could feel Meggani trying to gather her powers around her by the sensation of electricity in the air. "Don't let us fail, merciful God," Mtho prayed as he ran.

Everything seemed to slow, as if they needed to turn some kind of crank to make the scene match the normal pace of real life.

The effect forced them into experiencing each moment with pained agony.

"It will be too late," she called after him. They both whimpered knowing horribly that there was nothing they could do.

A motorcycle had pulled to the front of the throng on a direct course for the child. The tinted plastic of the driver's helmet would make seeing the boy dressed in dark clothes almost impossible. When it appeared they were about to collide, the lad held up his hand and crouched down. As soon as he did, the bike flew into the air over him, never touching a hair on his head and crash landed beyond him.

This is what standing inside of an American action movie would feel like, Meggani thought.

Brushing off his form, the child stood up, and finished crossing the avenue with a confident saunter. He acted as if he did this kind of thing every day.

He never even bothered to look at the wreck he'd left behind.

Other drivers swerved around the motorcyclist and the crashed bike; returning to their own swift routes.

"I guess that would be called a sign." Meggani beamed, as she rocked back and forth.

Mtho watched from the street corner as the driver of the motorcycle stood and limped over to his crumpled bike. The front wheel had been folded neatly in half, as if it were a piece of paper that someone had discarded. "That's not a sign," he admonished her. "That's a Kiddisti."

CHAPTER THIRTY-SIX

"Where there is unity there is always victory."
—Publilius Syrus

They were required to go on Danger's run to multiple villages. Their stop was out of the bandits' way and would have to come last. Each one was the same. The people were waiting for the supplies that were stored in the truck. In every location they left some food or medicinal item, taking something else with them. The exchanges were done in the bright sun. This was no clandestine, shadow-bound operation. Josephus felt it behooved him to point out to the others that the villagers were all ecstatic when they arrived.

Jack maintained with his dry sense of humor, that they were even happier when they left.

What these men were doing might not have been legal by human law—the human law of the country they were in—but it was certainly not against God's law. Even their token white man hesitated to fight the call of God.

After several weeks, they had time to work on their passenger's mission.

When they reached the coordinates that Josephus had determined could be the Ark's next resting place, it was worse than any other destination they had seen on the mercenaries' route. The landscape, as far as they could see, was either burned out husks or skeletal structures patched together with mud.

The men left behind by the wars and killing gangs were either under the age of three or over eighty.

Everyone suffered from illness.

Some nameless factory had polluted the only water source, which meant there was little hope these people would ever recover.

Josephus and his friends shrank as the smell of human and animal waste hit them in the face, with a powerful undercurrent of death. It coated the backs of their throats and made them gag. Their eyes watered as if they were trying to disperse it, without conscious choice. Despair was the only emotion they could feel or see as they gazed around them.

"This is a place where hope doesn't even have a chance to be born, much less grow." Jack's observation was meant for himself but Danger heard it anyway.

Father Josephus, Rhonda, and Jack looked around at a society gasping its final breaths. Danger exited the vehicle, holding the baby and handing her to Rhonda.

Look at her, Baba. She is no longer a baby. Their marked one had grown up before his eyes.

Taking the child in her arms, the Professor looked down at her astonished, and turned to Father Josephus for some kind of direction. "She's moving. It's been so long since she did anything. I was beginning to think I hallucinated what I saw on the Elephantine."

"We must be in the right place then." Josephus grinned. He took his charge from Rhonda and placed her on the ground, holding her against his body to keep her upright. His other hand reached into his pocket and he withdrew his paper and pen.

Jack rushed to set up the video camera equipment, with some help from Danger. It took only a few seconds, and then the adults all froze as they waited for the blessed one to show them the way.

The expectation was so heavy in the air that it created a palpable haze that was thick with hope.

She seemed to wait for some sign.

A sunbeam pierced through the gloom above them and embraced her as if a benediction from God.

She walked forward a few steps and threw her hands up to the sky. Tears streamed from her eyes, each sparkling as it traveled down her face. Rhonda took a few steps to help her, but Father Josephus held up his hand to prevent her from touching her skin. "She has reacted like this before. Give her some time, Rhonda. We will care for her when she is ready for it."

Danger gazed uneasily between the little one and his three adult passengers. If there was something here of value, he would use it. He always took what his people needed. These strangers might not like his methods, but he did help people. Jack kept back, his camera trained on the girl's face.

"The journey weakened the children, and strengthened the Covenant. It could feel itself getting closer to the torch. The torch's path called to it. The promise of this possible new land made it swarm with power. They found only despair in this place, the people and the land rejecting it, as if they were oil and water."

The child collapsed to the ground, and Father Josephus dropped his pad and paper to rush over to her side. Rhonda brought over a bottle of water from the truck. "She looks thirsty."

Josephus gave a small smile as the woman fed a few drops of liquid into the blessed one's mouth. "You have a natural way with the little one."

"Little one? It's a good name for her."

Rhonda ignored Jack's praise. "Father, isn't it enough? Let's wrap her up and put her back in the truck."

Her body pulled away from them and stood up as if she were in pain; hunched over like an arthritic old woman at the end of her life. Her sweat-soaked face shone in the sun.

"I don't think she's done," Josephus cautioned his friends.

A group of people from the village had moved to join the newcomers. Their dusty faces and haunted, devastated eyes made the visitors shudder with empathy. Jack peered nervously around at the circle that had penned them in. "Let's just hope that won't be a problem."

Without another word, the Little One took off running to the far side of the village. The others followed her, including every member of the town they had invaded. She moved beyond the buildings until she found a large series of fields. The sandy earth had clearly once fed the entire neighborhood, but was now pure beach. There was a harsh miasma of chemicals that emanated from below their feet. Whoever had done this to the people had intended it to be permanent.

She held her hands up at the perimeter and turned around in a circle. *"They have forgotten the rules of abundance and drained the earth of all life and energy. Poisoned their Holy Mother. They knew not the need for balance in all things and places. The people have made it so all that can grow here is death."* She gave the spectators such a scathing look it made them back up in fear as if it scalded their souls. *"This planet is our mother and must be cherished and cared for in order to allow its children to flourish."*

Josephus apprehensively looked between the villagers and his companions. What his charge was saying condemned their actions. How would they react? What would they do? The audience they had gathered seemed content to watch her actions, and not judge them. He felt sure that they had developed trust with the bandits, but even that would only go a limited distance. This could quickly become a very frightening situation.

Pulling out the crystal that she found on Mount Sinai, she held it parallel to the earth. When she began to moan, once again Rhonda jerked forward to tend to her. Josephus caught her arm and held it tight to prevent her. "No," he roared at the professor.

Rhonda tried to dart away from his hold, "It sounds like she is hurt."

"That is close to the noise I heard at the Dome of the Rock." He was slow to release her arm, even when he was sure she would obey him.

Whatever was about to happen needed to run its course. They had no right to interfere.

Suddenly, all around them, hundreds of plants began to shoot out of the earth. As the fields become burdened with crops the choking smell of chemicals dissipated. People around them smiled reverently, their eyes lightened by the miracle. The plants continued to grow until they were looking at a field of ripe and ready to harvest wheat. Laden with healthy buds, the smell of life wrapped around the villagers and visitor's senses.

Father Josephus fell to his knees, crossed himself, and lowered his head. "Our Father, who art in heaven … hallowed be thy name …"

His prayers were drowned out as the emaciated and devastated villagers began to laugh and sing. Rhonda wiped tears of joy from her face as the people went running through the fields, their hands stretched out to touch the plants to be sure they were real. Their happiness created a light of joy that illuminated everything around them. Voices joining in song and prayer, they were wrapped up in the glory of the moment.

Only Jack managed to secure the image of the child lying on the ground, her body exhausted from the miracles she had just delivered.

Forgotten and alone.

He was the one who moved her away from the rejoicing people and the praying priest. He gave her some water and covered her with a blanket. Wiping away his tears, he sat beside her and tried to think of something to say.

Bowing over her frail form, he folded his hands together to pray. "There is a price for what you are doing, child. I hope that God has prepared you to pay the bill."

CHAPTER THIRTY-SEVEN

"Snake at your feet – a stick in your hand."
—Ethiopian Proverb

For the first time in her travels with her robed companion, Meggani wanted to complain. Brother Mtho sending Kiddisti to the school with his mother had angered her. His insistence they stay in Eritrea made her see red. Now they were walking down a long garbage-strewn alleyway in the middle of the night. The smell, a blending of rotting food and excrement, made her eyes water.

Her stomach hurt. Something here was foul, and it was invading her soul.

She was officially ready to explode.

"Why are we here?" Meggani yanked on his hand and planted her feet against the pavement.

"Come. We are late, Meggani." Mtho tried pulling her but she was not budging. "There is something we need to do."

"What?"

"Later, Meggani," the monk shrank at the tone of his voice. It was the first time he snapped at her.

She wrenched her hand out of his grasp and folded her arms across her chest. "I'm not going any place until you explain."

"Meggani," Mtho tried to capture her arm but she evaded him. Seeing that force was not going to work, he sighed heavily. Crouching so that he could look up into her sweet face, contorted with rage, he snorted at the mutinous expression in her eyes. "When you told me what happened to you after you left the freak show, I got angry. I had to do something. I managed to contact the same people that had you prisoner. The villains you escaped from almost cost you your life. They are still doing the same things to other kids."

She began to shake at the danger he was inviting into their lives. "Why would you do this?"

"Because they need to be stopped," he reminded her while stroking her cheek with a gentle hand. "They need to know that children are not possessions that are easy to replace. They are not things to be used and discarded with the trash. When I began to speak with them, I found out that they were selling a girl with extraordinary abilities, a girl just like you. The difference is, she is too young to save herself."

"I am afraid." Meggani took a deep breath as she buried her hands in her pockets. "You made me forget what that felt like. I don't like that you have brought it all back." Her resentment was evident in her tone and the hurt reflected in her eyes.

"My mistake. I should have left you at the hotel." Mtho felt at war with himself. He had a responsibility to protect her childhood and to respect her independence, as well as her need to help. How could he do both in a situation like this, he wondered.

The two stared deep into each other's eyes as they fought their own battles, locked in silence. Meggani realized that no matter how frightened she was of where they were going, there was no way she would allow him to leave her behind.

She could not stand the thought of missing out on something, anything, good or bad.

"I would have just followed you," she countered.

Mtho looked between the far-off doorway where they were headed and the relative safety of the lit thoroughfare at the opposite end of the alley. "This is no place for a child."

"Or a monk," her voice came out hoarse with her building terror.

Realizing there were no easy answers in this situation, Mtho grabbed her hand. They continued down the alley toward the doorway that had a single red light beside it. He checked the number on the door from a piece of paper in his hand. "This is it," he stated, nervous and unsure. Kneeling once more he gazed into her eyes with steady confidence, "I will have your promise once more, Meggani."

"I swear to stay by your side at all times, and if we get separated I will run as fast as I can for the nearest well-lit street." She held up her hand as she gave him her word in the same patronizing exaggerated patience of all children.

Mtho held a finger to her nose and tweaked it. "Make sure you remember."

The lobby of the abandoned building has been set up as a reception area. There were two men, both with heavy muscles and well-armed, standing guard over the hallway to the other rooms, with a clear sense of menace. The area was clear from the debris outside, and the incense and cigarette smoke filling the area cut the exterior stench.

A woman with fingernails so long they defied imagination was sitting behind a table working on a laptop computer with absolute concentration.

Talon-lady stood to greet them. "You are the one here for the girl?"

"I am," Mtho's answer was curt and dismissive.

The female reached out to touch Meggani's face. The nails on her hand were so long and painted blood red they resembled the claws of a rapacious beast. Mtho shoved Meggani behind his body in the blink of an eye.

Whatever happened, he was determined that this vile creature would not besmirch the one he protected.

He had directed her to come disguised. Meggani was dressed in jeans and a bulky shirt, her hair covered by a skullcap. He had tried to make her look as much like a boy as possible. It had been his hope that the change would conceal her beauty, but the woman noticed something she liked anyway.

"I would trade." Her voice was a petulant whine, and he felt Meggani's shudder of revulsion.

"Not interested." Mtho squeezed Meggani's arm to try and given her some of his strength.

The woman shrugged, her claws swiping at the air. "Pity. I am sure she would be perfect for my stable."

Mtho made sure to enunciate, his stare hard as stone. "She is not for sale."

Shrugging once more, the Talon-Lady managed to snap her fingers at one of the guards. "Go get the problem."

One of the men rushed to do her bidding. He disappeared down the hallway they guarded. His partner moved to cover the opening by himself. The woman faced Mtho once more. "You have the money, yes?"

Mtho withdrew a pouch from the inside of his robes. "I do."

She weighed it in her hand judging its contents. "You are very trusting to carry so many gold coins."

"I have some very strong protection."

"You must." She slid the payment into one of the desk drawers as she continued to stare at Mtho, trying to gage his mettle.

The guard returned, dragging a small captive behind him by a long piece of rope that had been tied around her neck. She was dressed in rags, and covered in bruises. Mtho bristled with rage. "I demanded she not be hurt."

"She needed to be taught a lesson." The woman shrugged, as she gestured to her man to release the prisoner.

Meggani went into a rage at the damage done to the child before them. Her face was covered in purple bruises, her arm held at a strange angle to the rest of her body. The few steps that she took away from her captors were achieved with great pain. Her gait made it clear that this was not the first abuse she had withstood.

"You monsters," Meggani screeched. A series of curses followed this statement that made Mtho blush. Meggani flew at the woman and kicked her several times in the legs before Mtho managed to catch her and drag her back.

The evil one hissed, "I should just take her from you and teach her some respect."

"She will learn all the respect she needs at my feet," he thundered.

"You should leave before I decide to demand the right to watch these lessons," she spat. "I am an expert at such discipline."

Mtho ignored the threat. "When we are ready. Think of the girl," he instructed Meggani. He could not bend down to look in her eyes. His attention had to stay glued to the people threatening them. Pitching his voice low enough for her ears alone, he hoped his terseness would remind her how dire their situation was, how much care she must take. "Help the girl. Your anger does nothing but delay us in this place. What is it you prefer? To stay here or find some way to make this better for her?"

When Meggani's stopped struggling, Mtho barked a command at Talon-Lady's guard. "Release our new charge now or my 'protection' will make my umbrage clear to you all."

The woman gave a curt nod and the guard let go of his captive.

As soon as the rope dropped, the prisoner flew toward them like a whirlwind. Meggani stepped forward and took the little one in her arms to soothe her. Resistant to any touching at first, Meggani's gentle hand on her back calmed her.

Once she had her settled, Meggani lifted her in her embrace and moved to stand beside Mtho once more. She took care to keep from jostling the baby's arm.

"Business is done." Mtho ignored her mutinous expression, and dragged her by the shoulder to the alley. He was mindful of any kind of bulwark he could put between the children and the evil that was so close. He kept them moving as quickly as possible, determined to keep her breathless so she wouldn't have the voice to fight his decision.

Mtho wanted them safely away from the slavers.

"You're just leaving them to continue this atrocity?"

Mtho winced at the abhorrence in her voice. "I am getting you both to safety."

"What of the other children they have in that hole?" She tried to stop their exit, but he picked her up to keep them moving. Holding the two children was easy, they were each so light. Mtho pledged he would start to stuff them with food as early as he could. There were other hurts to address first. He steeled in his soul to ignore his newcomer's mewls of distress. His pace was so brisk it was hard for him to answer Meggani's scathing questions. When they were near the street he put them down.

"Can you manage the girl? I'll take her from you in a moment."

"After being in that place do you really think she would let you touch her? Do you really think she will let anyone touch her, ever again?" Meggani hid her face in the little one's shoulder not willing for him to see her tears.

"She's letting you."

Meggani kept up with him. When she realized he kept glancing at her, she guessed she had better explain herself. If he tried to take the younger girl away Meggani knew they would both go crazy. "She knows we are two of a kind."

"Because you are both reincarnated guardians."

"No," Meggani laughed hoarsely. *Why did she always feel so discarded? So like trash? Would she ever feel new again?* "That's not why." Meggani hid her deadened eyes against the girl's shoulder, allowing the monk to guide them both. She had sworn to lock the truth of her past in a place no one would ever see.

They rounded the corner, and stopped before a half a dozen police cars. Mtho took a direct path to a man in a suit that was giving instructions to the multiple agencies present for the arrest. Meggani could tell by the different colored badges each wore on chains around their necks that they came from many places and countries.

"It is just as we were told. Three guards. Very little firepower. It looked like they were carrying large handguns under their shirts."

The captain gave him a curt nod. "We'll take it from here, Brother Mtho."

"I'll be at the hotel if you have any more questions."

Meggani regarded her friend with newfound respect and appreciation. He had saved the Guardian and taken down the trafficking ring, all in one sweep. It was brilliant. He might have spent most of his life living in a monastery, but her friend had some real hidden talents.

"It's a privilege to meet you, sir." The captain shook the monk's hand and gave him a respectful nod. "This wouldn't have happened without you."

At a silent motion from the captain, the officers all rushed to their vehicles and took off at full speed toward where the threesome had just escaped. The cars' sirens surrounded the building with ear-splitting wails, overflowing the alley. Whatever had been taking place in the abandoned structure would no longer be given a chance - no matter what.

"I should have trusted you." Meggani begrudged her offered admission, so she whispered it.

Mtho chuckled. He used his finger to raise her head to look him in the eyes. "Yes, you should have."

"This is why we've been here for over a week?"

"It is."

Meggani gestured to the half asleep girl in her arms. "She is one of us, isn't she?"

"I think so." Mtho gently extricated the rope from the girl's neck and cast it into the gutter where it belonged. "I have heard only a rumor, though. We will have to wait and see."

Meggani shrugged without disturbing the girl. "I'll find out tomorrow."

"We have some time," he warned her. "We can't leave until I finish giving my testimony against that woman and those meager examples of humanity." Looking at the two girls, he remembered the hurt state of the newcomer. "I think we should visit the hospital to have your new charge checked out. Her arm may be broken."

"I have supplies from Mani at the suite. They should take care of it."

"Are you sure?"

The two of them walked down the street back to their temporary home, the hurt one making soft snoring sounds each step of the way. "Positive. What will happen next?"

Mtho would not lie to her. "If all goes well, those people will spend a great deal of time in a hole far worse than they ever put you children."

"Good." Meggani beamed, as they continued their trek toward their hotel. At least it was a nice place. They even had room service. Meggani loved her bedroom in the suite of rooms Mtho had taken. "Now I don't feel bad about kicking the Talon-Lady where it hurts."

Mtho tried to stop the laugh that burst out at her statement. "One does not kick women where it hurts."

"Believe me, brother, when I kick … it hurts."

CHAPTER THIRTY-EIGHT

"When spider webs unite, they can tie up a lion."
—Ethiopian Proverb

At that moment the sun rising over the village represented so much more to Josephus than the start of a new day. This little Sudanese hamlet had changed completely. Life could flourish here once more. The food in the fields had been joined by gardens in front of each of the newly repaired cottages, bursting with multi-colored fruits and vegetables. Its people were walking around brimming with good health, the sick well on the road to recovery.

Their eyes filled with the hopeful light of endless possibilities.

Josephus stood with Danger as he surveyed all that the last few weeks had wrought. "Your men were the key to this, you know."

"It is only through the good fortune of meeting you and the Little One that we now get to tell people we helped make a miracle."

"You should be most proud of the man you are."

"I take it you no longer fear us?"

"That was never I." Josephus looked at the two Americans standing nearby, patient and calm, while they waited for him. "I have always known that God would lead me to be in the right place at the right time."

Suddenly, the air filled with laughter. The children of the town were pushing at a patched soccer ball, manipulating it around the newly constructed buildings with expert ease. Their footwork would do David Beckham proud. All the adults had to smile at the sheer exuberance the young ones displayed. Their bodies were bursting with health. Each of them wore clothing that was fresh, laundered and repaired. The mercenaries' last gift to the town had been a few bolts of fabric.

It would have to last until they could get them some linen and sheep.

Father Josephus patted Danger on the back as he moved to Rhonda and Jack. They were watching a replay of something on the video camera.

Jack stubbornly shook his head. "I don't get it. I have never heard that the Ark was used as a weapon. I thought it was only mentioned being taken into battle to encourage the Jewish soldiers. They would parade it around to embolden them, and frighten the enemy."

"I certainly never heard about an Ark Maiden."

"Moses demanded his sister take over care of the Ark."

Father Josephus jumped in, "Miriam would have been the first Ark Maiden. It is also recorded that she was fighting with her brother at the time, for marrying an Ethiopian woman."

The two laughed at the priest's eagerness to include his country into any reference to the Ark and the prophet that helped form it. Jack rolled his eyes, "Not that we're surprised."

Rhonda continued her story, "When she refused, he had it inflict her with horrible boils. Afterwards, it cured her, only after she agreed to take over the task." Rhonda shrugged. "That is the only mention in the Bible I know of."

"So you think this girl is connected to these Ark Maidens?"

Rhonda looked at him exasperated. "What else would you call it?"

"Coincidence," he offered lamely.

Josephus interrupted before they began debating. Once these two started meshing out a point, all else would stop. They would be in this village for another year if they had their way.

"There are numerous references to the Ark leaving Jerusalem. It could not have left so many times. So if the better-documented occurrences are true, then it makes sense that there might have been something like an Ark Maiden. That way, the different components of the Ark could have left in staggered waves, making sense of the history we still have."

"What would that be?" Jack smiled, as he realized he got the question in before Rhonda could.

"I believe that Menelik, the Queen of Sheba's son with Solomon, somehow took the Maiden. It says in the Bible that she went of her own free will. The only things with free will are human beings. Next, under the reign of King Manasseh, who filled the temple with pagan idols, the actual Ark was lost. This is the time I believe that the faithful took the box we know as the Seat of God, or the Ark. Finally, I believe the remaining components of the tabernacle, mainly the ceremonial pieces, would have been hidden under the direction of the prophet Josiah. All were considered part of the Ark, so all could be true."

"What is the torch?"

Josephus smiled at the American male's question. He was a religious man, but not a spiritual one. Confusion was normal.

"The torch is the spirit of God," Rhonda explained.

"Which is what I believe our little one now carries within her," Josephus added reverently.

Jack shook his head. "No one is going to believe this."

"This is why we need to be very cautious about how we handle it all." Rhonda ejected the tape from the camera and handed it to Jack.

"Speaking of handling ... when are we leaving?"

Rhonda shared a grin with the priest. "We have been meaning to discuss that with you."

"I know Danger and his men are leaving." Jack growled when he saw the impish look in Rhonda's eyes.

Josephus held up his hand to stop Jack from erupting, "We are going with them, I promise."

"Promise," she added.

Her gaze regretful, Rhonda knew that he could guess what she had been thinking.

"You're not returning to the States are you?" Jack ignored Josephus, staring hard at his only female friend.

"I need to go to Ethiopia." Rhonda moved forward and clasped Jack's hands between hers.

"She is not your family, Rhonda."

Rhonda flinched at his reminder that she must look like she was making a fool of herself over someone else's daughter. "I know that, Jack. I also know that this girl is bringing me the closest that I have ever been to proving my husband's and my life's work. The father cannot care for her without some help."

"It is assistance that I can give her with ease."

"You support this lunacy?" He asked Josephus.

"I'm grateful for her support, Jack."

Danger approached with the girl in his arms. "I believe this Little One could use some care."

"I should get her some lunch." Rhonda took the child from the mercenary and rushed off with her to the cabin they had been using over the last few weeks.

"Thank you for watching her," Josephus commended the man. "You are very good with her."

"What she's done here is extraordinary."

The three men looked around them at this small pocket of heaven inside a very real, man-made hell. "The food and the water seem to be curing the people of the disease they were suffering from. It looks like we're done here."

"I am honored to have traveled with you." Danger bowed his head to them both.

Jack smiled, feeling deep regret over his earlier misgivings. All he had witnessed since meeting this man was integrity and honor. He was ashamed of his assumptions. "I heard you are moving your family here?"

"We all are. Together we can protect this place from the Janjaweed."

The *devils on horseback* were nothing but killing gangs assembled by the Sudanese government. They were well known for their brutality.

This sanctified genocide was one of the greatest tragedies of the world. One which few outside of the African continent were willing to acknowledge, much less do something to stop.

It was inconceivable to Josephus what the bandits were willing to take on.

Though he would do no less for his own homeland.

Jack coughed, "Are you sure you comprehend the trouble you are inviting into your lives?"

"Someone must stop it. Someone must stand up. We have the knowledge and the equipment." Danger nodded, "This place is blessed now. I wish my family to enjoy it. I wish my children to feel the magic of the universe once more."

"Yes," Josephus nodded and smiled, "she has that effect on people."

CHAPTER THIRTY-NINE

"She who does not yet know how to walk, cannot climb a ladder."
—Ethiopian Proverb

When he woke that morning, Mtho found Meggani crouching in the suite's large sitting area, beside a small bundle of blankets. He regarded at it with his eyes wide. Looking around, he could not see the little girl they had brought back with them the previous night, and with a sinking heart, he realized that she was wrapped in the bed covering that Meggani guarded with absolute diligence. "When we got back last night it was my hope you both would use the bedroom. What went wrong? That was why I asked for a suite, your room does have two beds."

"You shut your door and fell asleep." Meggani scowled. "Keberwa had some other ideas."

Mtho stepped closer. "Is that she?"

"I hope so." Meggani saw the cloth shimmy, as the child beneath started to tremble. "Otherwise, this hotel has some pretty big rats."

Mtho stepped closer, towering over the lump. "Maybe we should just unwrap her."

A soft keening began as the bundle quaked with terror.

"Guess not." He stepped back from the two children.

Meggani felt so defeated. She had just gotten this close and now the girl was wailing again. "Maybe you should go get us some food."

"I'll pick up more than that." Mtho left and closed the door behind him, making sure not to let it bang.

"He's gone now."

Keberwa peeked out from the blanket taking an apprehensive look at her.

"I promise I will never lie to you."

The girl kept most of her body beneath the covering. Meggani guessed that she was making headway when the child did not put her head back under. Her actions reminded her of a turtle, if their shells were made from blankets and hotel towels. "What does he want?"

"He wants to take us to a school for kids like us."

"Kids who scare their parents?" Keberwa's eyes glistened.

"Yup." Meggani smiled. The child had black curling hair that reflected so many colors in its shine it reminded her of oil on water. Her eyes were like the onyx stone she had seen in a jewelry store window the day Mtho and she shopped for new clothes for her. "Among other things."

"What else does he want?"

Meggani sighed heavily when she saw the girl's eyes narrow with suspicion. She recognized these signs. Keberwa's spirit may not be broken, but it was obvious that her emotional scars were quite deep. She tried to make her voice as reassuring as possible. "I worried about the same thing, but I've been with him for months and he's never done anything."

"I want to believe." The girl disappeared underneath the covering; the only thing exposed was a single lock of hair. "But I have heard these words before."

Meggani sighed again. She understood this stranger's desire to stay safe in her protective cover. Looking at her wild hair, Meggani had a pure and instinctual female idea. Dashing to her backpack she brought over her new comb and a set of the beads that she had coveted. "Why don't we work on your hair?"

The girl retreated under the blankets.

"You don't have to come out. I can braid your hair while you stay under there."

Just her head emerged, but Meggani felt it was safe to proceed. "Mtho bought these for me. I remember my Mama putting them in my hair when I was littler than you. She would explain what each of the beads represented."

"What do you mean?"

The whisper was a notch above a butterfly's wings but Meggani still heard it. "This one," she selected a bead, which was carved with an eye, "is for protection." A glass bead that had gold and green stripes was next. "This is for beauty. Each one means something else and gives you a special power."

Silence reigned as Meggani handled the child's hair with all the care a collector would show to an antique vase. The comb's rhythmic pulls and the tugs of braiding soon had the girl relaxed and much more ready to listen, rather than just react in fear.

"Look. I'll make you my very own personal vow."

Keberwa snorted, "You're not gonna tell me I won't be hurt, will you?"

"Nope. I'm gonna promise that if someone hurts you in the future, you will always be able to do something about it."

This pronouncement earned her the emergence of both Keberwa's head and shoulders. "What do you mean?"

Meggani gloated smugly. She didn't care. This kid needed some of those emotions. Not to mention it was the only thing to drive away the terror. She pulled her knife from her waistband and waved it back and forth in front of her charge's face with a mesmerizing rhythm. "I stole one for you last night, Keberwa. I'm gonna teach you how to use it."

Keberwa reached out to touch it, a slow smile of appreciation crossing her face. The fear receded from her eyes, as her pupils followed the blade as if glued to it.

"Call me Kebbie," the girl whispered, as she crawled out of her shell in more ways than one.

Meggani smiled, as she watched her turtle change into a fox.

CHAPTER FORTY

"He who digs too deep for a fish, may come out with a snake."
—Ethiopian Proverb

The heavy drapes and thick windows muffled the sounds of the busy city as Michael watched Jerusalem change from day to night. The energy here never failed to mesmerize and repulse him. He had arrived to present his report. His heart was far away in his thoughts for his plans that evening.

Michael had not liked what his duty asked of him.

He couldn't see the answer for a reconciliation between his heart, his mind, and most important, his faith.

The cardinal closed the file drumming his fingers against the desk. "So he does not seem to be searching for the actual Ark."

"He just carts the child from place to place."

"These things that happen where the girl goes ..."

Michael sat forward. "You mean the miracles?"

"They are only miracles if the Holy Father declares them to be so." The cardinal's voice was thundered, his eyes narrowed with rage.

"Of course." Michael grinned placatingly.

The cardinal looked at a crystal orb on his desk, his mind quickly processing the possibilities. "Where do they go next?"

Michael swallowed with difficulty. He did not like this game. It had rules that he did not understand. *I am honor bound to obey the cardinal's wishes no matter what*, he reminded himself. *Until he found a clearer sign from God that the cardinal's way was not for heaven, but hell, he would obey.* "They will be traveling to Ethiopia."

"Have you a way to follow?"

The office was wrapped in a tense silence. Michael wiped his hands on his pants. He had done many things for this religious leader in the past, but they had always been against evil people. The line between right and wrong had been an easy one in the past. He saw no light and dark here. There was only gray in this situation. "I understand you wanted the Ark confiscated if it was found here. I do not see how that is possible now. The Ark is a national historic treasure to the Ethiopians."

Michael lifted his head and shoulders and glared at his mentor, "I do not think it is right to take it from them."

He pounded his fist against the desk, making a boom that reminded them both of a gunshot. "I do not pay you to think and I have no need of your thoughts." The cardinal's eyes narrowed with apoplexy. "What are you saying?"

"Are you sure you are prepared for the repercussions if we take the Ark from them? God must want it with them. The Ethiopians have guarded the Covenant for thousands of years. They have done well with it."

"I know they think they have the Ark in Axum."

Michael released a deep sigh. *He's not hearing me, and he's not respecting these people.* Michael's thoughts whirled. *I bound myself to God first*, he reminded himself. *If this representative chooses not to follow a righteous path, I owe him no further loyalty.* Shrugging, he returned to the conversation. "Timkat is an annual celebration for the Ark that the entire country enjoys."

"That does not mean they have it," the cardinal snapped.

"What does it mean, your grace?"

"It means you will continue to follow the priest and take the Ark if he should find it."

"And what of the child?" Michael asked, his question sharp. His tone did not matter. The man before him would see it as eagerness to make another kill.

The cardinal waved his hand, his smile gloating, his teeth glistening in the lamp light. "We shall decide that later, my son." He allowed himself to chortle, not caring that Michael avoided making direct eye contact with him. "Trust me."

CHAPTER FORTY-ONE

"Do not try to fight a lion if you are not one yourself."
—Ethiopian Proverb

When Mtho returned to the hotel suite, he found the situation had gone from bad to worse. He had left Keberwa a huddled lump of fear, with Meggani gently coaxing her out. Upon returning from his errands, he found the two girls standing by the couch, practicing their knife throwing. They had drawn a target on the opposite wall, about the height of a man's torso. Each took turns throwing the knife at the red circle with all her might.

He saw the new girl seemed to be making as many good center shots as her eager teacher.

It was enough to make him long for a suit of armor.

"What are you two doing?"

At Mtho's loud bellow, Kebbie froze where she was. Meggani beamed her approval when she saw that, though the girl was shaking with terror, she was not diving under anything to hide. "Good job, Kebbie."

He collapsed onto the couch, his hand covering his eyes. "Meggani, what have you done?"

"She needs to know she can protect herself." Meggani rocked back and forth on her heels, smiling with pleasure.

Kebbie stood silently, watching the two forces who were deciding her life.

He pointed at the blade the girl was cleaning with a washcloth. "Did you have to give her a knife?"

"It worked," Meggani pointed out.

"Where did you even get her such a thing?" Mtho's eyes narrowed suspiciously.

"I stole it from a room service tray."

Mtho tried to stand, but collapsed back on the couch. "What?"

"I figured she would need it."

Mtho staggered over to the target, pulled the remaining blade out, and glowered at her. "Do you have any idea how much this will cost?"

"Not a thing," Meggani strutted over to the wall where the landscape that had hung before he left, was leaning on its side on the floor. She picked up the large picture and hung it back in its place. Their target had been drawn within the outlines on purpose. When the painting was straight on its hook, it masked all of the damage behind it. The hotel had provided them with the perfect camouflage to hide their activities. "See?"

"What am I going to do with you?"

Kebbie stood next to Meggani and took her hand. "We're sorry."

Meggani looked down at her new friend and back at the monk. "Actually, we're not."

A chuckle escaped his lips as he met the girl's unrepentant, proud stare. She had done what she needed to, he reminded himself. She had helped the girl. How could anything ever compare with that? "No, you are not," he agreed easily. "And I should not expect you to be."

Kebbie moved forward to stand in front of her new friend. "Don't send Meggani away."

"How could I possibly do that?" Mtho asked, keeping his voice calm, modulated and even.

"We were bad," the child stated looking at her new friend for assistance.

Mtho's smiled only slightly, worried that she would misunderstand even that overture. "That doesn't mean I will ever send her away."

Kebbie froze, and stared at Mtho with a deep knowing. He could sense something change in the air, just as it did when Meggani called forces to lift a heavy object. Keberwa's head tilted and her eyes took a dreamy cast. "You won't," she stated, clearly astonished. Receiving another encouraging smile from Meggani, Kebbie stepped forward and took Mtho's hand. The smile she gave him smote his heart. He wiped away his tears with his free hand.

"Looks like you just got the sign of approval," Meggani praised.

"I am honored." Mtho continued to keep his voice soft, refusing to lose his progress.

"I am Kebbie," the child piped. "Nice to meet you, honored."

"Hey," the light in Meggani's eyes would have lit a dark room, "who knew she got jokes?"

Mtho squeezed the little girl's hand before rising from his chair. "Well, get your stuff. We need to go."

"Where?"

"Eventually, to the school."

"Found another kid?" Meggani asked eagerly.

"No. First we need to get your friend here her own knife - one that isn't stolen. You will be returning the one you took in a few minutes."

Meggani scowled, "You're going to make me apologize, aren't you?"

"That's why I am the monk," he reminded her.

"Most monk's wouldn't like me teaching little kids about knives," Meggani pointed out.

"I'm a very smart monk and you are not normal little kids."

She turned to Keberwa and boasted. "Told you we could trust him."

"I shall do just as you say from now on," Kebbie promised her new idol.

Mtho groaned. "Two Megganis." He rubbed his hand over his face. "I'm doomed."

Kebbie's face twisted, "I thought your name was honored."

As their giggles danced through the air he changed *doomed* to *blessed* inside of his mind.

CHAPTER FORTY-TWO

"There is no one who became rich because he broke a holiday, and no one who became fat because he broke a fast."
—Ethiopian Proverb

The lake glistened like a polished crystal, straight from the cutter's table. Heat soaked into their bones as the cool breeze from the waters eased any discomfort. It was the perfect balance. The islands that they could see from the shore were havens of green and white against the endless sea of blue. Lake Tana had been a refuge for the Ethiopian religious community for hundreds of years. Also a generous provider of food for the surrounding villages whose residents used small reed boats called tankwa to navigate the choppy waves.

Evidence of God's continued favor for the region no matter how much the surrounding area turned into the driest of deserts.

If Ethiopia was the world to its countrymen, Lake Tana was the center of that world - a beating living heart that kept the rest of the body in good health.

One they would protect.

Father Josephus breathed in deep the air that seemed to be soothing his heart and soul. Smells of fish, flowers and life were everywhere. This place had always been a favorite of his, and he was looking forward to sharing it with his new companions. He turned back to watch as Rhonda continued to hover, trying to step into the tankwa that their new friend, Michael, was holding steady for her.

She was frozen with fear.

The American woman, so confident and able to handle even the hardest mercenary with a unique aplomb, looked to the priest for reassurance. "Father, are you sure about this? I mean, really sure?"

He soothed, "The boats are fine."

She ran her hand over the end of the ship and shuddered. "They feel more like bundled newspapers. Newspaper gets soaked and sinks. I don't swim very well. In fact, I am a lot like newspaper in that respect. I will go down fast." Rhonda grimaced at the bobbing craft. "I'll sink almost as fast as this craft."

"It is safe," Josephus and Michael repeated simultaneously.

Rhonda bit her lip, her eyes returning reluctantly to her nemesis. "So you keep telling me," she muttered.

"I promise I will be careful," Michael swore, his eyes brimming with mirth.

Josephus moved the sleeping little one into his craft like the expert he was, and lashed her to two different kinds of life preservers for safekeeping. The waves were so cold and choppy, going into the water was not an option, but it relieved Rhonda's mind to see them. As he worked, he glanced at the young man that had joined them when they arrived at the lake. "I don't know what we would have done without you, Michael. It was a lucky thing we bumped into you at Bahar Dar."

"I'm just happy you needed a helping hand."

"We appreciate your desire to see my home." Josephus finished securing the girl, and threw the rest of their bags into his vessel.

Michael tried to conceal his exasperation when he saw Rhonda backing away from the boat once more. "It's not going to bite you, woman."

"Only kill me," she muttered.

Seeing Josephus watching him, he shrugged. "Ethiopia and the Ark have been a bit of an obsession with my uncle for years. I am only trying to fulfill his dream."

"And so you will," Josephus assured him.

Before Michael could say anything, Rhonda moaned as a couple paddled by. Noticing the men looking at her with twin expressions of patronizing disbelief, she pointed at the craft, "It looks like they are taking a ride on a paper airplane. This is not how I expected to get to an Ark stronghold. There has to be a better way … doesn't there?"

"No more accurate way in historic terms, however," Josephus pointed out. Her eyes flared and her hands began to open and close. He was happy the enticement proved too much for her academic brain to resist.

Rhonda crossed herself several times, and dove into the boat. Michael barely had time to brace the craft for the change in weight. "Why do we have to do this, again?" She asked while her knuckles grew white as she gripped the sides in a death hold.

Once they were as settled as possible, Josephus got into his craft and the two boats pushed off from the shore.

They paddled for a few minutes. It took some time for them to grow accustomed to the pull of the currents and the rhythm of the waves. Smooth strokes were the key, with an ability to wait for the coast to do much of the work for you. It was rather what Michael imagined riding a dragon might have been like—if such things existed. Once Josephus was sure that Michael had the movement down, he returned to his favorite subject. "These islands have been the last defense for the Ark since it came to this country in ancient times. Whether war or any form of strife, the emperor sent the relic to the monasteries on the islands for safekeeping. This is the best place for the final proof from the Little One."

Michael studied the silent little girl, who looked like she was sleeping. "Are you sure you don't want to go to Daga Stephanos? I read a lot about these islands and if you're looking for an Ark nexus, that's more talked about."

"I think Tana Kirkos is a better idea." Josephus counseled. *There was far more going on than their new friend realized. He had a lifetime of research to base his actions on. Actually, he had his entire family's lifetimes to base his path.*

Michael gave Rhonda a concerned look. "Tana Kirkos is much farther."

"Couldn't we take a motorboat?" Rhonda glanced back at the marina where the few diesel engine ships for hire waited at dock.

Both men could not resist a long snicker at her expense. "What's the fun of that?" Michael asked.

Josephus felt badly when he saw her crestfallen expression. "Buck up, Rhonda. It will be over soon."

"You just watch out for the Little One. She's been showing more and more signs of life." Rhonda snapped. "What if she goes into one of her trances and tries to get up to walk around? I bet you'll wish we had one of those *for lease* boats then."

He rolled his eyes, "Yes, mom."

Michael and Josephus both laughed when she growled in frustration.

"She could also get chilled. We should have put her back into the blanket."

Both men continued paddling.

"You two just pay attention to what you're doing," she cautioned.

"Nag, nag, nag." Michael teased.

CHAPTER FORTY-THREE

The day's good weather held for them. Josephus hid his joy at the realization that they were going to make it to the islands without one of the sudden storms popping up that the lake was famous for. He didn't think Rhonda's nerves would survive one. If he were alone he would have spent some time exploring the water. No matter how many times he was in this area he always found something else to rejoice in. Marvel. He could spend days in one of these boats. Paddling himself around the many islands and taking the time to speak with the few fishermen left.

But it was not wise to delay when you were on a path for God.

Coming up to Tana Kirkos with a smooth glide, they docked the vessels on the wood planks that the residents maintained diligently. Michael, younger and more agile, saw to it that both their vessels were tied to the posts. "Wait for me," he called to Josephus and Rhonda. He secured his own first, and then assisted the priest by tying off the ropes that would keep his steady.

Josephus examined everything he could from his perch.

Look, Baba, do you see how beautiful it all is? We are so much closer now, aren't we? I can feel you with me, Baba. Each time I peer into the marked child's eyes I can see you looking back at me.

Josephus wondered how, after decades of living without him, he could still feel the ache of his loss, as if it were new.

He noticed with satisfaction that three monks were rushing forward to meet them. The island was just as he remembered. Its landscape bursting with lush greenery. He heard the calls of the birds filling the air. The sweet perfume of the fruits and flowers reminded him of the beauty of God's work and hunger for life.

Josephus jumped to the dock and embraced the monks. "My brothers."

While Josephus greeted his friends, Michael helped Rhonda out of the tankwa. Her caution demonstrated her continued fear. He chose not to mention the woman's shaking and the manner she clasped the pylon that held the dock against the constant onslaught of the waves. When he tried to guide her to shore, she refused his assistance. "Help the girl."

"You have journeyed long." One of the monks commented.

Another brother noticed the girl in Michael's arms. "But it has been successful."

"I have," Josephus enthused. "This is Rhonda Sith and a friend, Michael Leone." He took the girl from Michael.

"All are welcome to Tana Kirkos," the three monks chorused.

Rhonda nodded with pleasure to each brother. She had been well-prepared by Josephus before her arrival and knew not to physically approach any of these men. They would tolerate her because of Josephus' approval. They would not allow any contact. "It's nice to meet you."

"You have a beautiful home." Michael warmly shook each of their hands.

Josephus turned to one of the brothers, "Why don't you show Michael around the island?"

The smallest and youngest monk stepped forward and ushered Michael away from their little group. Josephus had managed to get a warning message to the island that morning through a friend who still fished here. He had no need for outside witnesses to the events that he hoped would unfold. The others knew to keep Michael distracted and far from their activities. Josephus hid his approval of this. Just because he had allowed the boy to travel with them did not mean that he was going to witness more than Josephus would permit.

He was a priest but he was not naive.

Or stupid.

Michael's inclusion in their small group had seemed as unreal as it was unlikely. He bore watching.

His motives were at question.

The other monk moved to unload the bags stowed in their boats. The remaining monk gazed at the couple and the small girl with satisfaction. "We did not know how to prepare for your coming."

"You needed to do little but what you have done." Josephus nodded at the path where the other man had taken Michael. "Whatever happens is up to God, my brother. I am just here to follow where he directs."

The monk clasped his forearm, "You are ever wise, my friend."

"How should we begin," another brother asked.

Josephus waved his concerns aside. "The girl shall lead us."

He set her down on the ground, anticipation making his palms itch. He unwrapped her from the life preservers and the blanket. As soon as the girl's bare feet touched the soil she stood up with a beaming smile.

Catching the breeze in her nose, her mouth fell open joyfully.

Surprised, the adults watched as the child went tearing into the hills, without once stopping or turning back.

Realizing they were about to lose her, they dashed forward to follow.

CHAPTER FORTY-FOUR

"Everybody has been young before, but not everybody has been old
before."
—African Proverb

Their return was heralded only due to their fortuitous timing.
Father Mtho opened the gate for Meggani and Keberwa to enter
the main yard, just when the school had broken for some post-lunch
playtime. It was a merry time to arrive. The children gamboled around
the emerald swath of grass in a game of tag that used their watching
adults as home base. Laughter rang out over the sound of their calls to
each other. The grown-ups ranged from Jake's parents, dressed in jeans
and shirts, to the monks who wore spotless robes in a variety of earth-
based tones.

As soon as they entered, Kebbie ran into the midst of the other
students, radiant with pleasure.

The others accepted her.

No questions or hesitation.

She was drafted into Ani's team, as if she had been in the school for years, and was busy chasing Jake around his mother before they could even say hello.

Meggani held back as Father Mtho moved to confer with Kwai. She noticed Peter sitting by the now-completed barrier, his legs sprawled in a most undignified position. "You took over the fence building from Kwai. I see Ani came in handy while I was away."

He looked up, as she shifted back and forth on her feet. Peter let out a deep breath and patted the ground next to him.

She collapsed in a heap without waiting to be told twice.

"I commend your progress. You did a good job with her. Mtho told us when he called, how hurt she was." He continued to keep his eyes focused on the children, whose laughter called to his soul

"You did a good job with the school."

Peter couldn't prevent the snort of laughter from escaping his lips. They quivered with his mirth. He turned to study her, his eyebrows rising so high they disappeared inside his turban. "Praise, child? From you?"

"Maybe." Her impish grin met one of his own.

"I give you my most humble thanks."

The two lapsed into a comfortable silence that friends usually took years to reach. The breeze rustled through the trees surrounding them. One of the first things the monks had done was plant a variety of trees. They believed that it would only be through reforestation that the country's soil would begin to heal itself. They felt it vital to lead by example in everything they did. It was quite clear to them that the trees' roots aided mineral balance and water retention. The sun seemed to wrap them with its comfortable warmth on the outside, while the children's mirth made them feel contented inside.

She took a deep breath before broaching the peace they had found. "I'm sorry I took your place, traveling with Mtho."

"You have nothing to apologize for, Meggani."

His earnest gaze overflowed with kindness. For the first time since meeting him, Meggani could see the monk beneath the man. "I don't want you to dislike me," she whispered.

"I don't." His quick denial and shocked expression put her at ease for the first time since meeting him.

"To be honest with you, I've taught some of them how to protect themselves." She shifted the blade in her ankle sheath with a fidgeting hand.

"I know." Peter chuckled. "I saw their knives."

"You're not mad?" She turned to him, with open-mouthed.

He shrugged. "I was glad to see how much comfort it gave them."

"I will teach all of them soon." She winced that she had said that. It went with her earlier compulsion to make sure that this bristling stranger understood her in a full and complete way.

Peter laughed again, recognizing what she was doing. He approved. It was good to know that she was both honest and honorable; that such rare qualities were intrinsic to her personality. It was one thing to build a school for the reincarnated guardians of their homeland. It was quite pleasing to discover that, in spite of the darkness these children had been exposed to, they were still inherently creatures of light. "I approve ... but how about we buy them their knives from now on?"

"That's what Brother Mtho said," she admitted ruefully.

"Who knew he was so wise?"

Jake and Mani brought out a soccer ball and began kicking it back and forth.

One of the monks had brought out the sports equipment they kept in a shed. He was trying to explain cricket to the rest of the children while keeping some kind of dignity. It was harder to run in his robes and keep them from getting dirty than he seemed to realize. The laughter of children and adults built up, drowning out their talk.

As the laughter calmed, Meggani took a deep breath, shaking her head. "They're so happy."

Peter heard the awe and astonishment in her voice and glanced at her, curiously. "Of course they are."

She looked between him and the others trying to understand. "Why are they so happy?"

"They know they are safe and loved. Why wouldn't they be happy?"

"I've never felt that before," she disclosed.

"Give it time, child." He patted her arm with gentle awkwardness that showed how unaccustomed he was to showing affection to children in general. "All wounds heal. In time, they heal."

"Some wounds kill you, brother."

Peter placed his arm around Meggani as the two continued to watch over the others in silence. She was right.

Many wounds killed you; he knew that better than most.

There was an illness inside him. He had felt it growing.

Peter did not feel he had made penance for the crimes he committed in his life so he refused to ask these children for assistance. The Church was here to help them, not the other way around. He didn't want to share his troubles with others. He didn't want to die in a clinic somewhere, or in a monastery.

He didn't know what he wanted; he only knew what he would rather avoid. "Please God," he prayed in his heart. "If I have made recompense for the sins of my past, please make my end quick. It is the only way I will know peace. It is the only way I will be free. Just give me enough time to make a difference here. Just a little chance to help, one more time."

Meggani felt his sadness. Words failing her, she laid her hand on the monk's. They watched the other residents laugh and play, content with their silent vigil.

CHAPTER FORTY-FIVE

"Our deepest fear is that we are powerful beyond measure."
—Nelson Mandela

T he child had kept ahead of the others, moving up the path with ease, climbing as if she were a goat, leaping from stone to stone with a casual grace. It was clear that somehow the small girl knew the route as well as the back of her hand. Josephus and Rhonda had some trouble keeping up, so one monk kept even with the lass and the other two stayed by their sides to assist them over each obstacle. As soon as she gained the crest she froze, peering over the verdant landscape with a luminous smile. The hill gave them a view of the entire island and the surrounding waters.

His Little One held up her hands to the sky and stood so frozen in the moment, the very molecules that made up the universe stilled, awaiting her gesture that they could move once more.

Turning to her audience she gestured to the island itself. *"Here it came to rest. Here they placed it within a tabernacle again, the heavy cloths confining its power. The land fed the Covenant, and the Covenant left them in* peace at last. Not all was good. The torch could not be found, but the people remembered enough to know that the Covenant could not be destroyed. It could only be guarded."

Josephus grimaced as he heard the priests of the island begin to pray. They were causing a bigger stir here than they had in the Sudan.

His charge continued her lesson. "The Covenant kept the land healthy, but could not stop the destruction brought by the children. They grew proud. They grew bold. They were careless. The way was forgotten. Hate was taken into their hearts. Balance was demeaned. The Covenant knew that one day, one day much too soon, the land would start to die, drained by greed, fear and hatred; the very things that created it in the first place."

Rhonda gasped and looked around astonished.

Violets. The professor smelled violets on the air as if someone had just spilled the oil nearby. Her rational brain churning, she realized the scent seemed to be coming from the girl.

What could make such a strong scent of flowers?

The girl took in a quivering breath, "It wept for its people. Its sorrow took the moisture from every living thing."

Josephus blanched. Drought had often been a problem here. Now he knew why.

The blessed one collapsed to the dirt, her eyes blank, staring helplessly up at them. "I remember before that. I remember who I once was."

"I remember what it is to be the torch," she whispered as their audience fell to their knees and bowed their heads.

The monks all gasped, and made the sign of the cross on their chests.

Even Josephus and Rhonda were forced to wipe the tears from their eyes, their little one's tale was so moving.

Her body shook with the effort to continue the tale.

"The flame of the Covenant followed her heart." The child sat up and looked toward Aswan, her eyes pensive with her many memories.

"I remember the caravan that came. It took years, and the baby camels that were born were placed on the backs of the camels walking before their mothers; so they would know that its child was well. I remember how the men laughed, keeping their spirits up and trying to erase the sound of their families' *weeping from their hearts. I remember the shame of our soon to be king when he realized what my love had done. I remember the smell of the highlands as we traveled into the mountains. Cool green shadows that eased your skin and eyes. The change was a glorious release from the heat and light. I remember the feeling of the stone steps as I entered the palace. The palace that was chosen to be my new home."*

She looked at them, and Josephus held his breath sensing she was about to tell them the one thing he wanted the most to hear. *"I remember so many things. Each lifetime that the torch lived, all of the knowledge of the Covenant is in me. I remember it all now. Each piece is like a beautiful crystal hanging in my mind, capturing the light and reflecting God's glory back to me."*

"It is all possible, Father," she whispered, "every dream and image from your imagination. It can all be done."

Josephus felt his mouth fall open. *Baba, did you hear her? Are you in heaven right now, laughing and singing with my parents? Do you sit near Mother Mary rejoicing at your children's resurrection?*

Shall we now rise from the ashes? New, reformed into something stronger than ever achieved in the past.

Her face grew slick with her tears as she shared a journey that happened before the beginning of time. Rhonda rushed over with her bottle of water to return some fluid into her body before she grew dehydrated. Josephus knelt beside her to wipe the tears and perspiration from her sweet visage; the head monk watching, feeling helpless.

They all gasped when she blinked several times and broadly smiled. She shook her head as if clearing it. When she spoke, they gasped, for rather than using the singsong voice of someone fresh to language, her voice was adult-like in the way it pronounced each consonant and vowel.

"I remember so much now. I even remember me."

CHAPTER FORTY-SIX

"Evil enters like a needle and spreads like an oak tree."
—Ethiopian Proverb

A haven of greens and bright vivid color in the sea of sand and browns made up the color scheme of Jerusalem. The small garden was his refuge. Few would dare to disturb him when he was spending his meditation time amid the plants and flowers that came from his country. He fingered a khat leaf, releasing its sticky sweet smell to tease his nose and soothe his senses.

The archbishop smiled as he remembered how hard he had to work to have this item included in his new home. He had a friend sneak it into the country, and even now it was masked from the main path by larger shrubs. Most countries banned his beloved khat due to its psychotropic properties when chewed.

What they did not understand was how key reaching that state could be in some of the less-known rituals of his Church.

His assistant brought the cardinal to him. The archbishop watched silently from his seat next to the ebony tree. Its veined leaves made a pleasant fluttering sound in the wind that he found more soothing than any wind chime. He remembered planting it himself, vowing that he would see his land saved before he moved it from that spot. Returning his attention to his visitor, he sighed. "This is a surprise," he offered, as if beginning a pleasant conversation, though his eyes were as guarded as his soul.

"I thought to return the courtesy." The cardinal strutted through the flowerbeds with the ego of a man who had never existed in a drought-ravaged country.

There was no reason for archbishop to look up at his former friend, sarcasm dripping from his words as honey from a spoon. He chose instead to give a regal incline of his head. "Indeed." He gestured to the neighboring bench, "Sit and join me, why don't you? I find time in nature to be a delightful restorative and strengthener for my spirit. It also instills respect for God's beauty."

He was not surprised when the cardinal never once looked at the plants he had walked on. "I am told your priest has made some progress," he stated while sitting.

"Indeed," the archbishop confirmed.

"You will not stop him?" The cardinal did not realize that his eyes had narrowed with rage.

"Father Josephus is no longer working for the Church."

The cardinal jerked back at this staggering news.

He was a man who did not like surprises. "You mean he is not working for you in any official capacity," he scoffed. "I highly doubt such a thing."

"Does it matter, in truth?" The archbishop once more stroked the khat plant beside him, aware that his companion did not care for the smell. Robeson thought it was dirty. Disordered. His friend had never understood.

The archbishop found the plant to be rather like his people. There are as many different kinds of black men as there are different lands where khat can be found. More than he could remember, offhand. The difference for him was that nowhere did either grow as strong or as true - as in his homeland.

His countrymen and this plant were hard to comprehend. The

thing was, that once you really understood them, grasped their allure, you could not help becoming captivated. Khat was just beginning to be explored, its healing properties only now being considered.

Also, just like his country.

They were rising slower than the tides to gain respect from the rest of the world.

"Father Josephus is following a different master now." The archbishop hid his amusement at his comment. This cardinal would never appreciate that his student was following God's signs and not any illusion of blind ambition.

"I could have him stopped." The cardinal's threat was said with a menacing growl.

The archbishop smiled, knowing his amusement would incense the Roman Catholic even more. "You have tossed your threats around before."

"Do you dare to doubt my resolve?"

"I doubt your faith." He sighed heavily. "Not your resolve."

Robeson sneered. The archbishop had no right to rebuke him, and that was what he had just done. Ambition for the church could never be evil, and if it was for his cause, it must be blessed.

"And yet you do nothing to stop your man," he spat at him.

"My man, as you call him, is following the calling of his vows to his country, family and to God. I have no right to even consider stopping him."

"I notice you did not put God first," the cardinal observed.

The archbishop tired of this uncalled-for audience and felt a growing irritation that his precious meditation time had been so thoroughly disturbed. He felt as if his beloved garden had been tainted somehow. As if the cardinal's fearful resentment had infected his precious plants and flowers.

Rather than angry, it only made him sad. For them both.

"What is it you want, Robert?"

He reeled. It has been years since the archbishop had used his former name.

It took all of his concentration to muster his righteous outrage once more.

"To warn you that I would not allow this to continue for very long."

"You are walking a very treacherous path, my friend." He shook his head, sad for a man who could not see that the route to God's glory never elevated your own. For when you stand within heaven's light there was no higher place to be.

"I am walking the path of the righteous."

"Why is it that the cruelest, most wicked men in history always use that excuse?" He addressed his question to the sky that sheltered him, with absolute confidence that his former friend would not begin to know how to answer him.

"For we are the ones who win," the cardinal responded with a smug smile.

"Not in the long run." The archbishop stood and gestured to the nearby exit. He was done with this man and this conversation. His friend would discover the truth in the end. The truth he understood now was that it would be too late for Cardinal Robeson.

Too late for Robert, his friend.

"You do not understand, cardinal. Love will always win, for God is love. It is the only fact that is true and real in the world."

Robeson's mouth opened and closed, as if he were a landed fish fighting for air.

The archbishop gestured to the exit once more, "Good-bye."

As he watched the black robes flair around his friend's exit, he could not stop the heaviness in his heart. He prayed for him first, and then added one more truth. "You will never be the one who wins in heaven," he whispered, as Robert walked away from him for the last time.

"That is the saddest part of all."

CHAPTER FORTY-SEVEN

"You cannot build a house for last year's summer."
—Ethiopian Proverb

Digging shovels slowly extricating the dirt from the hole were the only noises on the top of the hill. It was as if even the animals and birds had abandoned the area. There was no wind to caress their skin. Even the sun had disappeared behind a cloud to hide from the events unfolding. The monks had not said a word in protest when Father Josephus had directed them to dig.

His Blessed One had told their leader it was important.

So they would let the little child lead them.

Father Josephus and Rhonda Sith flanked the girl, their hands on her shoulders, supporting her slight weight. She refused to sit or let them carry her. After so many months of being locked in a waking death, they really could not blame her resistance. Her body seemed that of a healthy six year old, though her demeanor belonged to a much older person. It was as if the flame of God she had carried for so long had aged her faster than usual, leaving behind the soul of a wise old woman locked inside the body of one with few years.

It was not long before the sound of their tools hitting something hard rang through the area. With an impish grin, the child looked at the adults around her in triumph. "We found it," the monk whispered in awe.

The priests jumped out of the hole to give the Blessed One room. Josephus lowered her inside it. She knew just what to do. They opened the box, and inside they could see a woven basket of grains. Dried to mere dust now, the outline of a cloth package was visible in the granules. The girl dug out the bundle and clutched it to her chest. Extending her hands, Josephus and Rhonda lifted her.

She stood before the adults with her prize.

"What have we found?" One of the priests muttered.

The child crouched on the grass and set her surprise down. She unwrapped it from the fraying and delicate cloth. "Behold the shamir," she proclaimed. Displaying a device that appeared to be an ancient-looking stone sculpture that resembled a cross between a gun and a crude version of a laser, the adults jumped back. "What is wrong? It is safe." She looked around at the others, bewildered by their hesitation. Holding it out, she glowed with pride. "It has always been a good thing."

Josephus held out a shaking hand that he withdrew before touching it. "Dear Lord, this is the tool that Solomon designed to split stone at the behest of the Ark Maiden."

"If we have some water it should still work," she informed them.

Without waiting for permission, Rhonda stepped forward to hand the girl her ever-present bottle of water. She was tired of their hesitation with the lass, now that she had woken up. She had the required items handy; their professor was a great believer in staying hydrated. The girl instantly poured the fluid over the device until it glistened like marble. She then loaded more water into what appeared to be the barrel portion. Josephus shifted with uncomfortably when he realized the relic reminded him of a weapon

"How does it work?" Rhonda asked, her curiosity pushing away her unease.

The child chuckled, "It's easy."

She pointed the device at a boulder and moved a lever on the side. A sonic wave burst from it that made her witnesses flinch.

They gasped with awe when they saw the result. The rock was split into two clean pieces. No work. No strain. There was not even smoke to indicate the miracle she had just performed.

"It's also fun. How do you think Solomon broke the rocks for his mines? This was a gift of both the ancient's knowledge and God's own bounty."

Father Josephus led the others to their knees as they all lowered their heads to pray. They ignored everyone and everything in order to show their appreciation to the most High.

The Blessed One looked at them, confused. She lowered the shamir to her side, shifting with discomfort in the dirt. She looked down to watch her toes seeking purchase in the soil so that they could not see that they hurt her. When it appeared they would be a while, she slowly sat down to rest her head on her fist.

Rhonda sat beside her and put her arms around the child, gentle and kind. "They are not upset with you."

She shrugged, "It's fine."

"Child," she took a deep breath. Rhonda reached out a single finger to touch the device cradled in the girl's lap. "This is proof of a beloved story that is part history and part myth for them. It is their way to halt what they are doing so that they can give thanks to God.

This is why they live set apart from the world on this island. They are overwhelmed with gratitude."

"It can grow dangerous." The girl stated in a strained whisper. "Did you bring the basket of grain?"

Rhonda reached the requested item from her position and pulled it closer to them. The girl buried the item inside the rice. When it was immersed, she handed the basket back to the woman. "It never stops working." The child shrugged. "If you put it into anything that is conductive it will split the container, just like the rock. I guess I shouldn't have turned it on, but I couldn't resist. Father Josephus and you have been so patient with me."

When Rhonda gave her an amazed look, she shrugged. "I

remember you taking care of me. I remember loads now. I'm surprised my head hasn't split open from it all."

"Little One, we'll help you," Rhonda counseled. "Do not fear."

"I know." The girl played with the fringe that went around the bottom of her shirt. "I fear you are feeling your way, just as much as I am."

"What do you mean?"

"It's not like anyone has done this for thousands of years."

"True," Rhonda patted her arm, "but we'll manage."

"I appreciate that, professor," the girl looked up at her with eyes that were older than the hill where they sat. "You all still flinch when I speak or do things."

"Honey," Rhonda tucked a curl of her hair behind her ear with a gentle look. "You have been unconscious for months. I have been traveling with you for months and you were always in that strange sleep. I never expected you to wake up so ... so ...."

The girl chuckled when the woman found it impossible to finish her sentence. "Normal?" she provided trying to be helpful.

"Well, if you wish me to be honest, yes. I thought you would recover. Father Josephus promised us you would. I just thought you would be like you were when you were hit by the lightning. I don't know a lot about kids. How old are you, by the way?"

"I'm not sure, really." She crunched her face as she tried to remember. "I think I'm six."

"Honey, even with your extraordinary abilities, you would still be special for six."

"I have always been ahead for my age."

The woman laughed, a full rich sound, and hugged her close. It was then she smelled the violets; it came from her curls. The girl had only been awake for a few days but already she had fallen in love with her. How could she not? The little one's humor and quiet assured aspect of omniscience, awed her on a regular basis.

As they watched, the men rose as one unit. The lass knew that they had heard some of their conversation and offered them the basket without a word.

Three of the monks bowed their heads with thanks. The first

brother took the liberty of speaking for them all. "We will keep this safe in the Makda from now on."

"Makda?" Rhonda asked.

"Sanctuary vault," Josephus explained. The brother's ability with English had been his gift to them, one that Rhonda found herself to be quite grateful for. It was rare that she needed assistance with a word, but he was happy to provide it. She had already started to learn the native languages with an ease that humbled him.

The brothers all bowed their heads to the girl. "Thank you, child," one stated. Another finished for him, "This is a gift beyond measure." The three men took their treasure toward the group of buildings that they had tried to be polite about keeping the women from, during their sojourn.

"You have done very well," Josephus, praised the girl.

"I don't understand, Father. I can remember so many things, from this life and my last ones. There are all sorts of facts about the Ark's life in my head, but I can't seem to recall my own name. I can't even tell you my exact age."

Rhonda squeezed her shoulder. "I think your brain has so much information that it is just taking a while to adjust to it all. Give it time honey. It will come to you."

"I'm trying," she sighed. Her voice was heavy as she dealt with her visible frustration.

Josephus sat down beside the two females. "You are doing very well."

The Little One got a faraway look in her eyes.

It was an expression that the two adults had learned fast to recognize over the last few days.

"We are gonna have to leave soon."

"I know. We have taken enough hospitality from these good men."

"No, that's not why."

Rhonda and Father Josephus look at her with surprise.

"You'll find out," she informed them. Standing up, she went skipping down the hill toward the shoreline. They were sure she was happily scheming how to con Michael into playing with the monk's soccer ball.

He was the only one able to teach her the tricks of the footwork.

She would be with other kids soon, and wanted to show off. In her dreams, she often saw her fellow students playing games like these. It was for this reason she was so determined to catch up.

"Perhaps we should ask," Rhonda questioned the priest.

Josephus shook his head. "She will tell us in her own time," he advised.

On the outside he was confident, but within his heart he still clung to the sanctuary of his grandfather's memory. *Baba, can you hear me? Make this be the right choice, Baba. She has given me so much already. How will I ever be able to provide her with any kind of repayment? How will I keep this soul that is so close to heaven safe in this often-cruel world?*

Can I be good enough for her, Baba? Could anyone?

"There is so much that I wish we could protect her from."

"We will have to rely on God's protection." Josephus chuckled at her doubtful look. He understood that she was an academician, but this was ridiculous. What could help her give up her old thought patterns? "After everything you have seen, you can't tell me that you still have some qualms."

Rhonda could not resist a chuckle of her own. "What can I say? I'm an American woman."

Their laughter echoed down the hill reaching the girl. She was glad they were happy. The child knew that there were dangers near them, and people hunting them. She just didn't know if they were all one in the same.

Life would always be fraught with danger.

Great change always came with a very high price.

All she could do was trust in the universal force that had brought her to this point in the first place.

For in truth ... she had no other choice.

CHAPTER FORTY-EIGHT

"If the heart is sad, tears will follow."
—Ethiopian Proverb

The schoolroom was an expansive well-lit chamber, with large windows looking out at nature. Electric lighting was above, and in strategically placed lamps. There were three different sources of heat and air-cooling to make sure that the space was a comfortable one at all times. This room was for when they were all together, students and teachers, though there were smaller chambers surrounding it for one-to-one instruction.

It had been decreed by Josephus that this unstructured curriculum would be key. This was one of the first rules the priest had set down for the brothers. A democratic education was best.

They had no way of predicting how these children would wish to learn or how they would choose to share. The architecture gave them the freedom to make allowances for any changes that the kids decided.

Rohan's mother had taken over the cleaning of its cleaning. They tried to keep it tidy, but she insisted on scrubbing it once a week.

Brother Mtho was sitting at one of the desks, grading papers. Though the children could not fail, the tests they gave them each month insured that their progress was monitored. The days were divided between the children being instructed about the world, and the adults gaining knowledge from the children. These tests made sure that, when completed, the guardians would have an education that rivaled the best boarding schools in the world.

He had a small cup of coffee next to him, and a plate with a variety of sliced fruits on it. Jake had been experimenting again. They would show him a description of a plant, and somehow the boy could call the produce from the earth as if they were his pets that found him to be a beloved master. Since he had missed lunch, one of the other brothers had brought him the snack to tide him over until dinner.

Meggani came running in dragging Kebbie behind her, so he put aside his pen and papers to be polite. This show of haste was not like either child. "What's wrong?"

"Where's Brother Peter?"

Mtho scowled. He was in no mood to be dragged into the Meggani and Peter feud. "We got a report on another kid late last night. He left to find him."

"I am so sorry, Meggie," Kebbie gasped. Her eyes shone with tears.

Meggani patted the child's back to calm her. "It's okay Kebbie," she soothed.

He sat forward. "What's going on, ladies?"

Meggani's eyes shone with her held back tears. "He won't make it back, Brother Mtho. The child he is going after is not good. He's learned to use his ability to punish the world for the pain he feels. Brother Peter will not know how to recognize it. He will not know how to stop it."

"That is not all," Kebbie added her voice soft with pain. "He asked God for a gift and he is about to get it."

Meggani knelt before the girl and held both of her hands. "It is not a good gift is it?" She had felt the change when she was near her former nemesis. Peter had become more relaxed; easier to approach. He was resigned for something, and they all knew it.

They just did not know how to fight it for him, when he was unwilling to do so for himself.

"Not if you like Brother Peter, it isn't."

Mtho drew Meggani back from Kebbie. "Keberwa, did you see this in a vision?"

"How'd you know?" Meggani asked suspiciously.

"It's her ability, Meggani." Mtho tried to remind himself to stay patient. He had spent years researching and learning about the guardians under the Abbé's direction. This girl did not understand that. Why should she? They may have ancient souls, but they were still children. "I thought you would understand I knew that by now."

Kebbie's eyes glazed over, turning molten silver in the noon sun. "Father Peter drowns with the boy. The waters rush him away. They wash away his past crimes, just as he requested from the Lord. He will never return to our school."

"I warned him it was the rainy season." Mtho shook his head recognizing that there was nothing they could do. "I begged him to let me go."

"What do we do?" Meggani asked, her anguish clear.

Mtho puts his arms around both girls and rested his cheek against Meggani's hair to hide his tears. "We must pray, girls. We must pray very hard."

"That he returns," Meggani asked in a small voice.

His answer could not be yes, he knew. To say that would negate his belief and even possibly the power of Keberwa's gift.

Desperately, Mtho searched for a way through this quagmire that had opened before him like the yaw of some invisible monster. It was such a sudden dilemma that he reeled within his soul. He could see the appeal in Kebbie's eyes and felt his heart break. There was no way out. No alternative.

"No," he admitted. "We must pray very hard that Peter remembers how much we love him. How much we need him."

Kebbie nodded with great sadness. "He'll know," she promised. "He just won't be able to help from here anymore."

"I'm so sorry," Meggani began to sob.

"For what?"

She looked at Mtho. Her friend. The first adult she had given her trust to without reservation. The first man she found she could be comfortable with sharing her complete soul, including her ability.

"I should have been able to stop him. I should have helped Kebbie with her dreams. I should have made sure he didn't go."

"You are not God, child." Mtho squeezed her shoulders.

"No." Meggani's agreement was hoarse with her emotional turmoil. "Just his messenger." *No matter what Mtho said she would never stop believing that she should have helped Peter.*

She should have kept him and the child alive.

The others had discussed healing him. They had even begun to suspect they could heal others without touching or use of salves.

She had refused that option.

It was her intuition that they were meant to let the monk find his own way. He had found it, but it took him farther from them rather than closer. She was about to lose someone she liked, again. Her efforts to help and protect had failed.

Once more, she was simply not enough.

CHAPTER FORTY-NINE

"Whatever accomplishment you boast of in the world, there will
always be someone better than you."
—African Proverb

He was so tired. Peter was surprised at how much he hated
traveling. It always looked so glamorous and fun when his
brothers took off on their quests. He had been forced to stay behind at
the school. Mtho went to search for the children. Kwai went for
supplies and shipments. Peter had no interest in teaching. The only
time he cooked he seemed to excel at making people ill. Other than
leading the other brothers in prayer, he had no function at the facility.

It had gotten more interesting since some of the children had joined
them. The feats they accomplished without physical effort were
thrilling to witness. Mere thought brought their tasks to fruition. Peter
was still frustrated by his inability to help.

Help anyone. He felt like a fifth wheel.

This was his chance to change things. He did not want to mess up.
The messenger from a small town outside of the city of Harar came at

midnight. A center for the Muslim religion, it was a shock to receive a note for the Ethiopian Church. He was the only one up to receive the man, bedraggled from his travels. A terse note, written on crumpled and stained paper, had filled him with dread. The muezzin who wrote to them was sure that soon the child in question would be in danger.

Villagers do not like those that are different.

This poor and depressed hamlet was ready to cut out that difference. The depths of poverty shocked him when he entered its boundaries, considering that it was in walking distance from the gates of Harar.

Harar is a center of learning and prosperity. He found the escarpment overlooking the surrounding plains a romantic sight. The smell of eucalyptus scented the cool air from the higher climate. Peter had taken a break to visit some of the stained glass on display, which caught his breath. He had made good time since he had taken the railroad and then caught a ride with some tourists in their air-conditioned sedan.

It was drumming in his ears that time was wasting. The muezzin had been specific. Speed was of the essence.

His destination was a mirror image to the haven of Harar.

A small village, lost and forgotten by the mapmakers of the world. The place filled Brother Peter with dread. People he could see here were sullen, unclean, and starving; casting him looks of resentment.

He had been praying since he came to this place.

Whatever was at work here was not the same beautiful light he basked in at the school.

This was shadow. Darkness.

After dealing with Meggani for the brief time when they first met, Peter had not been sure of how to face this arrogant boy. He was eleven years old, filled with the swagger and bravado of a twenty year old. His long dark hair was oiled so heavily the monk could smell the odor of the liquid used from across the room. The child's eyes glittered with rage and a constant fire. He had caught the boy striking out at others several times, uncaring at the impact that his violence and rage might cause.

That was not even what worried him.

Peter was aware of one thing: the boy was not like the other students he had met.

Something had broken in him.

There was no place he saw more evidence of this than the way the other villagers looked at the child. They were afraid.

It was contagious.

The stories of young Abdullah's feats had curdled Peter's blood. The boy's parents had died under mysterious circumstances. Screaming. Others in the village had met similar strange ends, that were brutal and without mercy.

"If you have said your good-byes, we should go."

Abdullah glowered at the monk who dared to question him. "I am eating."

Peter looked around with concern. "If that is the last of the food, you should leave it for the others. I will get you more to eat on the road."

The child proceeded to shove as much of the bread, cheese and fruit onto his plate, glaring at him. "If I wish to eat it they give it to me. I do not need to wait. I do not like to do so. You have no say over me."

He recoiled from the boy's belligerence.

Abdullah laughed with an evil slickness that churned the monk's stomach. "You are weak. Sick."

He released a deep sigh, striving to find some words that would break past the child's protective barriers. "Abdullah, I know that you have been alone since your family died. I understand that these people have not given you any support or guidance. This is my vow, the place I am taking you to will be filled with other souls just as powerful as you. You will be able to learn and grow. You will increase your knowledge of the world."

"There is no one as powerful as me."

Peter shook his head, his eyes glued to Abdullah's face. "There are children like you. My friend, Father Josephus, is bringing a girl that is more powerful than all the other kids you are about to meet, combined."

Abdullah stood and threw his plate against the wall. It shattered into dust. The boy added his earthenware mug to the destruction. He smiled at the cries of distress his action caused. The water mingled with the plate's remains to become a brown paste. It made Peter think of blood, for some reason. The woman who owned the house gave a choked cry as she fled in tears from the building.

"You must think of how others feel," he reached out to the boy, who looked at his hand as if it were a snake ready to bite.

The child sneered, "Soon you shall know what my strength feels like, monk."

Peter managed to get them on the road only with a constant application of prayer and patience. Abdullah continued to stew. The steam seemed to puff from his ears with each step they took. Peter was nervous at their timing. They were crossing an old riverbed. Once standing on this bank, he would have looked down into a deep blue relentless stream of water from the mountains. It had been so long since the waters fled these shores that Peter could see the fossils in the rocks.

"I do not wish to go to this school," Abdullah tugged on his hand.

"You have no choice," Peter snapped.

Abdullah folded his arms over his chest. "I have all the choices in the world," he boasted. A crack of thunder split the air, lightning following, and the smell of electricity burned his nostrils. There was another series of strikes. Peter looked around with surprise as he realized that a cloud had formed around them.

They were standing in the middle of a storm cloud. He turned his head and was not surprised to see a smile splitting the boy's face.

Abdullah had called this miracle.

Or was it a nightmare?

Peter's sense of awe left on winged feet. The cloud grew larger. The water accumulation grew denser. The sound of the thunder and the smell of the electricity made it impossible to know which direction to turn. He could not see. He could not think.

"See," Abdullah called, "there is no one stronger than me."

The monk fell to his knees. "Abdullah, child, you must stop this insanity."

"I am the most powerful force in the world."

"No one is stronger than God," Peter yelled to him.

"Worship me," Abdullah called before throwing his hands up to the sky.

Peter began to pray and felt a large beam of sunlight embrace him. The warmth banished the chill of the storm cloud that surrounded him, and eased the ice of the rain that soaked him. The monk's devotion was rewarded. He looked up into heaven and found a welcoming face. His smile was light as air; the cataclysm raging around him meant nothing any more. His prayers were heard. His prayers were answered.

He was finally able to go home.

Peter sobbed, as he realized he was welcome. He was loved.

The boy was still screaming about his power when the waters he had called down washed their bodies away.

CHAPTER FIFTY

"I'm from a place where there's only love, where the sun comes home every morning."
—Sizzla

S taying on Tana Kirkos for a few weeks was like taking a small vacation. The island's priests were eager to finish learning all that they could from the small girl who continued to grapple with her memory loss. It was all scattered pieces in her mind, ones she could not put together. Rhonda and Josephus kept assuring her that it would return when it was supposed to, but they knew she had nightmares. The only thing she seemed confident of was that she had family.

It was the one thing neither of the adults wished to hear.

The child spoke of a feeling of love and security from the people in her life. When Josephus tried to suggest that it was her family looking down from heaven, she announced in her far away voice that her parents were still alive.

No matter what they said, the blessed one spoke of people that

G. J. PHOENIX

were healthy. Looking for her. Loving. Caring. No matter what Josephus suggested to the contrary, she would not be swayed.

Rhonda maintained that if the Little One didn't remember what had happened at St. Catherine's, it was a good thing. She could recall it all or be told when she was ready. Josephus could not understand when anyone could feel prepared to hear that a mysterious lightning bolt had killed your parents - in an act so weird it had to be of heaven's origins.

Surveying the tankwas, Josephus made sure they had collected all of their belongings. Michael came from the woods with a swagger and the camera bag in his arms. He had become a trusted friend to Josephus and Rhonda, after the Blessed One had insisted that his heart was pure. The monks had loved sharing their religion and beliefs with the young Italian with hair like the sun.

Michael gestured to the Eden that surrounded them. "Are you sure you don't want to stay a few more days?"

"It is time for us to go." Josephus smiled as he watched the girl kicking a soccer ball with one of the younger monks. "Women are not meant to be here."

"They didn't act like they minded." Michael secured their luggage in the vessel.

Josephus chuckled, "They would not do such a thing."

"You know, Father, we were here for a long time. Not once did one of the local clergy tell me his name. Why is that?"

He smiled at Michael's question. "It's their way."

"What is?"

"Complete release to God." Josephus gestured to the island that teemed with life. "When the brothers give themselves to life in this citadel, they relinquish all hold on everything from the mainland. Family, possessions, ambitions and even their names."

Michael shook his head. "Why don't they take new names like in other priesthoods?"

"Ethiopians have a unique way of looking at faith, Michael. They give themselves in totality; without abandon. So you see, they have no use of individual names."

"How do they know who should respond when someone needs them," Michael quipped.

Josephus chuckled, "They seem to manage, son."

One of the brothers came over with Rhonda. The two had been working on changing the medicinal herbs, per the girl's instructions over the last week, and had developed a tentative friendship. When they reached the two men, the priest turned to gesture to the giggling girl. "The things that young one has taught us are beyond measure, my friend."

"Thank you all for hosting us for so very long." Josephus gave a deep, respectful bow. They all smiled when her laughter grew louder. "The girl is bursting with health, I am sure that you and your brothers will be grateful for some peace and quiet."

"It is true that she has kept things interesting." The father offered them an apologetic smile.

Rhonda inserted, "The news from the school is the only reason we are leaving."

The priest shook his head with great sadness. "It is tragic that Father Peter and the child were lost."

"I don't understand why they tried crossing the river during a flood." Josephus blinked his eyes to clear them of the tears that threatened.

The others all gave him a moment to recover.

"You could stay," their host offered.

"She wishes to see the school. Also there are plenty of more places she says need trees."

"Traveling the country and making full-grown trees grow from dust. I almost envy you."

"Moringa is our heritage and can easily be our people's salvation."

"So much knowledge lost."

Rhonda could not help asking them something that troubled her. "What will you do with what the Little One has taught you? Will you tell the world about it all?"

Michael nodded with eagerness. "It would help many people."

Josephus and the monk shared a knowing smile. They were not Ethiopian. They could not understand. There was no separation for them between church and secular matters. There was no question of the power of God's love. "We have always believed that should the question be asked, the answer would be given."

"That's it?"

"It is just our way," Josephus answered enjoying his cloak of enigmatic charm.

"You must do more with it," Michael protested.

"This information could change the world." Rhonda's voice grew impatient at their attitude.

"Only if it is ready to be changed," Josephus reminded them.

CHAPTER FIFTY-ONE

"A blade will not cut another blade; a cheat will not cheat another cheat."
—Ethiopian Proverb

C hess had always fascinated him. He never played the game. Its history with war was too ingrained for his peaceful nature to allow a close association. The game did provide some powerful lessons of deft movements useful to maneuver through this growing political world. As the archbishop surveyed the article about a recent championship, he considered the moves he had been forced to make of late.

In this game there was a pawn.

He was a pawn though, that could become king.

It was yet to be seen if the pawn would accept that greater destiny..

Turning to his laptop, he tried to write some sermon notes at his desk while finishing his afternoon tea. "It is in God's hands," he reminded himself. "All you can do now is wait. Be patient and have faith. Your prayers will be heard." A knock on the door sounded, and his assistant led in a smiling Michael Leone. The archbishop immediately rose to greet Michael with a warm hug. "It is good to see you."

"Same here, my friend," Michael glowed with his joy at being in the presence of this holy man. His reputation was pristine.

"Let us sit," the archbishop gestured to the nearby couch. When they were both comfortable he looked over at his assistant. "Would you care for tea?"

Michael quickly shook his head. "No thank you."

The assistant nodded and left them alone, shutting the door behind him. The two men regarded each other, from the opposite ends of the couch.

"So, my good friend has returned to his school?"

"He has," Michael responded. "Father Josephus is a holy man."

"I am glad that you could spend so much time with him." The archbishop plucked at the folds of his robe. "Tell me, how is the Blessed One?"

"She is … she is … I'm not sure of the word."

"I have not met her," he admitted reluctantly, "but it would seem she does wondrous works."

Michael nodded eagerly. "Yes it does. The things she can do, archbishop …"

The archbishop gazed at him with deep concentration and understanding. He knew much of Michael; he was not a child of privilege. He had been born into one of the worst Italian orphanages, and had known much hardship. What Michael had, he had gotten through hard work and perseverance.

But Michael was also a white man.

How could he ever understand what it was to be an African in this world of commerce and progress? He wondered if Michael could even begin to comprehend what this child represented. "Think carefully of what this Blessed One means to my people, Michael."

The man turned to the window and stared out, intent with his thoughts. Michael knew that his next step would be a last choice. His heart beat like thunder within his chest. He would not be able to unmake the decision. It would mean everything for both his future and his faith. "I did," he vowed to the waiting archbishop. "I do."

"I take it that I have no need to fear for my priest."

"No." Michael could not help his snort of amusement at the question. "I could never harm such a holy man."

"What will you do?" The archbishop asked the question with feigned mild curiosity. Michael's answer would be very important if his plan were to work. Strike that. His plan had to work. If this young man took his path, he could be sure that his country would be on the road to recovery in a permanent way. They would be free from the yoke of certain death.

"I do not know, archbishop."

"Michael, I cannot support your mission for the cardinal."

He watched the young man's face until he was positive that he grasped the strength of the words he was about to speak. "But I can support you."

"Money means nothing to me, archbishop. I was paid well in the past. Even if I never work again, it will affect me very little.

"I meant that I could provide you with family. Faith. A higher purpose."

Michael smiled. "That I will always need."

"So be it," the archbishop intoned, with a triumphant clap of approval. "There is something I should warn you about, sir." Michael swallowed several times as he gathered his courage to make his final break. This was it. There could be no turning back after this. Cardinal Robeson would never take him back to the fold after he had betrayed him.

"What is it?"

"There are others chasing your priest and the child. These hunters are not working with the Church."

"So we shall have to pray, and pray very hard." As an Ethiopian, one of the most underestimated African countries in the Union, he rejoiced in the shock that crossed his new student's face. His white friend had not expected him to take the pious route. Little did he understand that was the only path the archbishop would ever choose.

"Archbishop, I could stop these threats. I would be honored to protect the child and the priest."

"No, Michael. That is not our way."

"You are very different from the Roman Catholic Church." Michael released the breath he was holding, not caring that the older man heard it. This felt right. This was the way he wished to go. It made all the dreams he had been having makes sense. His heart filled with joy and his spirit lightened.

"We are different from Cardinal Robeson. The good cardinal is not the Roman Catholic Church. The man has forgotten his own way, much less ours."

"I shall like your way."

"You shall, Michael. Indeed you shall."

The archbishop smiled, as the boy left. Michael had come as the pawn.

He had left his presence as a king.

CHAPTER FIFTY-TWO

"A partner in the business will not put an obstacle to it."
–Ethiopian Proverb

The clearing at the end of the fence had been decided as the meeting place. In the Middle Ages, European villages would use market day as a chance to make money and share their talents. Meggani had insisted that working with real people was the only practical utilization of the students' abilities. The more they used them, the more they gave them away, the more they themselves had.

It was a glorious way to spend the day. And it was also the brothers favorite time of each week.

At first the citizens of Axum were unhappy at the news that there would be a gathering. They had no intention of going anywhere near the strange school in the hills. It was the property of the Church. They would never violate the sanctity of the holy institution that was the fulcrum of all their lives. As with most things they did, it was the children that made it a success.

Not the students of the school, but the ones that lived in the village.

Two girls brought their sick baby brother. Meggani arranged for him to be healed.

Another boy brought a camel, ill with festering sores. Mani cleared them.

A male teenager came with tales of woe that his family's small farm no longer produced anything. They were starving. Jake, Rohan and Meggani went home with the boy. While the family watched, Jake called the crops to come out from their hiding. After Jake assisted the boy's father in understanding how to keep the soil balanced so that they would no longer face the same problem. Rohan added his encouragement for the family to return some trees to the farm's outskirts. He was already the monks' star pupil and right hand.

Rohan was the one who spent the most time with them for the Guardian students tended to drift off by themselves when the mood struck them.

On the next village day there were some adults. Most were young mothers. The women came with babies that had fevers. Or their bellies were bloated from parasites. They were seen by Jake, Mani and Ani; prescribed food or tonics. Restless sleepers were soothed by one of Tera's songs.

And then, just as they did not expect it, the miracle happened.

For on the next village day, everyone came. The fathers. Grandparents. Mothers, young and old. Youths of all ages and sexes.

The brothers stood back to watch and learn. They relished the glow of pride they felt as the people marveled at the accomplishments of their students. Though none had ever had children of their own, they watched over the boys and girls as if they had sprung from their loins.

When all that could be done in the clearing was finished, the monks broke off into different directions. They were to travel with the kids to the various homes and farms to deal with the matters that could not be dispatched without a visit.

Mtho stood on the side, making sure that none of the children left unsupervised. He was always careful that the young ones were protected from any negativity or fear that could slow their progress.

"Your children," one of the Axum elders spoke, his voice a gruff growl, "they are wondrous gifts."

"This is why we protect them," Mtho explained.

"It is good. We shall assist you."

Mtho did not wish the kindness of the children, or the villagers' energy, to interfere with the school's course. In their pursuit of protecting the school, the people of Axum could bring far too much attention to their secluded location. It was isolated for a reason. "That is not required. They are happy to help you."

"How can we repay their assistance?"

"We are secluded for a reason," Mtho explained his voice pitched low so that the others would not hear. "We need to stay that way."

The man nodded, understanding what was being requested of him. "They must grow and learn where none can cast doubt. Or make them feel wrong. They must be able to explore what they are without anyone holding them back, or trying to capitalize on what they can do."

"I agree," the villager nodded with eagerness. "I will tell the others."

"They need to be protected. If you see any of them wandering alone," Mtho added thinking of Meggani and her habit of disappearing, "I would appreciate you keeping an eye out."

"They shall be guarded as we would our own flesh."

Mtho released a deep sigh, happy to feel the tension that had gripped him ease with this news. He understood. The children would be safe. All that mattered was that the students would be left alone.

"We will never tell anyone the truth of this place," the man continued his vow. "It is ours, and only our right. We shall protect it just as we do the Ark."

CHAPTER FIFTY-THREE

Brother Mtho and Kwai were on gardening duty all morning. Mtho found the act of pruning the fruit trees that lined the main courtyard a soothing chore that approached a meditative state. They had been working for three hours, when Kwai stopped suddenly and looked around curiously. "Where are the children?"

"Meggani is giving them a self-protection lesson." Mtho snipped off a few stray twigs.

Kwai scowled into the mulch he was tamping down. "You mean a knife lesson."

"It comforts them, brother."

"All this play with weapons … it can't be healthy." Kwai started to gather some of the twigs to use in their fireplace that night. It got quite cold in the evenings this time of year.

Mtho shrugged. "The children don't seem to mind."

"Of course not, they follow Meggani around like besotted puppies."

"They followed you around when you gave them their robes." Mtho grinned at the disgruntled look that crossed his friend's face. The children had taken to their robes that were like the monks, with an enthusiasm that had shocked them. Mtho thought it made them feel good to have the new clothes.

One of the abbé's visiting monks snapped that it was because the boys liked not wearing underwear.

"I thought they would like to feel a part of a unit," Kwai muttered.

Mtho threw his head back with his deep resonant laughter. "Half the time they finish each other's sentences. They are already a unit, brother; what you did was give them a chance to feel like a family. A concept that most of our charges have never known, before our little haven accepted them into our midst."

Kwai looked away from him, both uncomfortable with the praise and desiring to be honest.

When it did not look as if he would say anything, Mtho nudged his shoulder. Kwai stood and ran his hands over the branches from a finished baby tree. "I could not give clothes to the abused ones without hurting the ones who came from loving families. It was a way to help the kids find an equal footing."

"I know that Kwai, and I approve." Mtho put his hand on his friend's shoulder and squeezed.

At the sound of the bell ringing out that they'd attached to the gate lock, the two turned to their fence. Father Josephus, Rhonda, and the child each stepped through the gate. The priest paused as he looked around at the school's grounds and all the progress that had been accomplished while he was gone. Rhonda looked with polite interest, the end of the child's mouth twitched as if she were fighting a smile. When Mtho and Kwai saw them, they both rushed to their side, and gave Josephus a warm embrace.

Following their greeting, Josephus brought forward the females with him. "This is Rhonda Sith, a Professor from America University. She will be helping us."

The two monks shook her hand, and then knelt so that they could look directly into the girl's eyes.

Josephus could not help glowing with pride. "This is our Blessed One."

"I prefer Little One for now," the girl admitted to them ruefully. "My name seems to be slow in returning to my mind."

"A privilege to meet you," Mtho enthused, while pumping her hand up and down.

Kwai leaned forward to kiss the girl's sandal-covered feet. "We are honored."

The girl immediately pulled the monk up from his kneeling position, shaking her head. Her eyes wide with discomfort over his actions. This was not the way things were meant to be. "Please, please don't do that. I'm just a little girl."

"One who happens to carry the knowledge of the ancients, the Ark, the Ark Maiden and many others," Rhonda reminded her. They had discussed last night what kind of reception she might receive upon their arrival at the school. The professor had been concerned that the brother's reverence might make the little girl uncomfortable. For all of her abilities she was very down to earth.

"Good thing I have a big head," she proclaimed, "or it wouldn't all fit."

Josephus could not prevent a dramatic roll of his eyes. "It's apparent that her sense of humor has returned."

The doors to the classroom building suddenly flew open. From inside came a queue of students, each one dressed in their eggplant colored robes, with the hoods up to cover their heads, though Mtho was sure he could still identify them.

He was that close to each of the souls he'd guided to these gates.

First one out was Meggani, who had her marbles levitating around her head moving as if they were planets and she the sun. The next was Jake. As he walked, flowers bloomed in his steps, creating a runner of fragrant blossoms. Mani followed him with a jar of his healing powder cradled in his hands. Ani followed him, though she was levitating several feet above her classmates. Tera came after her, playing his reed pipe, with a thick-billed raven sitting on his shoulder and nodding along.

Each of the children walked with some sign of their gift or ability. Kebbie carried the crystal glass she had taken to using for her prophecies and Kiddisti carried a small energy ball that crackled with silver lightning in the middle of his palms.

Mtho realized Meggani was carrying an extra set of robes. Clothing he himself had never seen before. Someone had taken the time to include a gold band on the arm.

He was positive this was not something they had rehearsed.

It was a moment that had been scripted from the time they were born.

He said a soft prayer beneath his breath, he was so moved by the spectacle.

The adults all stepped forward to discuss what the kids were doing, but the Blessed One beat them to it. She moved in front until she was more than halfway between her adult protectors and the coming schoolchildren.

Rhonda asked the two resident brothers she had already met, "What do you think this is all about?"

"I don't know." Mtho smiled at the solemn expressions on the kids' faces.

Josephus chuckled. "They are welcoming her."

How magnificent they are, Baba, he thought while blinking his eyes to clear the tears. *They know her. She is as much a part of them as their arms and legs. We did it, Baba. Azarius' descendants did not fail, after all.*

How could I have ever doubted you, Baba?

How could I have doubted myself?

When the kids had reached the Blessed One they circled her in a clock-wise direction with slow, sedate steps. They added their voices to harmonize with the tune from Tera's flute. A low chanting began that wrapped them in peace. Josephus smiled, recognizing the song from the Dome of the Rock.

Kwai turned to Mtho. "Did they tell you about this?"

"I don't think this was practiced," he admitted.

Josephus tapped his chin. "It wouldn't have to be. They are all connected in a way I doubt that we will ever understand.

"I've never seen children act this way." Rhonda shook her head, amazed.

Father Josephus snickered. "I suspect we will say that often, over the years to come."

As the children made a complete circle around their new leader,

Meggani stepped forward to bow her head and hand her the garment. "Welcome to your school."

Little One took the robe and put it on over her shorts and tank top. "You mean welcome to our home." She reached forward to hug Meggani. The children all laughed with abandon, as they clambered over each other to embrace the new addition.

It was a circle of love. One where the adults did not belong.

Josephus nodded with satisfaction. "What next?" he asked the others.

"The archbishop contacted us to warn you that someone is hunting the child." Mtho's confession was said just an octave above a whisper.

Rhonda snorted. "She's mentioned it. We think it's her relatives."

"What if they take her away?"

They could all see Kwai's nervousness that they might lose the Blessed One after going through so much. Josephus shook his head. "I do not believe God would have us find her, only to take her away again."

Kwai smoothed his turban with a shaking hand. "We were warned that the hunter is dangerous."

"God will protect us." Josephus patted his shoulder.

"If God won't," Mtho joked. "Meggani will."

CHAPTER FIFTY-FOUR

"No one tests the depth of a river with both feet."
—African Proverb

I t would be difficult to survive, but Michael was determined. He had liquidated most of his accounts and redistributed the funds to keep them safe. His camp had been easy to build in the mountains overlooking the school's compound. He had a central fire pit, with a small pile of logs to keep it well stocked. The only other things he needed were an animal stockade and a tent where he could sleep. There was no need for him to have any guards; there was nothing in the camp that was worth protection. He had created an image of slight poverty, with a purpose. Michael was sure that if he turned up on their doorstop, Josephus would take him in.

His intent was never to become a burden to them. He would only play that card if he felt it would enable him to be more protective of the good priest's charges. He had the resources to be so much more.

Donning the robes of a Bedouin made it easier for him to fit in to the sea of dark faces that populated the town. The hood was a godsend. He kept it up all the time. His pale white skin and long blonde hair made him stand out too much, otherwise. If he were to protect what he held most dear, he needed to be like a wraith.

He had the training.

From the moment he had entered the town, he decided to be a silent ghost. The one who protected the school and the precious children who found a haven in its confines. He did his job with absolute vigilance.

Michael made sure to further his hold on the townspeople to protect the academy by visiting often and buying supplies. He appreciated that he could come every day and find food from the many women eager to make extra money.

Life on the road had never taught him much about cooking.

Purchasing some doro wat, a spicy chicken dish, injera, and kitfo, a dish of freshly ground raw beef from one of the village woman he murmured, "Shokran" to her in thanks. The call of "ala el rahib wa el saa," which meant you're welcome in her language, echoed past him as he left. He was stuck conversing in Arabic since he hadn't mastered Amharic yet.

The Amharan tribe was a treat to him. Michael liked the people in their white robes, and the friendly nature of their children. He found the food delicious, and the people open to everything. They showed such deference for their priests when they walked through the streets in their colorful robes. He felt, for the first time in his life, as if he had found his way home.

Watching over these children made him remember his own origin.

Growing up in the orphanage had been hell. Escape had been the only option. Running away was a desperate plea that started in the hearts of all the residents when they reached their early teens. It was like night to day in comparison to the life that was led in the Ethiopian complex.

He occasionally saw the Blessed One with the others. His favorite time of the month was during the school's village days. Michael watched from the shadows of the trees. Students and villagers passed him without discerning his presence. Michael's eyes were always locked on their leader. The little one was a constant source of ease to his troubled heart. Her laughter would ring out over his small camp like a cool breeze on a summer day.

There was one other he had taken to noticing: she was called Meggani.

Her hair was always braided, shining with the beads that she tended with such care. Michael was surprised at how drawn he felt to her. She was a baby. It was indecent. Still. Something in this one female called to him, and made him hunger to teach her to smile and laugh with the same freedom as her schoolmates. The shadows that haunted her eyes made him ache to find the demons that had put them there and slay them for her.

Michael had found out the hunters were drawing near.

He had spread enough money through the town to make sure that they would find their next stop a dead end. The people were no more willing to see danger come to the special ones' home, than he was willing to allow it. Michael was an expert at subterfuge, and the town was eager to learn.

They would give the coming party of foreigner's indirect answers or simple silence. It would not be a simple task for them to find out about the unique children that lived and grew far in the hills that surrounded them.

If one of them should push regarding the priest traveling with a child, Michael had given them leave to discuss the death of Brother Peter in the loosest terms.

Misdirection was the second best way to hide.

The hunters would go off, crushed, but sure that whoever they searched for had died in a flash flood. It would be as he decreed. He was doing God's work. For the first time, Michael found his life filled with ease and contentment. It had started after his initial audience with the archbishop. He was changed. The nightmares from his childhood were gone. Guilt from his past erased. The Ethiopian Church's piety had been well known to him in rumor, but the actual experience defied his imagination.

The archbishop had been specific with his instructions.

He was to do only what his conscience guided him to.

Michael laughed to himself. The holy man that empowered him on this quest did not understand one thing. His conscience allowed him a great deal of freedom.

That was what happened when you did not have one.

CHAPTER FIFTY-FIVE

Axum was once the capital of the lands of Kush. The tiny hamlet that was the center of the hurricane that is the Ethiopian Church was surrounded by ruins of many different ages. Mtho had taken the children in small groups through the stele park, with its intricately carved stone monoliths. Some of them looked like a luxury hotel to the students, complete with people on all different floors pursuing varied recreational pursuits. They had attended services at the Church dedicated to Saint Mary, mother of the prophet Jesus. He had even insisted they make homage of flowers and fruits to the sanctuary for the Ark of the Covenant, though most of them believed the holy tabot was no longer in residence.

Since the citizens came to the school so often, Mtho wanted the students to be seen visiting the town.

There was an abundance of things to be seen.

Josephus had chosen to build the school in the hills that overlooked the fulcrum of his faith, on purpose. It would have a regular influx of people that were in need of his students' services. He liked the area and was confident of their reception, and he had also received the large plot of land, where they had built the school, in his cousin's will.

Meggani adored the town and begged to go on any errand into the village, no matter who was making it. Mtho allowed her to go whenever he went. He sensed her frustration at the walls of the school. Meggani was a wild creature, untamed and free. Feral. She needed to roam occasionally, no matter how much it might endanger her.

The errands at an end, they were on their way back, when he noticed her lagging steps. "I realize you don't wish to go back to the school but this box is getting heavy."

Meggani glanced resentfully at the packages overflowing from the crate. "I could carry it. No problem."

"What's wrong, child?"

"Sometimes, it just gets to be too much."

He didn't understand. "What," he asked her, his voice gentle.

"The school, teachers, the kids … all of it."

Mtho bit at his lower lip. "You have been on your own for a long time."

"I guess I just need a time out from it all, every now and again."

"You have been working the others very hard, and yourself."

She smiled at the mention of the knife training he had allowed in spite of everyone else's protest. Rhonda had been especially vehement in her refusal to be comfortable with the children each carrying their own dagger. "They know all they need to now," she admitted.

"Is it really that bad?" His voice was teasing. They had been together for such a long time. He knew that her twelfth birthday would be any day now.

"No. Most of the time it's great. It's just that sometime it all builds up and I need to get away for a moment."

He nodded. "That's why you go on the hikes."

"I like exploring," she blurted, feeling defensive.

A sigh of resignation escaped him. He was going to get into a whole lot of trouble for this. "If you promise, really promise, to be back by dark … you can stay and explore on your own."

She threw her arms around his waist, much to his surprise. "Thank you."

The monk watched the girl scamper off with a bemused expression. He was comfortable with her need to wander. It was safe. The residents were dependent on the school's good will; they would keep an eye out for her. Axum was such a small town.

Nothing ever happened here. There were never that many strangers.

After walking through the marketplace for an hour, Meggani was ready to return home. She was going to do just that when she heard a strain of music she recognized all too well. At first she thought she might have been followed by Tera for some reason. As the next oldest he had been trying to copy the things she did, without understanding them all the time. It made her laugh. This was not he, though. She was sure.

The song did not have the same hypnotic pull as the first time she had met him. It was a lamentation, making her want to weep for something vital that was missing, some aspect of her soul that was intrinsic to her capacity to thrive.

Each note made her want to sit down and wail.

Meggani did not notice the man who watched her. Michael had seen the girl often in the town. He had never approached this close before. Her eyes were that of a wounded creature. The small sweet face tugged at his heart and made his breath catch. When she took off running toward the ruins, he felt compelled to follow.

She kept moving, following the music as if a puppet on a string. Meggani was sure this was not the song of another child, a fellow guardian. It was, however, very close.

This tune was unique.

Reaching the ruins, she dashed up the few steps and stopped in the center of a forest of broken pillars. This was the palace she had visited so often in her exploration. In the center of the Queen of Sheba's once great home, sat a woman. She had long honey gold hair that glinted with red and white highlights. To Meggani she looked like she had melted strawberries and sunlight in her hair, and it whipped in the breeze. She knelt on the ground, a harp under each hand. The instrument was one that was quite popular with the villagers. Seeing her face, Meggani's breath caught. The woman was crying. Tears streamed down her face, glinting like crystals in the sun, she was weeping as if her world had ended that day.

Surely, no human could display such grief if it were not true.

Village women nearby commented the woman was an American, traveling with two men. Meggani moved around the pillars, flitting from column to column, trying to keep a distance between herself and the other members of the audience. The song continued; the weeping unabated. She played the instruments so quickly, and with such force, that the child could see the woman's fingers bled.

A small group of villagers gathered to watch the crazy American female with the creamy skin, as she wept with sorrow and filled their hearts with her remorse.

Meggani felt someone watching her. She had thought everyone had direct focus on the crying lady who was performing a once-in-a-lifetime musical experience. Her body became damp with sweat. Mtho's warnings echoed through her mind. Meggani covered her head with her hood glancing around. She did not like being nervous. It had been a long time since she had lived in this manner.

Two men came dashing into the ruins and approached the woman. Meggani guessed they were her friends by the concerned looks on their faces. They were too far away for her to hear them over the playing, but she noticed that the one black man kept the white man from stopping the woman. It was a good thing he did. Ethiopians recognized someone taken with the Holy Spirit. There was no way they would allow any interruption of whatever God was trying to communicate through this lady's song.

When she finished her lament, her head fell forward slowly. The lady staggered to her feet as if waking from a daze. She saw Meggani in the distance and reached out a shaking hand. "Keda?"

Her two friends flanked her. "Jasmine," the white man shook her, trying to gain her attention.

The black man shook his head, saddened. "It was too much for her, Gabriel."

"I don't care what you think, Raffe," he shouted at his friend. "Jasmine, it will be fine."

The woman named Jasmine took a few more steps toward Meggani, her eyes wide as the full moon and her body trembling with fear and possible hope. "Keda," she cried, again.

Meggani was still nervous from the feeling she was being watched, and now this woman was looking at her with a strange urgency and calling her some odd name. She had promised Mtho and the brothers she would stay safe.

Unseen.

This was not the way.

She took off running, toward the safety of the school, easily leaving the odd group of people behind her. In her heart, Meggani wished she could do the same with her fears, but they stayed rooted in her soul with an unbreakable hold.

CHAPTER FIFTY-SIX

Meggani burst through the garden gate as if a rampaging army were on her heels. The school was in recess, so the yard was packed with the other pupils who were playing or just sitting down to talk. She dashed through them all to shout a warning to the teacher watching over them. When she saw that the monk went inside to speak with the other adults, Meggani moved to Rohan.

They had a plan.

They knew what they were going to do.

As a group, they had been training for this day for a long time.

This was the moment they were warned about in their dreams.

Her pursuers come through the gate right behind her. The woman was first. Her hands held out from her body, it was obvious she was in great distress. The two men followed, their eyes agonized and tormented for their friend.

As soon as the students caught sight of the strangers, they froze. One by one, those that did not have their heads covered by their hoods, pulled them up to hide their faces.

The woman looked around wildly searching. "Keda?"

Her white friend pulled her into his arms. She pushed away from him and once more called again, "Keda?"

She watched in anguish as the shrouded children assembled themselves into ranks of equal numbers. None had yet to claim the name she cried with such pure desperation. The Ethiopian with her nudged the white man with a teasing smile, "How many nieces was she searching for?"

"Please ... please ... one of you must be Keda. Please be her."

Meggani was taken aback when the Blessed One was the first to start the response. If this woman was related to their leader, she would have to prove herself. The call was the test. "I am Keda," the girl called out. Meggani was quick to add her own voice, "I am Keda." One by one, each of the children, boys as well as girls, added their own words to the test.

"Choose with care, Jasmine," the white man advised the woman. "I do not think you will get a second chance."

The Ethiopian had spotted the knives in some of the sleeves of the kids. "I do not think any of us will," he muttered.

Jasmine started to head to the middle row, but suddenly turned to the last one.

The monk that watched over the children playing had warned the adults. Brother Mtho, Father Josephus, Brother Kwai and Rhonda came out from the main school building, each deeply concerned at the news. Strangers made them uneasy. No villagers would come to the academic complex. This would have to be a danger to their school's future.

Each of the religious men drew their hoods up to cover their heads. Rhonda bit at her lip as her eyes grew large with concern, and shone with unshed tears. The woman must be searching for their blessed one. Meggani had explained the test might be needed.

This was the time.

Her sorrow and fear were like a knife, slicing from her stomach to her heart. She had come to look at the Little One as if she were her own child. There could be no mistaking the look on the woman's face. This was Keda's mother.

All the professor's dreams and hopes for the future were dying.

The Ethiopian stranger softly cursed, "This may have just gotten more complicated."

Walking down the lane, the American woman came to the last robed form in the row. She stopped and slowly knelt before the child. This was the moment she had dreamt of for so long. With shaking hands, she uncovered the Little One's face. "Keda," she called out with a joyful tone as she gathered the girl into her arms.

"I knew you could do it, Aunt Jasmine," Keda called out as she threw her arms around her aunt's neck.

Jasmine began to kiss every inch of the girl's face. "I swore I would not stop looking for you until we got you back. I will never let you go again. Everything will be fine. We are taking you home."

The other eleven children in the clearing pulled out their knives and pointed them at Jasmine. She hissed when some of them pressed against her bare skin. Others she could feel through her clothing. The white man started into their midst to pull Jasmine and Keda to safety, but his black friend held him back.

"Do not move."

Jasmine could barely contain herself from rolling her eyes at this unnecessary advice. "As if I would."

Father Josephus rushed over to them. "Only a mother would find a child with such unerring accuracy."

The Ethiopian stranger's brows rose. "Excuse me?"

At Josephus's comment, the children withdrew their knives and slipped them back beneath their robes. Without needing to consult each other, the students chose to leave the situation in the priest's hands. They allowed the adults to stay alone, trusting them to protect their leader, and moved nearby to return to their play.

Meggani lingered behind.

She was like a mother to all of them. It was her job to protect each of her charges. She did not trust this white woman who claimed to have a bond with her leader. If she took Keda away, their mission would fail. How dared she interfere? Meggani was determined to guard all of them, no matter what.

Keda looked after her friends with great longing. "Aunt Jazzy, if I promise to be where you can see me, can I go play?"

"Make her promise to stay closer than that," the white man requested.

Jasmine nodded her permission while her eyes stayed glued to Josephus' face. Keda dashed off to join her friends as Jasmine stood. The priest broke into a broad grin, not recognizing the glitter of rage in her eyes. "John?" she whispered. "John Prester? You are the one who took Keda? How could you do this to me? How could you do this to her? What in God's name were you thinking?"

The strange Ethiopian rubbed his hands together. "This definitely just got interesting."

Everyone else ignored him.

"They call me Father Josephus now. It is good to see you Jasmine Rose; it has been a very long time."

He barely finished his sentence before Jasmine flew at him and slapped him across the face with her open palm. Kwai, Mtho, Rhonda, and Meggani rushed over to him, but he held his hand up to keep them from doing anything. "I take it you are not glad to see me?" He fingered his stinging, bright red, cheek with unease.

Others were not as sanguine in their response.

Mtho put his hand on Meggani's shoulder to keep her from throwing her knife.

"You left me," the American female wailed at him. "I searched everywhere for you."

"Gabriel, looks like she's needed the great CIA hunter, for a while." The Ethiopian joked to his friend.

The white man rolled his eyes, "Quiet, Raffe."

Jasmine could not get past her bitter disappointment in the man before her. "You just disappeared off the face of the earth. I thought I meant more than that to you. You left me seven years ago, alone and pregnant."

"Pregnant?" Josephus was more staggered by this news than the blow she'd landed earlier. "You were pregnant? Seven years ago?"

At this news, Mtho picked up Meggani and strode away from the others. Realizing what the girl had witnessed, Kwai joined them, to try and help make it clear for her. They were all quite sensitive to Meggani's need to be a mother to the others. No one expected that role to be supplanted by the woman who had actually given birth to Keda. This event could be inconceivable for her.

They feared they could lose her as well.

CHAPTER FIFTY-SEVEN

Mtho held Meggani close as they went behind the main school building and set her down. It alarmed him that the girl made no move to fight his touch. He held her in place against the cedar shingles of the wall. "It will be fine, child."

"She will take Keda away."

He could hear the tears choking her voice, making it sound as if she were being strangled. Beneath his palms clasping her shoulders, he could feel her tremble with terror. The one thing they had never counted on was this. After giving the children a home for the first time, anything jeopardizing that place could send them into this freefall of panic.

Light, he reminded himself. You can only banish darkness with light.

What else is love ... but light?

Kwai was breathing heavy when he joined them. "Father Josephus will not allow it."

"It won't matter," Meggani muttered. Her eyes streamed tears, and the two monks could see the shadows of nightmares she had survived move underneath their obsidian surface. "Keda will go and there will not be any reason for the school anymore. You will all go to your monastery and we will be left ...

"Alone," she moaned.

They had no words they thought might comfort her.

Meggani took a shuddering breath, "Again."

Both men took a moment to wipe their eyes as they empathized with her. Taking a deep breath, they remembered that this, right here and now, was why these children needed them.

Relied on them.

Light.

Mtho knelt in the grass, his fingers clutching at her arms. "No, child. Never again. You will never be alone again."

Kwai wished he could reach her, but words escaped him. There had never been training in his history for a moment such as this. "Meggani, the school was never meant for just Keda. It was always developed to be a fortress for children such as yourself. It may be harder for us to reach our goals without her, but we would still manage." When his logic made no change, he tried emotion as well. "You will never be alone again."

"Well done, brother," Mtho's soft praise made his friend glow with pride. "Meggani, listen to him."

"I am afraid," she confessed as if it were a crime against her nature.

"You have a right to be," Kwai pointed out.

Mtho smiled at her. "Meggani, do you understand why you were born first? Why you are so much older than the others? You were meant to be an example to us all of why this place is so vital for our future. This school will not go away. You and the others will be able to live, learn and grow here. Safe. You will explore everything you can do without any criticism or censure. When you are strong and independent, and ready to leave, we will send you with our love and good will.

"The time of darkness is over, child."

"We are the light," Kebbie stated, as she joined them.

Meggani tried to collect herself when she saw the youngest child standing by Kwai's side. "I'll be right there," she called to Keberwa.

"No cry, Meggani. No be scared. Go look."

Brother Mtho peeked around the side of the building, his eyes widening. "I do believe it is time we joined the others."

"I can't," she confessed.

Shooing Kwai and Kebbie away, Mtho sat on the ground and guided Meggani down beside him. "We'll be there in a moment," he explained.

When they were alone, Mtho pulled Meggani's blade out from her sleeve. When she glowered, he shrugged. "It is not that I don't trust you, child. It is just that I understand how these things can go. It would be better if you were not armed when we rejoin Keda and meet her friends. I could hardly blame you just because those strangers said something that provoked you. So let's have me hold this until we are sure they can be trusted."

He was secretly amused when he heard her admit that it was wise.

CHAPTER FIFTY-EIGHT

eggani sighed and wiped guiltily at her tears. They were a sign of her lack of faith, and made her feel ashamed. Looking up at Mtho, he shimmered through the moisture in her eyes, though his smile was steadfast and calm. "Let me get you a drink," he offered as he rose, "and perhaps a cloth."

"I'm sorry that I cry."

"God doesn't mind a lapse in faith. Or questions. We always return to him sooner or later."

"I'm supposed to be better than that," she mumbled.

Mtho leaned over to squeeze her shoulder. "If you were any better you would no longer be human."

She smiled for the first time that day, "Me? An angel?"

His grin warmed her heart, a place that had grown cold from her biggest fears being manifested before her eyes. "Why not you, child?"

"Brother Mtho … have you been paying attention to who I am?"

"Yes, young one, I have. And I see more than you think."

When he left to go inside the kitchen, Meggani felt the same sense of unease she had detected earlier. A prickling on her neck told her that someone was near. Twitching restlessness shot through her arms and legs with the desire to flee.

Someone was watching.

Someone else.

Moving her legs up so that she clung to the deepest shadows of the building behind her, she steadied her breathing. *It's okay,* she reminded herself. *There were others nearby who would protect her. Nothing bad could get her here.*

Calm settled over her.

Looking up, she saw what she had felt watching her.

A man.

Hidden in the shadows as well, he stayed so still it was as if he had become a tree. It was his eyes that she recognized first. They were the clear blue of a summer sky and held such warmth in them that she felt no fear.

It was as if an angel had come to protect her.

His arm moved; slow and sure, making no noise; until he placed one finger in front of the straight line of his lips. *Don't speak,* his gesture instructed. Meggani was willing to give him a chance because of the ease she felt within. She nodded.

The first sign of danger though, and all bets were off.

Her visiting angel came out of the darkness and walked toward her. Bending down, still so slow it was as if he were the movement of the sun across the sky, he kept lowering his body until she only had to lean back a little bit to keep her eyes on his.

A single finger was extended until it touched her cheek.

Meggani did not move. She tried not to even breathe. She was positive this angelic visitation would flee at the first sign of her acknowledgement.

His touch was so gentle it made her lips twitch.

She was amazed that she still felt no fear.

As he pulled his finger away, Meggani smiled wider as she saw he had caught a single teardrop on the tip.

He stood up with the same steady pace; raising the teardrop until it was inside a single sunbeam that pierced the gloom. Her stranger smiled, a look of such sweet understanding, that it pierced Meggani's childlike veil, to hint at what it truly was to be a woman.

For the first time she liked it.

When he was sure he had her attention, he flicked the teardrop into the light, and grabbing as if to take it back. His fist held over her lap, he opened his clenched fingers to allow a single small diamond to fall into her palm.

Sounds of Mtho's return made her visitor turn and flee back into the shadows. Holding the diamond tight within her grasp, Meggani felt a flow of information fill her mind with all of the details of her visitor's life.

His name was Michael.

He was sent to guard them by the archbishop.

For the first time, she understood.

She was not the first of their kind to come.

Meggani was just the first of their kind to be found.

As the monk settled beside her again, she made herself not think about what just happened. She shoved the diamond into the deepest pocket of her robe. She would take it out later and examine it more closely.

Think about it.

Debate with herself what must be done.

What should be done.

Perhaps she would even discuss it with the other girls.

The one thing she would not tell them was how she felt inside. She was too young to understand what the stranger made her feel. Too inexperienced with the goodness in people to grasp what this feeling could mean.

First, they must settle what was to be done with Michael.

He had found them. It was time for them to find him as well.

"You almost ready to join the others?"

She was startled by Brother Mtho's question. Meggani had forgotten the drama that was taking place nearby. Michael had given her a greater gift than she had realized. "In a little while, Brother Mtho." Taking a sip of her drink, she smiled to show that she was recovering, faster than he realized. "Tell me again about Debra Damo."

CHAPTER FIFTY-NINE

When he and Meggani emerged from behind the building, Mtho cursed silently. Keda was gone. It was easy for him to see she girl had been taken home by the strangers. His hand clasped the girl's shoulder, uneasy what this could mean to her hard-won calm. "No matter what happens, Meggani, remember we will not leave you."

The eyes she turned to him were so devastated he took a step back before he knelt to hug her. Mtho knew she would take only so much physical contact in a day.

Josephus hurried out the gate, Kwai seeing Meggani's distress, joined her and Mtho.

"Will she return?"

Kwai nodded, "She just went home with her mother for dinner. She will be back, Meggani."

"They'll take her away," her strangled whisper still managed to reach them.

"No, child," Kwai knelt before her to take both of her hands.

"Everybody leaves."

Kebbie came running over to lean against Meggani. "I see it, Meggani."

"Tell her," Mtho encouraged.

"Keda comes home. Promise, Meggani."

"Which home?"

All three of them shook their heads at Meggani's stubborn insistence in imagining only the worst possible outcome. "You aren't acting very angelic, now," Mtho joked feebly.

Kebbie stamped her foot. "Only home, Meggani. Here home."

Meggani pulled the younger girl into her embrace and held her tightly. Rhonda joined them and sighed at the sadness in the girl's face. "Josephus went to finalize the plans to take Keda into the Ark sanctuary tonight. I believe in Kebbie, Meggani, and you should as well. Keda will come back to us. All the children agree."

"It is so easy to listen to your fears," Meggani's head dropped forward.

"Of course it is," Rohan pulled her braid before sliding to the other side of Kwai. "Doesn't mean you should do it."

"Shut up," Meggani's lips quirked at the corners, as she fought a smile.

"And the crisis is averted," Kwai proclaimed.

"I want to go to the sanctuary," Meggani asserted.

Mtho helped the other monk up. "I don't think that's a good idea."

Kebbie shook her head. "You no go, Meggani. Has to be Ani and Tera."

"Right," her head stayed down, as she scuffed the ground with her shoe.

"You help me with my braids," Kebbie decreed. The younger girl grabbed her hand and with a hard jerk, pulled Meggani away from the adults.

"Will she be okay?" Rhonda asked the monks.

"She'll be fine," Rohan answered. "No one can be sad around Kebbie. She sucks it right out of you."

The adults all laughed, as the boy went to join the others. "Well," Kwai surmised. "We've always been told a little child will lead us."

"But this many children?"

Rhonda laughed at the monks. "Who knew we could get so lucky?"

CHAPTER SIXTY

"Do not look where you fell, but where you slipped."
—African Proverb

As Josephus drew close to the Ark sanctuary, he took a deep breath. The scent of the azaleas brushed against his skin like a caress. His child. He was going to see his child, the marked child. He shook his head trying to clear it, aware that he held the hands of two other children whose parents trusted him to keep them safe.

It was his charges who reached Keda first. They wrapped themselves around her as if they would never let her go. He became conscious that any trepidation he felt at the potential to lose a child he had just gained paled in comparison to the souls who feared losing their leader.

Though Keda was one of the youngest at the school, there could be no doubt she was the leader.

Seeing the confusion on Jasmine's face, he pushed away a regret that once upon a time he had let this woman's words send him away without first gaining an understanding for her fear and begging her to let them confront it together.

But Baba, he whispered in his secret-heart, *we are where we are meant to be.*

Still, I learn at your feet.

Once he had watched his grandfather draw angels in the air. Now he realized Baba had been drawing Keda and the rest of the children living at the school.

Jasmine stared at the trio. "She was only gone a few hours."

Josephus's brow furrowed. "They're already a family. In ways we may never fully understand."

A black man in white robes swept out of the chapel. "Quickly," he said, encouraging them all. They followed without question, Keda leading the others as if it were her natural place. The Ark sanctuary was a small oblong building set in the shadows of the Saint Mary's church as if it were created to protect it.

Jasmine was going to step into the structure, but Josephus held her back. "You can't."

"Why not?"

"Females are not allowed," Raffe explained.

"It didn't seem like Moses had that problem. He demanded his sister tend the Ark."

"You're not Miriam," Josephus cautioned.

"I'm not letting my child go into danger," Jasmine swore.

"Her father will be with her."

She fisted her fingers in the fabric of his robe. "I swear to God above," she whispered, "if one hair gets harmed on my baby's head, I will kill you."

"Jasmine ... I love her as well."

"I. Will. Kill. You."

Josephus nodded. "I swear she'll be fine."

Not wishing to give Jasmine another chance to refuse the meeting he had worked so hard to get from the archbishop, he stepped inside of the holiest building of his religion.

Here he would find the final answers, he promised himself, his eyes closing in prayer as he committed a sacrilege, which could still get him beheaded by many of the wilder tribesmen who still dwelt in the hills that surrounded the ancient city. Entering the sanctuary, by the law of their country and the main religion.

When his eyes opened he found ... nothing.

The children held a stained piece of fabric that had clearly been pulled off of a carved box — and looked nothing like the Ark as it was described in the Bible. The archbishop had the Atang, in the corner, the ark guardian and the archbishop fiercely debated something in harsh whispers. "What did you expect, Father Josephus?"

He shook his head at Tera's question. "I'm not sure."

"Your Ark isn't here, Father."

Nodding at Keda, his eyes were glued to the gleaming wood, which matched the desk in the archbishop's Jerusalem office. "So where is it?"

The children rushed out of the room, and he followed.

Josephus threw his arms up. "So where is the Ark?"

Keda joined hands with the two other children, and they took several steps away from the sanctuary. The boy and girl moved with Keda as she turned in a slow circle. When they pivoted two hundred and seventy degrees, a smile began to build on Keda's face. "They hid you good," she whispered.

A sonic boom went off, and a light burst from the horizon and shot straight up into the sky.

"Is this where the aliens demand to be taken to your leader?" Raffe mock-whispered to Gabriel.

"Hush," Jasmine scolded.

The light came back down from the heavens to shower all three children.

"My quest began almost exactly the same way," Josephus cried with excitement.

When the light enveloped the three kids and pulled them up into the sky, no one dared move to stop it. With another boom of thunder the children were set back down. Everyone's ears rang from a series of deafening booms exploding above them. As she looked at the three,

Jasmine shook her head, trying to understand what was wrong. *Why did they look like they were turning red?*

Gabriel pointed up with his finger since he doubted anyone could hear. As the adults' eyes followed his direction, their mouths fell open. The sky looked like it was on fire. Churning flames covered the horizon as far as they could see.

"It's a cloud of fire," Josephus gasped. He and the archbishop knelt, made the sign of the cross, and began to pray.

The cloud of fire continued to boil across the heavens and descended as if it were going to crush them. Growing alarmed, Gabriel pulled Jasmine and Raffe to the ground. She twisted to make sure Josephus had helped the children and was glad to see Keda protected by her father's arms. The archbishop had the other two. Gabriel restricted Jasmine's movements when he buried her beneath him to protect her from the flames. The air grew scalding, and it was hard to breathe. Pressure built inside their bodies and made them scream in pain.

Just when it was about to consume the adults' heads, the cloud relented, rising skyward until it dissipated.

Raffe helped Gabriel and Jasmine to their feet. Jasmine flew to the children's sides as the men checked on Father Josephus and the archbishop. Another loud crack of noise made the earth shake, and all crouched down and peered up with unease.

"It's okay, Mommy." Keda patted Jasmine's arm. "Watch."

A rain began to fall. Gentle. Refreshing. The water seemed so enticing that Jasmine couldn't resist lifting her head to try and catch some of the drops on her tongue.

"No!" all three kids yelled.

They kept her head straight.

"Wait," Keda lectured.

The raindrops turned hard and biting. "Hail," Gabriel swore. He tried to grab Jasmine and Keda and rush them inside the sanctuary, but the archbishop wouldn't allow it.

Raffe instead hustled them to the thick branches of the nearby trees. "We should be fine under here," he hollered.

"Did you want me to wait and see the hail?" Jasmine asked Keda.

She giggled and shook her head. The girl beside her scooped up some of the hailstones and held them out to the adults. Father Josephus pulled out a flashlight so they could all see what the children were so happy and excited about. The items in the girl's hand were gray and clear, catching the light and sending back tiny prisms.

Gabriel gasped. "Are those …"

"Uncut diamonds?" Raffe finished.

"Rainbows," Keda corrected.

The other girl stepped forward, "God promised Noah he would never again use water to destroy the world. So he set down his bow and arrows and gave us rainbows."

"Here's a new kind of promise," Keda added.

"One of invincibility," the boy continued, "for us all."

Keda's face began a terrifying transformation without warning. Before her horrified eyes, Jasmine watched Keda turn into an ancient being caught in her child's body. Eying the two holy men with contempt, she sneered. "Did you think I belonged to you? Either of you? Did you think you could control us? Make us do your bidding? The curse is over, gentlemen. The legacy of Moses will fade away. What I am, and what I will do, is never going to be decided by either of you."

"We're heaven's now," the children intoned as one.

Josephus bowed his head in shame. "Please forgive me."

Keda leaned forward to whisper in his ear. "Your Baba says, thank you. Thank you, Mamush. Now be at peace. The prophecy has finally manifested, and it's all due to you holding steady to your vow."

As Josephus lifted his head, a relieved look on his face shone through his tears. Jasmine knew that those were the special nicknames that Josephus and his beloved grandfather had given to each other. For the first time since their reunion, she saw the man she had known in London who had taught her what love could truly be. When he rose to his feet, he did so with a new purpose and moved to stand between the children and the archbishop.

Josephus glowered as he faced his former mentor. "You said you wished to use the Ark to advance our financial prospects."

"This," the archbishop sputtered as he gestured to the field of uncut diamonds that was accumulating around them, "takes care of all of that—and more. Forget what I said. You'll have autonomy for your school, the children, all of it. I will see to it that nothing will ever threaten any of that again."

As they watched the archbishop dance his way to the church, Gabriel gave Raffe a pointed stare. "What?"

The Ethiopian shrugged, "I admitted he was my uncle. Doesn't make him perfect."

"I'm surprised you admit it."

"Only perfect one in my family is me."

"What did you see in there?" Gabriel asked the kids, choosing to ignore his friend.

"A memento created in a bygone age," the girl answered.

"Made to give hope to a people who were having their faith tested and needed something to cling to in the waves of uncertain times."

Keda smiled at the boy, who found speaking in English so difficult. Pointing at the sanctuary, she repeated, "That's not the Ark."

"Where is it?" Raffe asked eagerly.

"Far away." Keda stared up at Raffe, daring him to challenge her authority.

Disbelieving, Gabriel turned to his friend. "Why would you want to get the Ark now? The kids were hundreds of miles away from it and look what happened." He shook his head, marveling at what they had all witnessed. "How did the Ark make diamonds fall from the sky?"

"Pollution," Jasmine whispered. She picked up a handful of stones and let them slip through her fingers. "There is a ton of carbon in the air because of pollution. The cloud of fire and the pressure must have compressed the pollution in some way and formed the diamonds."

Josephus glowed with joy. "This is what I was trying to prove to you. Our child is a gift in more ways than I can explain."

"I still haven't chosen, Josephus," Jasmine said.

"Can I please take Keda back to the school?"

"You swear you'll be there in the morning?"

He drew himself up with such affronted dignity, she considered bowing her head in shame. "Whatever I have done or not done,

Jasmine, I have never been a man without honor. Please remember just what brought about our break."

She swallowed hard at the rebuke, nodded, and let him go.

Josephus took the girl's hands and hurried them back to the school, determined to confer with Mtho and Kwai over all he had witnessed.

CHAPTER SIXTY-ONE

The next morning, Mtho and Kwai joined Josephus under the shade of the lemon tree as yet another family was turned away from the gate. "They keep trying to give us the stones," Mtho explained to him.

"I wish I knew what to do," Josephus admitted.

"We keep telling them it is as God commands."

"Best we can do," Josephus shrugged. "The Mariam heir says his family has a plan for them. Perhaps his way will solve the problem."

"This is what Keda and Kebbie believe."

"I shudder to think what their teenage years will be like," Mtho admitted.

"How do you think I feel?" At Josephus's sardonic question, the three men all chuckled. When they saw Rhonda bringing Keda and Kiddisti, he motioned for them to get serious. Their role as spiritual guides didn't mean they couldn't laugh, he just preferred they not subject the children to frivolity. "Is something wrong?"

"No," Rhonda held out a piece of paper.

"We have a gift for Obed-edom's heir," Kiddisti explained.

It took Josephus a moment to remember that they meant Raffe Mariam. Then he fully took in the piece of paper and threw back his head with laughter. Wiping his streaming eyes he handed the crayon and pen drawing back to Rhonda. "Why don't you take this to them? You know where the house is and the children should get used to visiting the family."

"Do you really think this will work?"

"I'm sure of it," he promised the professor. "And it will cement the Mariam family's feelings about this place, which might be a very good thing."

Keda came wandering over, sat next to him, and tucked herself into his side. Josephus put his arm around her with care, worried she might rebuke the embrace, and then blinked back tears when the child accepted it so easily.

Rohan joined them, "I know where they live. It's the big fancy house by the stele."

Mtho brushed off his hands as he rose, "I'll go with him."

"Good," Rhonda gestured to the half-asleep Keda. "I fear the others are all exhausted after last night. I'll stay here with them."

"I'll get some extra supplies, while I'm there," Mtho promised them.

When the gate closed behind Rohan and Mtho, Josephus turned warm and appreciative eyes on Keda, marveling at what he had just learned. His family had searched for generations for this one soul. They had never expected her to be of their bloodline. *Oh Baba. Why didn't I see it? How could I not understand? Did you know all those years ago where the road you directed me to would lead? Do you love your great-granddaughter? Are you proud of her?*

Are you proud of me?

Perhaps I shall finally leave behind the moniker: 'the breaker of vows.'

For the first time Josephus reeled as he considered that this meant his Baba's bloodline would not die with him. His family was alive and flourishing under his own care. How could he have ever imagined such an event? *His bloodline, Baba, our bloodline, is meant to guard and lead this country to safety once more. Our future has an adorable smile, a mischievous look in her eyes as she watches her mother and new stepfather, and a cutting intelligence.*

Our tribe does indeed live.

It would live on through the spirit of the Blessed Child that they had been directed centuries before to protect.

He didn't know if he should feel proud, shocked, or just grateful.

So he chose a combination of all three.

It was well after lunch when he found himself again sitting underneath his favorite tree watching the children play.

He looked up with surprise, when he realized that Brother Mtho, Meggani, Keberwa and Brother Kwai were striding over with wide steps to join them.

Josephus smiled triumphantly at them. "All is well. It is too beautiful a day for another crisis."

"I hope." Rhonda could not seem to keep herself from being the resident skeptic.

Mtho folded his hands over his stomach as he rocked on his feet. "So what's next?"

"Now that we know the hunter we have been on the watch for is not a threat, what is next?" Kwai looked at the others.

"You mean, other than help the damaged kids heal, all of them gain an understanding of their abilities, and give them some kind of education?" Rhonda chuckled at the male talent for understatement and blinders.

Mtho could not keep from smiling at her sarcasm. "Other than all that, what is next?"

"Next, we save the world," Josephus shrugged.

"Oh, good," Kwai nodded. "I wouldn't have wanted to forget that one."

"And here I thought it would be hard." Mtho's comment was met by laughter from all the adults, as they returned to the classroom for their plans for world resurrection.

Their eagerness and enthusiasm was a good sign.

Due to that attitude, they did not notice that the children had eavesdropped on their planning. Or that they hurried away from the adults when it looked like they might be noticed. Some things, Meggani knew, were not for their ears.

Kebbie turned to her leader, Meggani, compelled to ask the same question. "What is next? Were the adults right?"

Jake, Keda, Mani, and Ani joined them. "Right about what?"

Kebbie answered them, since Meggani seemed transfixed by the closed gate. "The adults said that next we save the world."

"That's years from now," Ani joked.

"No," Meggani still had her faraway look. "Not years."

Mani held up his hand, unsure of when he should speak in the group without Ani's help. "I heard the brothers talk. They are not going to send anyone else out to search for others like us. They want to just focus on educating us."

Jake shook his head, "It's because of Brother Peter."

"This isn't right," Ani added.

"What do we do?" Jake asked the older kids.

Meggani's face lit with a smile so bright it made the others hold their breaths. In her pocket she played with the diamond. Handing it to Keda, she felt justified when the younger girl's expression matched her own inner turmoil. Some of the events in Michael's life that Keda saw as she held the stone were not easy to witness. Turning back to the others, she held up a hand to make them wait until the Blessed One was ready to respond. Meggani turned to Keda to find peace in the rightness of her choice. "They are right. The monks should not travel to find us anymore."

"Then you're just gonna leave the other kids out there? Even after what happened to Brother Peter?" Rohan had joined them, and was the one to voice the fear that the others would not speak aloud. "How can you do that?"

Meggani clasped Keda's palm to share some more of the information she had learned from her visitor with her leader. It was a new way of passing information that most of the others were still learning to use. By the time she finished, Keda's smile embraced them all.

They had much to do. They had even more to discuss.

Not everyone would be happy at this news.

"There is another," Keda explained. The others were called, to receive the news. Soon the yard filled with their talk as they debated the decision before them. This one was fraught with hazard. They could reach the others with their powers, but someone needed to protect them still.

Was Michael the answer? Or was he the problem?

CHAPTER SIXTY-TWO

"If you refuse to be made straight when you are green, you will not be
made straight when you are dry."
—African Proverb

I t was that very night that they came to him. The moon was full and
heavy in the sky, a large spotlight in a sea of midnight. He heard
the birds herald their arrival. Michael's observations of the academy
had taught him this was a sign. Some of the children relied on the
creatures of nature for protection.

Michael did not feel their proximity until he realized how still the
world had grown around him.

Looking up, he saw the trees surrounding him were full of all kinds
of birds. There were so many of them they obscured the branches
behind a sea of feathers and burning eyes. His mouth grew dry as fear
sent the blood coursing through his veins.

Predators and prey, all perched in the same tree, looking at one
thing.

Him.

In truth, he had never known fear until that very moment.

Michael started to stand, but when he saw the children in a large ring around him, he fell to his knees. Here was the holy moment he had been searching for, ever since he was a child, caught in a false religion's grasp. Tears filled his eyes and streaked down his cheeks.

Here was a moment he could feel God.

Here was the answer to all the questions in his soul.

Michael had been watching the school for so long he had grown able to spot the Blessed One even though she wore the same encompassing robes as the others. She was the one facing him. He guessed that the two on either side of her were the ones called Meggani and Rohan. He felt closest to Meggani. The boy had no abilities. He was still gifted with a tight bond to the others, so would be a frightening enemy to whomever caused the school pain. Michael had already developed a fondness for him.

The girl existed in a place inside his heart he thought he had lost the right to, after he had killed his first man.

He had been only a little older than these children were now.

Keda was the one who spoke. "You are the lost one," she informed him. Her voice was soft and yet seemed to echo through the rocks and earth around him. He felt something broken and dark inside him get ripped apart, flooding with light. It was as if every transgression he had made against the laws of God and men was wiped clean in that moment.

"You are the one who seeks redemption. You are the one who seeks our way."

"Protector of the guardians," a small voice called out from the side.

A male voice added his own statement with a sound so lyrical it had to be the Bedouin, "You are the one who watches over us."

"I am," Michael admitted.

Meggani stepped forward, Rohan quickly following. "We did not ask you to do this." Michael had become her unofficial guard when she had stopped traveling with Mtho. She had recognized that it was his surveillance she had felt during her explorations through the village and hills. Meggani had not seen him in person, other than the day when he had changed her tear into a diamond. Neither discussed it. In some natural and deep way, their pairing fit.

Michael shrugged. "You did not need to. It was something I just knew I had to do."

"So you shall be ours," Keda proclaimed. The other children began to stamp their feet in disagreement, their actions causing the ground to throb, making the light she carried wobble. Keda scowled at her friends, indignant that they would challenge her Keda knew they wanted him to make more recompense, but she could feel the sorrow and regret in this man's heart. *You did not have to scream an apology to mean it. You did not have to pay again, when your guilt was more than enough of a strain on your life.*

Even though they had been angels once, they needed to relearn grace.

"It shall be as I proclaim," she called to them.

"He is worthy. He shall prove himself," a different female cried out.

"I will serve as you wish," Michael offered.

Seeing Meggani's eyes flash with concern, he smiled gently. There was just something about her.

He felt her answering smile, even though her face was still in shadow. She kept her head covered, the hood close to mask her features, after the episode with the Americans. "He still has time," she explained to the others. "He must be given a chance. It is not his fault that he came first. His past means nothing. It is only tomorrow we tend."

A girl's voice carried out from the right side. "He has the darkness of the ones who hurt us."

"He has never hurt a child," a boy's voice answered.

Another girl explained, "I feel he was trying to use evil to fight evil."

"If you put darkness into darkness you get only more darkness."

Michael lowered his head at the Blessed One's reminder, and felt himself start to weep. She was right. He had just never realized it. In an attempt to end the evil destroying the world around him he had embraced evil, in turn. "I would like to serve you," he repeated to the girl he now knew was called Keda. "I should like to be the light."

She lowered her hood and leaned forward to whisper into his ear. "You already are."

The female voice that fought for him, spoke out once more. "We are children with souls of light, and faces of night. Here is our opposite. This wraith is a creature that strives to change his Essence. We should help him. We should rejoice in his entrance to our lives."

Meggani moved in front of him and presented a crystal held on a long strand. The translucent stone glittered with the light of the stars and reflected some of what was inside these special children. It hung on thin woven leather; he liked to think one of the kids had made it for this event.

"You shall be the seeker. You shall go and find the ones that are still lost. You are the one who shall guide them to this place where they can learn to use their abilities for good. They shall learn that they are a blessing for their difference, and not the curse that they fear they are."

A boy moved over and handed him a jeweled dagger with a solemn nod. Keda had brought it with her from Lake Tana for this eventuality.

Michael's breath caught as he realized the weapon was very old, and belonged in a museum. "You shall be the lost one's protector; for you yourself were once lost as well."

"I am now found," Michael responded.

"Yes, you are," Keda told him. She pressed her palm against his breastbone. He felt a burst of light shoot though him that made him collapse to the ground, unconscious. When he woke once more, he was not surprised to see that he was alone. Even the birds had departed. The only proof that the children had visited was the crystal hanging from the leather strand around his neck, and the dagger strapped to his arm.

He set out the next day. Michael was not clear on what he was supposed to do or where he was meant to go, so he just kept moving. It bewildered him, that no matter where he was, the dagger strapped to his arm was never noticed by others. Airport security was a real shock —not even the metal detectors could sense it.

Michael felt filled with a compulsive drive. One thing kept going through his head: he was once the lost. It was now his job to find the "lost ones."

It wasn't until he was in the desert one afternoon that he understood what the kids meant. He had been driving the entire day, determined to get to the other side of this sea of hot grit, one way or another. The Jeep was filled with petrol, to make sure he didn't get stranded in the center of one of the hottest and most desolate places in the world. The outpost people assured him there was a small town in the middle, where he could get some additional supplies if he needed. How there could be any kind of permanent dwelling in the hottest place on the entire planet, defied his imagination.

Still, for all the desert's harsh formidable conditions, people called it home.

The town was little more than three buildings. Michael chuckled when he saw the soda machine. It wasn't even plugged in. And it looked older than he was. It still had that distinctive red white and blue painted on the side. Americans had it wrong. If they truly wanted world domination they should focus on their soda pop companies. They managed a presence in places the CIA would never be able to reach.

All the buildings were noticeably empty. "Hey," he thought to himself. "The town in the desert is deserted." Michael took out his water bottle and drank from it. If he found that line that funny, he had to be delusional. He needed to stay healthy.

The lost ones would not find themselves.

A searing heat shot through him, and Michael pulled out his crystal.

It was glowing an iridescent blue.

Looking around, he was determined to understand what was going on. Tossing the bottle back inside the car, he shut it. Michael started to head over to the buildings but he felt the crystal cool. "Great," he muttered. "In any normal circumstance I would think a hot stone losing some of its heat would be a good thing. It is unfortunate that me and normal circumstances left company years before."

Michael pivoted and moved in the opposite direction, and the crystal grew hot once more. He held it away from his skin, "I need to look into getting an asbestos shirt."

Turning around, he headed away from the small town. The crystal resumed its nuclear level heat. Michael kept trying to shift it away. He didn't mind that he was moving into the hills, he just minded the blue-white heat burning his chest.

A twenty-minute walk later over two of the largest sand dunes he'd ever seen, Michael heard the distinctive sound of children laughing. The middle of the desert was not a place he expected to hear true joy. There was no doubt, however, that this was where he was supposed to be looking. His entire body pulsed confidently. Global warming and millions of years of continental drift meant it was quite common to find ancient lakebeds in unusual places. They were all over places like high deserts. He had visited a whole town once that was built inside one.

Over the next sand dune, Michael found himself looking down into one of those beds.

The only difference was, this one was filled with water.

Actually, only half of it was. The other half was covered with ice.

Michael slid down the side of the dune to reach out and put his hand on the glittering surface of the lake. Ice. He was touching ice while standing in the middle of the Sahara. It had to be real.

He was touching it.

He was touching ice.

The frozen surface came close to burning his skin. His smile was goofy he knew, but how else should he react? "We are not in Kansas anymore, Toto," he whispered. "I suspect you will often have moments like this."

A little boy around five years old came skipping over to him, his face beaming with a smile that outshone the sun reflecting off the surface of the body of water. He was well fed, his features chiseled and fine. The kid's beauty was so obvious; it was as if he were the offspring of an angel and a super model. "Hello," the child chirped, in English.

"Hello," Michael swallowed with difficulty.

Continuing to beam at Michael, the boy cocked his head. "You are the one who will be taking me to the school? The one that I dream about? The others have taught me all kinds of things in those dreams. This is how I can speak your language. The others explained you are new to working with one such as me. You needed an easy one for your first time out. I am he!" The last word was said with such pure joy, that Michael laughed with his new charge.

The crystal stopped trying to make him burst into flames. Michael reached out a shaking hand to take the boy's and give an official greeting. "I believe I am. I am the Lost One and was asked to find the others that needed assistance."

"I am found," the boy crowed to the adults who were observing them warily.

Michael wiped away the tears he was unashamed to feel streaking down his face. "I am too," he explained to the boy. "Welcome to the school."

"You do not use the dark anymore to fight the fear?"

"No, child," Michael swallowed past his tears. "I work only with light now."

"I'll get my things," the boy explained, before dashing over to the others who were enjoying his creation. The child skidded to a halt as he gazed back at Michael with an apologetic shrug. "I am sorry to not introduce myself. I am Aderaiki."

"Nice to meet you. I'm Michael."

The child bowed from the waist. "It is a pleasure to meet you, light worker."

Michael put his head back to let the sun embrace him. For the first time he felt as if he deserved its beneficence. The Ethiopian watching him from the far side of the lake kept hidden. Forces from beyond the school directed his appearance, and the man known as the Light Worker would have to face him another day.

For this moment, even the Ethiopian understood, was not to be interrupted.

CHAPTER SIXTY-THREE

The map they followed was penned in a combination of crayon and marker. The few words included had been spelled phonetically, at most. If the duo leading them were not as respected as they were, the men would have thought the entire expedition was a joke. Albeit one executed on a massive scale. The four Range Rovers drove through the hills piled high with camping gear on the outside. This was their cover should their movements draw any kind of comment. One look inside at the shovels and picks would create quite a stir. Each of the vehicles had four men, representatives of the different branches of the Mariam family tree. Only one sported a female in its midst.

When they stopped to check the GPS coordinates to the map, Gudit questioned their choices. "Why did we need to keep our good fortune from the papers?"

"Being overrun by fortune hunters and opportunists will cause more harm than good."

"Tourism dollars buy as much food as normal ones."

"We need to focus on industrial expansion," Raffe snapped. "Aren't you the one who handles our strategic planning?"

"Yes," Gudit sighed. "I just thought the miracle country would make a nice headline."

Raffe scowled, "We've had enough press for a lifetime. Being anonymous is valuable in this situation. It keeps the price of the diamonds ensured."

"Are you sure about this map?"

"As much as I can be, when following directions given to me by a little girl."

"She is a very advanced child," Gudit maintained.

It disturbed him that, within ten minutes of meeting Keda, his twin sister had gone through a complete personality change. He was going to have to be nice to her if she continued this calm mood. "We should be there now," he muttered to her.

"What's wrong?"

"I thought the ground would be disturbed in some way."

"That's why you rushed us out here."

"Exactly."

Gudit shrugged, "Somehow I would think after everything the Ark has done, it could handle landscaping."

Her brother chuckled. "There is another explanation."

"What?"

"The Ark might not be the only thing out here."

"Super. As if the Ark alone isn't enough for nightmares, you insist on making things worse."

"I am your brother, after all."

"Don't remind me." Gudit bumped his shoulder with hers before moving back to the car. "Get busy, already."

Raffe snapped his fingers for someone to bring the GPS and Keda's instructions. They had no idea what kind of condition the Ark might be in, but they were sure the child knew where it was. Raffe double checked the coordinates and scratched an 'x' in the dirt. Looking up, he was glad that they made sure to bring only first cousins with them. If there had been anyone else here, he'd feel concern for their safety.

It was rare someone uncovered the oldest relic of man. "You are sure," Gudit demanded.

"Do you dare to doubt Keda and her friends?" He didn't bother waiting for her to respond.

Looking over the area, Raffe was struck by how rich and green it appeared. Even the dirt was the deep color of soil that had not been baked into empty dust by the unforgiving sun. The high sides of the mountain plateau made a natural defensive position. Raffe imagined the men who once carried the Ark to this place must have been running from a great danger to pick such a difficult location to secret it.

Or, knowing the Ark, perhaps they were really trying to protect others from it.

Either way, here it had hidden for thousands of years and they were the only ones with the knowledge, will and power to retrieve it.

She started to snap her fingers for the others to begin digging when Raffe held up his hand. "We should think about this."

Representatives from each of the branches of the family came over and stood in an arc around him, to have the council. They had decided that in this, as in most things they did, there would be frank and open discussion among them all. His mother's brother put his hands on his hips, "Why do you stop?"

"I saw what this thing could do from hundreds of miles away."

"The children said if we followed the rules we could unearth it."

Father Josephus and his students had given all of them a detailed list of instructions if they chose to uncover the Ark from its ancient hiding place. Their digging implements were made from molded plastic or carved by wood. Even their clothing had to be altered, woven by the oldest female members of the family, so that there were no metals anywhere on their persons. None had fillings or surgical implants. Each had fasted for thirty days, repeating ritual prayers on a constant basis. Their bodies and minds were as clear of modern toxins and metals as they could accomplish. They even had a special Lucite box created for the Ark with sweet incense burners that would be supervised at all times.

Raffe shook his head, "What if we leave it where it is?"

"Why would we do that?"

He shrugged at his uncle's question. "It has been safe for hundreds of years where it's buried, and we have been safe from it. Why are we digging something up that sets the sky on fire?"

"It covered the countryside with diamonds."

"Think what else it might accomplish."

Raffe held up his hands when everyone started to jump in. "Keda was the one who was there to direct the energy, and she still needed two other kids to help her. What if that was it? What if that was the one good act this artifact had left in it?"

"You speak of the holy tabot," the youngest gasped.

"How can you show such sacrilege?"

"I am trying to protect us," Raffe yelled.

"As he always has," Gudit put her hand on her brother's shoulder to show her support. When everyone quieted at the unity of the Mariam twins, she turned to her sibling with an expectant air. "Tell us what you think we should do?"

"Bringing it up is a mistake."

"We can't just leave it there," one protested.

"Someone else could find it," another added.

Raffe looked over the landscape, his brow furrowed. "Maybe there is another way," he murmured. Hurrying to the car, he retrieved the maps and spread them out on the hood of the car. He noticed a strange smile on Gudit's face and was relieved that she spared him her usual biting remarks. "This land has a lot of natural defenses. We could build something here."

"What?"

He chuckled as he looked up at his twin. She guessed what he was thinking and nodded eagerly. Raffe took one of the shovels from a cousin and used it to bite down deep in the dirt. "I have officially broken ground on the Ethiopian Diamond Exchange."

"One problem," his cousin folded his arms over his chest, "we don't know who owns this land."

"That won't take long," Gudit assured them. She rushed to her laptop and used the satellite phone to connect to the Internet. One of the cousins took it from her so that she could type and browse with both hands. A few clicks later and she began to laugh.

"What?" everyone yelled.

She shrugged. "Somehow I don't think it will be difficult to get permission to build here."

"Why not?"

Gudit shook her head. "According to the registration office, our grandmother owns this land."

They shared triumphant smiles at the good news. Raffe turned to his cousins as he began to gesture to the area. "Think about it." He noticed Gudit take one of the guys to the side, as he continued enthusically. "We can put in a helicopter pad and ferry people in from throughout the country. It will be easy to keep the compound safe with very few men to maintain it, just like the ancient Israelis did when they were fighting the Romans at Masada."

"You mean like our ancestors did at Debra Damo."

"Whatever," Raffe clapped his hands. "It will be a fortress for the wealth of Ethiopia, both known and unknown. There can be no better plan." When all of the men nodded their wary acceptance, he beamed.

"Shall we get started?" Raffe asked.

"Funny," Gudit declared. "I thought we already had. Right now, David is calling our construction foreman to get the architects out here."

While the others grew distracted with their planning, Raffe double-checked the numbers that Gabriel had given him before they left. The tape from Keda's visit to the Dome of the Rock had been solved. They believed it was a set of longitude and latitude coordinates. After checking that it didn't match the location of Keda's school, Gabriel and Jasmine, now newly married, decided it was Raffe's responsibility to decipher it.

Gudit leaned over his shoulder. "We aren't there?"

"I am just as surprised as you."

"What do you think is at that place?"

"I don't know," he admitted. "But I am really looking forward to finding out."

Gudit watched her brother as he joined the other men. While he interacted with their family, she could still tell his mind was far away. A benefit of being a twin. Raffe was trying to decipher whatever the Dome of the Rock's tape was trying to tell them.

She was terrified she would not like what it said.

EPILOGUE

It waited.

Deep in the earth, protected from the passing of time. Placed by an ancient people who had fought over it. Dreamed about it. Coveted it. Passed it back and forth as the generations died and its legends were altered. None of them understood what it was. What it could do.

It knew.

The day was coming when a unique set of players would be given the cards to find it. Unearthed from its soil grave and put into the light. Put into use. They had accomplished one odyssey. Identifying and securing the most well known holy artifact of all time.

What they didn't know yet, was that it held even more power than they perceived.

Science had evolved; now its secrets could be unlocked. The puzzle that it represented would entice the inherent curiosity in people until they could figure out its mysteries. If found by the wrong cast of characters, its power would end the human race.

Now it only needed to bide the turning of the Earth until they set out on the path.

It had already waited thousands of years.

In a little while, it would be free once more.

ABOUT THE AUTHOR

G. J. Phoenix

Hi! I'm G. J. and I love books, yup, proud nerd, party of one. With a name like G. J. I guess I was always meant to be a writer, I mean seriously, my parents didn't even spell my abnormal name in a normal way. When I realized my childhood of constantly getting in trouble for "telling stories" is now considered on the job training, I saw how right it was to follow my dreams. So if you like a good story, love some adventure with a good dose of romance, you've found the "write" place to hang.

Check me out on social media, I'm everywhere or at least try to be, and I love to talk to my readers.

Learn more about the *Ethiopian Chronicles* at
www.gjphoenix.com or www.avalerionbooks.com

ALSO BY G. J. PHOENIX

Ethiopian Chronicles

Seat of God

A child marked by God's hand …

A woman willing to risk her life to save what's left of her family ...

A priest obsessed with an ancient prophecy ...

A man forced to face his past ...

Four people on a collision course with an earth-shattering destiny.

An Ethiopian priest, believing a little girl is the key to a biblical curse, kidnaps her. The girl's only surviving relative, Jasmine Rose, turns to former CIA operative—code name "the Hunter"—to help her find the child. The two must decipher a series of clues as they search from Israel to Egypt to Ethiopia to catch a holy man who always manages to stay one step ahead. What Jasmine doesn't know is that the Hunter's former boss is intent on having his revenge.

As the chase escalates, Jasmine finds herself becoming both hunter and prey. She is willing to pay anything, do anything, to secure the child. But will the child's mystical abilities save the world—or destroy them all? Jasmine must face the ultimate questions: Will finding the girl be a blessing or a curse? And what will she sacrifice to save the child?

Available in ebook and paperback